THE SPEED OF
LIGHTNING

THE
SPEED OF
LIGHTNING

JENNIE RICHMOND

Matador
9 Priory Business Park,
Wistow Road, Kibworth Beauchamp,
Leicestershire. LE8 0RX
Tel: 0116 279 2299
Email: books@troubador.co.uk
Web: www.troubador.co.uk/matador
Twitter: @matadorbooks

ISBN 978 1800464 605

British Library Cataloguing in Publication Data.
A catalogue record for this book is available from the British Library.

Printed and bound in Great Britain by 4edge Limited
Typeset in 11pt Minion Pro by Troubador Publishing Ltd, Leicester, UK

Matador is an imprint of Troubador Publishing Ltd

For Peter

PART ONE

YNYS MON
North Wales

1

1ST MARCH 1848

Dinas Farm, Ynys Mon, North Wales

The wind threw sea salt in William's face, as he led his dad's horse, Seren, into the farmyard. Across the Menai Straits, the snow-capped mountains were bathed in the gold of the rising sun. Their magnificence filled him with unbearable longing. He was desperate to be droving cattle through those mountain passes; sleeping beneath the moon; fording rivers; crossing the English border; making his fortune in the great cattle markets of London, two hundred and fifty miles away. He ached for the experience.

Dad came striding across the yard, his greatcoat flapping in the wind as he rammed his wide-brimmed hat on his head. With him was Owain, William's older brother, who went into the stable to fetch his own horse. Seizing the moment, William pulled Seren into Evan's path. "Seren is ready," he announced, sweeping his hand over the gleaming saddle which he had been polishing since before dawn.

"I should hope so." Dad snatched Seren's reins and heaved himself into the saddle without even commenting on William's handiwork.

"Wait, Dad!" said William, clinging like a limpet to Seren's bridle.

"We're in a hurry, William. What's the matter?"

"Please, take me with you. How can I learn to be a drover's boy if you don't give me the chance to learn?"

Dad looked down at William as if he were a weaner escaped from a pigsty, his weathered face full of annoyance. "Enough, William!" he thundered. "We've been through this a hundred times and I meant what I said. I am not taking you on the first drove of the season, when we all need our wits about us, and no one will have time to look after you. What's more, I need you to stay here this morning and do Owain's chores as well as your own. We've got supplies to buy in Beaumaris and men to hire for the drove. You'd only be in the way if you came. Now let us get on!" He kicked Seren forward with such force that William's fingers were wrenched from her bridle.

Owain, now waiting by the gate on his own horse, added to William's humiliation. "Don't forget to muck out the stables, little brother. Leave those cattle in the top field. I'll move them up to the Hughes' farm when I get back."

William felt trapped as a chained bull as he watched them go. Evan's back, rocking in Seren's saddle, blocked his view of the mountains, through which they would soon be travelling without him, like a great oak door. Ever since he could remember, William had wanted to be a drover's boy – to learn how to drove cattle to London and sell them in Smithfield Market. To be part of the glorious welcome when

4

the drovers returned, boasting about their adventures and the money they'd made. Before each new drove, William begged Dad to take him, but Dad always found an excuse not to: William wasn't sensible enough, he was needed on the farm, he was too young. But this year William was fourteen – the same age that Owain had been when he went on his first drove – and William thought it only fair that he should be given the same chance.

He dug his hands into the pockets of his breeches and stomped around the yard kicking up stones. Instead of being a drover's boy, he had to be a slave: collecting eggs, feeding pigs, mucking out stables and doing all the other boring jobs that Owain didn't want to do. Except… William stopped short. What about the jobs that Owain did want to do? Didn't he say he was going to move the cattle up to the Hughes' farm when he got back? Well, William could do that.

Grinning, he kicked a stone so hard that it clanged against the water butt, setting Mab barking. Why shouldn't he? If he showed Dad that he could herd cattle by himself, Dad would have to take him seriously.

William scanned the yard for trouble. He knew the rest of the family were busy for now. Mam and Margaret were in the dairy, churning butter for the market and Anne was getting ready for school. When he was sure he was alone, he ran over to Mab's kennel. As soon as he unleashed her, she jumped up and covered his face with slobbery kisses and doggy breath.

"Calm down." William cupped her chestnut-coloured head in his hands, flattening her ears. "I need your help." Mab panted and writhed in William's grasp as he slid one hand firmly down her back, ruffling her fur. "Now listen,

Mab. I'm sick of Dad treating me like Owain's stupid little brother. We're going to show him that we can handle cattle. We can do that, can't we? We've practised enough. Come on!" He brought Mab to heel and strode out of the yard and across a field with the dog prancing beside him.

The cattle were in the top field, which was a good thing because it meant that he could bring them down the back lane without being seen from the farm. It hadn't rained for three days, so the ground was firm, and the world was bathed in spring sunshine. What more did he need? He reached the gate with Mab hard on his heels and vaulted over it as she squeezed underneath. Then he adjusted his cap, squared his shoulders and set to work with a grin.

The herd was several hundred yards away, scattered on the rise: brawny black Ynys Mon cattle, as familiar to him as the grass under his feet. On his first command, Mab raced across the field towards them, her white tail dancing in the breeze. With perfect timing, he whistled through his teeth with the keening 'bring them here' whistle that he had heard since he was born. Mab raced around the back of the herd, weaving backwards and forwards, rounding them up and chivvying them towards him. William scanned their heads, looking for Big Beast, the herd leader. He knew that if he got Big Beast on his side, the rest would follow. He chose twelve animals: a small, select group that he and Mab could easily manage.

Big Beast was easy to spot, being taller than the other oxen by half a head. William saw him jogging to the front of the herd, as he had expected, and whistled to Mab. Her response was instant, but William was nervous because he could never completely trust her to do the right thing. This time, however, she didn't let him down. With her ears flattened and her tail lowered, she crept little by little towards Big Beast. When she reached him, she separated him from the herd and directed him towards the gate.

Success, thought William.

Now, he sent her to cut off a small group of oxen from the rest of the herd. As she worked, he whistled commands and crooned, "Come by, come by," as Dad had taught him. Thinking about Dad made him anxious. He hated to think what Dad would do to him if this all went wrong.

He ushered the selected cattle through the gate and banged it shut behind them before any of the others could follow. The animals at the front of the remaining herd rested their chins on the gate and licked their nostrils with huge, pink tongues.

William felt pleased with himself as he began what now seemed an easy task. All he had to do was drive his selected herd down the lane, through the village and into the fields of Robert Hughes, Dad's deputy drover. Mr Hughes farmed a smallholding with his wife, Gwen, who also ran the village shop with their daughter, Lizzie, William's friend.

The lane was bordered by a stream on one side and a hedge on the other, so the cattle couldn't stray. Each time one stopped to graze, William moved it on with a flick of his stick. As his confidence grew, he pushed his flat cap to the back of his head and pulled from his pocket a plug of tobacco, cadged from Owain's supplies. He put it in his mouth and chewed like a cow, until the bitter juice ran down his chin, then spat it out with a grimace. All drovers chewed tobacco, but he didn't like it yet. He supposed he would, in time.

When they neared the end of the lane, he had to turn the animals so he could drive them over the bridge and into the main street. He and Mab had already practised turning Big Beast on his own, and that experience now enabled William to send all the oxen in the right direction. Even though this was only a small success, it filled him with delight. Momentarily, he pictured himself driving Dad's entire herd of cattle all the way to London by himself.

As a result, when he crossed the bridge and saw something that would normally have alarmed him, he wasn't bothered at all. Peering over the wall, he saw a human head topped by a shock of black curly hair. The head's owner was crouching at the edge of the stream with one arm up to the elbow in water. When he heard William he looked up, his mouth slashed open with fury. Then he sprang to his feet and shinned up the bank. Soon he was towering over William with his feet set apart and his arms folded across his powerful chest.

Cade Jones.

Although just one year older than William, Cade was a lot bigger and had fists like rocks. On this occasion, however, William was so puffed up with his new-found droving skills that he didn't feel intimidated by his enemy and dared to confront him.

"Poaching again are you, Cade?" he teased.

"What are you talking about?" snarled Cade, rubbing his hands on his trousers to wipe off the scales from the trout he'd been tickling. "And what are you doing with this lot?" He pointed at the cattle ambling up the hill through the village.

William was about to reply, when the voice of Old Griff rang out from the woods beyond. "I know what you're up to, Cade Jones. Get yourself home! And you, William Evans. Get those animals off the road. I don't want my cabbages trampled. Go on the pair of you!"

8

Cade shoved his face into William's. "You'd better watch out, William Evans. That trout was going to be my breakfast. I'll get you for this." He dived into the woods, shaking his fist at William as he went.

2

1ST MARCH 1848

Pontarcarrog village, Ynys Mon, North Wales

Cade's threat did not bother William in the least. He even congratulated himself on standing up to the bully, as he hurried after the herd between the grey-stone houses that lined both sides of the street. The villagers of Pontarcarrog were carrying out their daily routines: hoeing the vegetable patch, baking bread, cleaning. They waved as William went by. He breathed in the crisp spring air as he drove the cattle up the hill to the village shop, his task almost done. All he had to do was get them safely into Mr Hughes' field.

But as they drew level with the village shop, where Mr and Mrs Hughes and Lizzie were peacefully serving customers, pandemonium broke out! Big Beast suddenly leapt into the air, bellowing, with all four legs leaving the ground at once. He flipped around as he landed, tossing his head and scattering the herd in all directions. Mab rushed at him, barking and nipping at his forelegs. Big Beast dipped his head to hook the dog with his horns, missed, turned his sinewy loins and kicked her in the side. She yelped as the impact sent her skidding across the square amongst the legs of the other oxen. William attempted to head off Big Beast, but the raging animal escaped him and bucked his way towards the woods on the far side of the village square.

William watched with horror as the rest of the cattle scattered around the square, back down the hill and into people's gardens. Old Griff, on his morning stroll, found himself surrounded by confused animals and lashed out ineffectually with his stick, to clear a path.

"Keep them away from the shop!" Mr Hughes' voice boomed out as he and Mrs Hughes exploded through the shop door, slamming it behind them, and their daughter, Lizzie, ran out of the dairy. "Open the gate, Gwen. I'll drive this bunch into the field. Lizzie, get that mad dog out of the way – help her, William."

The sound of his name brought William back to his senses and he lunged at Mab, who was rushing past, slowing her down long enough for Lizzie to grab her collar and shut her in the shop.

"Head those oxen off, William. Don't let them go into the woods," shouted Mr Hughes.

Across the square, Big Beast and two faithful followers were about to do just that. Big Beast was bellowing and rolling the whites of his eyes. Any sudden movement would send him off again. William crossed the square cautiously, with his eyes fixed on the ox, but as he got nearer, he caught a glimpse of Lizzie running towards him. He slowed her down with a backward wave of one hand, so that she tied up her skirts and tucked strands of auburn hair under her white cap, ready to help him.

"I didn't know you could herd cattle," said William when she caught him up.

"And I didn't know you couldn't," teased Lizzie.

She left William to deal with Big Beast and tackled the other two oxen heading towards the woods, sending them trundling towards her dad's field. William was a bit put out at how easily she did this. He hadn't counted cattle-droving as one of her many skills.

But this was no time to be thinking about Lizzie. Big Beast was only a few yards away, snorting dangerously. William crept towards him. "Come by, come by," he crooned. Big Beast stopped mooing when he heard William's voice, but teetered at the edge of the woods, swinging his head and twitching his tail. Beads of sweat dripped into William's eyes, but he continued to advance, in spite of his fear of being gored by the curved white horns that quivered in front of him. Eventually, he got close enough to lay a hand on Big Beast's rump and began to coax him towards the field. But as he started to move in the right direction, Lizzie, excited by her own success, came carelessly flying back across the square.

Her sudden arrival, at this crucial moment, was too much for Big Beast. With a bellow, he twisted around and disappeared amongst the trees, passing so close to Lizzie that she jumped backwards and fell over a log with a cry.

"We'll never catch him now," said William.

"I'm sorry, I'm sorry. That was so stupid of me. I didn't think. Ouch!" said Lizzie, rubbing her ankle.

William bent over her. "Are you all right?"

"I think it's just a bruise," said Lizzie.

12

William grabbed her hand and pulled her up, wrinkling his nose as she fell against him. "Mm, you smell of sour milk."

"And you smell of cow dung." Lizzie shoved William away with a grin which quickly faded when she looked over his shoulder. "Oh no, William. There's your dad."

William followed her gaze. Tearing down the road from Beaumaris, he saw Rhett, Dad's dog, followed closely on horseback by Owain and Dad himself.

"William! What are you doing here? What in heaven's name is going on?" Dad didn't wait for an answer. He slid off Seren and sent Rhett after the oxen that were still lumbering around the square. Villagers looked on with admiration as he, Evan Evans – the most respected drover in Ynys Mon – soothed the frightened beasts and sent them over to Mr Hughes.

William shuffled slowly backwards, hoping to get away unnoticed, but he was too slow.

"That's how it's done, William," called Dad, pointing his stick first at the cattle and then at William. "Now come here." William reluctantly obeyed. "Tell me, who gave you permission to drive my cattle through the village? I certainly didn't. Somebody could have been killed."

"Don't be too hard on him, Evan. The boy was only trying to help," said Mrs Hughes, as she came around the corner from her kitchen garden, carrying a trampled cabbage. But Evan ignored her. "I'll make us all a drink," she said with a sigh.

But this was a bad idea, because as soon as she opened the shop door, Mab bounded joyfully through it with a chunk of stolen ham in her mouth. She saw William and raced towards him, startling the last ox going through the gate and causing it to charge back down the road.

"Now look what your dog's done, William. This is the last straw!" shouted Evan. He kicked Mab out of the way with an oath, grabbed William and raised his cattle-stick.

"I was trying to save you a job," cried William, squirming in Dad's iron grip as the first stinging blow lashed his backside.

"Mr Evans, Mr Evans, please don't beat William. He was only trying to help," cried Lizzie. As William tensed himself for the next blow, she flung herself at his dad, clinging to his raised arm. William, still firmly wedged under Dad's other arm, could feel him trying to shake her off.

But it wasn't Lizzie's pleas that saved him from further punishment: he was unexpectedly rescued by the arrival of Mostyn Jones. "Caught up with you at last, Evan Evans," Mostyn called as he came up behind Dad. "Didn't you see me in the hiring fair, at Beaumaris, this morning?"

At the sound of Mostyn's voice, Dad dropped William and finally shook Lizzie off. "I'll deal with you later," he said, scowling. "Yes, Mostyn Jones, I saw you at the fair. What do you want?"

Mostyn Jones stank of stale beer and he looked dreadful as well. He was wearing a filthy, ragged coat and a battered drover's hat. Lank hair covered his ears and his face bristled with spit-encrusted stubble. He thrust his face close to Dad's. "What do you think I want? I need work. I know we've had our differences, Evan, but we're old mates, aren't we? Give me and Cade jobs on your drove. You know we're good with cattle. I'll take a boy's wage with my son, if you like, but in the name of God give us jobs. The family are all but starving."

Evan folded his arms across his chest and looked at

Mostyn coldly. "I can't believe you're asking me to take you on, after last year. Have you forgotten that I caught you stealing Sir Edward's best cattle?" he said.

"I wasn't stealing them. I was moving them to better grazing," mumbled Mostyn, staring at his feet.

You were most certainly stealing," said Evan. "I'll never trust you again, Mostyn Jones. Anyway, just look at you. Have you no pride, man? I don't want a drunk handling my cattle. If you're so keen to help your family, why are you wasting every ha'penny you've got on beer? On your way! I've got no time for you."

"Don't you insult me," Mostyn raised his fist, but when Evan didn't even flinch, he turned to the crowd of villagers who had gathered. "He won't give me a job," he said, opening his arms for sympathy. But he met only stony glares. Mostyn Jones was well known for his wild ways. "You'll be sorry for this," he said to Evan, as he backed away. "Me and my boy, Cade – we'll make sure of that."

William thought how foolish Dad was to make an enemy of Mostyn Jones, as he watched the drover shuffle off. Then he realised that here was a golden opportunity. Dad was still holding his stick, but William was so desperate to go on the drove that he was prepared to risk a second thrashing. He sidled up to Dad, keeping just out of reach.

"You'll be short of help now, without Mr Jones, Dad. Can you take me instead?"

"May God give me strength!" Dad's stick twitched in his hand but this time he kept his temper. "How dare you ask me that, boy, after the way you've just treated my cattle?"

"But I was just practising, and it was an accident," said William. "Everyone has accidents when they're learning. I bet Owain had accidents and you took him droving when he was my age, so why won't you take me?"

"Enough! Get yourself home, boy, and take that idiot dog with you," bellowed Evan.

William didn't wait to be told twice, but as he ran over to collect Mab from Lizzie, he remembered Big Beast with a twang of fear. How long would it be before Dad realised his prize ox was missing? "Lizzie! Big Beast's still in the woods," he whispered.

Lizzie clapped her hand to her mouth. "Oh no! I'd forgotten that." She grabbed William's arm. "Look. Old Griff's coming over. Ask him to help."

"It was a stone that scared them oxen, boy. Someone threw a stone," said Old Griff as he reached William.

But William hardly heard. "Big Beast's still in the woods. What shall we do?" he said.

Old Griff winked at Lizzie. "We'll find him, lad, don't worry. You'll help me, lass, won't you? I can see you've got the makings of a cowgirl."

"I'll do my best," said Lizzie, pulling a nervous face at William.

"I told you to go home, William. And if you know what's good for you, you'll keep out of my sight for the rest of the day," Dad shouted across the square.

"Go along, William. We'll manage," said Old Griff.

William needed no further encouragement. With Mab in tow, he ran down the hill past villagers who bawled out grievances about squashed cabbages and trampled potatoes. Then he raced to the safety of the old barn with his backside stinging and his face glowing with embarrassment.

3

1ST MARCH 1848

Dinas Farm, Ynys Mon, North Wales

The old barn was William's favourite hideout. In a corner at the back was a forgotten pile of straw where he and Mab now huddled. William rubbed his sore backside and then ran his hands over Mab's body, feeling for lumps and bumps from Big Beast's attack. The dog winced a bit, but nothing seemed to be broken.

"What am I going to do with you, Mabyn?" William murmured, as he picked clots of mud from her matted fur. He had put Mab through her paces as a true working dog, so many times. He had taught her to nip an ox's ankle and then leap clear and on to the next one without getting a hoof in the belly. He thought he had taught her obedience.

"Whatever made you bite Big Beast like that? I've never seen him so mad." Mab nuzzled William's hand and threshed the hay with her tail, making him cough on the chaff. "Don't you try to get around me," he said when he'd recovered. "And you're a thief. Stealing Mrs Hughes' best ham." He grabbed Mab's ears and pulled her head from side to side, reciting. "I'll – have – to – pay – for – that." Mab licked his face adoringly, but William shoved her away. "Maybe Dad and Owain are right. You haven't got what it takes to be a drover's dog."

He rolled on his front and buried his face in the straw, remembering how he had rescued Mab from an early death because she was the runt of a litter. He'd fed her day and night as a pup, cradling the tiny, wriggling body whilst she licked milk off his fingers. He'd refused to let her be taken away when Dad said she was too weak and spoilt to be of any use on the farm. Drovers' dogs needed to be independent, hungry and tough. No dog would risk its life for its master and run hundreds of miles on a scant diet, if love and pampering were an option.

William turned on to his back and gazed miserably at the bird droppings on the rafters. He'd defied Dad and given Mab all the love she wanted and now look what had happened: she'd spoilt his chance to show Dad he could handle cattle. If Mab had guided the cattle as he'd taught her, Dad might have agreed to take him droving… well, he wasn't going to give up. He'd just have to think up another plan.

He was still staring blankly at the rafters, sometime later, when he smelt rabbit pie.

"Where are you, William?" called Lizzie.

William sat bolt upright, hastily combing straw out of his hair with his fingers. "Over here," he muttered, not wanting Lizzie to see him like this. Mab ran over to her, barking, and jumped for the pie, which Lizzie held out of her reach, laughing.

"Get away you, thief, you've already had a free ham today. Here, William, my mam sent you this."

As William took the pie, Mab's rank breath warmed his ear. "Lie down over there!" he commanded, and Mab slunk into a corner with her tail between her legs.

The sweet smell of rabbit meat and warm pastry made William ravenous. He sank his teeth into it over and over again until he had eaten it all and had gravy running down his chin. "I was hungry." He grinned and wiped his chin with back of his hand.

"I can see that." Lizzie snorted with laughter. "I'm not surprised, after that shambles. I know it wasn't funny when the cattle stampeded, William. But it did look comical when old Griff was dodging about in the middle of the square, trying to get out of the way."

The mention of Old Griff reminded William of Big Beast. "Did Old Griff manage to find Big Beast in the woods?"

"He did – with a little help from me," boasted Lizzie. "Don't worry, we got him into the field. Anyway, William, what did you think you were you doing – driving those cattle through the village on your own? Even an experienced drover doesn't do that. It's dangerous. I'm not surprised your dad got so angry."

Now she was talking to William like his mother. "You didn't have to rescue me from Dad. I'd have got away myself if you hadn't interfered," he grumbled.

"If you say so." Lizzie shrugged and stuck her nose in the air.

"Everything went wrong this morning," continued William. "I was trying to show Dad I would make a good drover's boy, so that he'd take me on this next trip to London. Now, I doubt if he'll ever take me anywhere again."

"Don't be daft. He'll change his mind eventually. One day he'll need you." Lizzie slid the almost empty pie dish over to

Mab, who was creeping slowly towards them on her belly, salivating. "Anyway, I've got some news for you. Old Griff doesn't think Mab caused the stampede. He wants us to meet him up on my dad's field to have a look at Big Beast's leg. He thinks someone threw a stone at the herd. Will you come?"

"I certainly will," said William. As he stood up, he remembered Cade Jones shaking his fist at him after he'd caught him poaching that morning. What was it Cade had said? 'I'll get you for this.'

When they reached the field, Big Beast and Dad's other oxen were grazing peacefully alongside Mr Hughes' own cattle. On the far side of the Menai Straits, the snow on the mountain tops whitened the twilight. There would be a frost that night. William turned up his collar and Lizzie tucked her home-spun shawl around her ears.

Old Griff was leaning on the gate, puffing on his clay pipe, his dog sitting obediently at his feet. He really did seem 'as old as the hills' to William. Everything about him was grey and craggy. He had a grey beard, spiked with grease, and one jagged tooth left in his bottom jaw. But he knew his trade. In days gone by, he had worked as a drover for the father of the local squire and landowner, Sir Edward Ellis-Lloyd, the man who now employed William's dad.

"Evening, William. Glad you've come. Need to sort this out." Old Griff took his clay pipe out of his mouth, cleared his throat and spat.

"I thought Big Beast went mad because Mab bit him on the leg, but Lizzie says someone threw a stone," said William.

"Someone certainly did, young man. I was just thinking I'd go into the village shop for a plug of baccy when, all of a sudden, a stone flies past and hits the big ox clean on the leg.

After that it was like watching them all dance a jig on hot coals." This comical vision made Old Griff cough and chortle.

"Did you see who threw it?" asked William.

"'I did not. But whoever chucked it had a damn good aim. Let's go and look for the damage." As soon as Old Griff had walked through the gate, the target of the stone-thrower caught his attention.

"What do you call this one?" he asked.

"Big Beast," said William.

"Well, he's certainly that. A fine specimen. He'll fetch a good price in London. Now, you take this rope, boy, and slip it over his head when I've caught him. Lizzie, you stand by in case William needs help." Old Griff whistled softly and his dog set off, creeping low and bursting into short runs. Soon he was driving Big Beast steadily towards them. When the ox reached them, Lizzie and William slipped the rope over his head and kept him calm whilst Old Griff cast an expert eye over his legs.

"Look here, boy," he said after a bit. "Does that look like a dog's bite?"

William inspected the wound. He had expected tooth marks but found a straight gash, two inches long and quite deep. He shook his head. "No, you're right, the wound's the wrong shape for that. It could have been done by a stone."

Old Griff steadied himself on his gnarled walking stick, as the three of them left the field. "It's a crying shame, what happened today," he said, pointing the mouthpiece of his pipe at William and nudging Lizzie's arm. "He's got the makings of a drover, this one. I saw him driving those cattle through the village this morning before they went on the rampage. Steady as flying geese they were. I can tell he's Evan Evan's son – no mistaking that."

So Old Griff thought he was good at droving. This was the best thing William had heard all day. He gave Lizzie a triumphant grin and strutted along the lane as if he was performing in a play at the village fair.

"You'll need to do something about that wild dog, though," continued Old Griff, bringing him back down to earth. "She went crazy when Big Beast jumped. Made the whole thing worse. And she's a thief. Gwen Hughes will send you the bill for that ham, I'll be bound." He stuck his pipe back in his mouth with a wheezy chuckle. When they reached his garden gate, he clamped his hand on William's shoulder and gave him a piercing look. "One last thing, boy – where do you think that stone came from? Have you got an enemy?"

William's heart thumped. He'd forgotten, until then, that Old Griff had seen him and Cade together down by the river, that morning. He tried to look innocent. "Not that I know of," he said.

"Well, have a good think," said Old Griff, meaningfully. "We don't want people in this village to get away with throwing stones at cattle, do we?"

"I wonder if Old Griff suspects Cade Jones?" said Lizzie, as they walked home. "He's got a reputation for stone throwing and he's well known for hitting his mark. Have you done something to annoy him, William?"

"Of course not," lied William.

They walked on in silence for a few minutes, but they were nearing Lizzie's house now and William had to make sure she was on his side. "What if I did annoy Cade? It wouldn't prove he threw the stone," he said, blocking Lizzie's path.

"I knew it," said Lizzie, planting her hands on her hips. "What's the matter with you two, William? You can't leave each other alone. What happened?"

"Nothing important," said William.

"Huh!"

William put his hands on Lizzie's shoulders and gazed into her cynical blue eyes. "Please don't tell anyone. Dad's already fallen out with Mostyn Jones. If he finds out that I annoyed Cade, he'll be angry with me all over again."

4

14TH MARCH 1848

Dinas Farm, Ynys Mon, North Wales

Two weeks later, the day came for Noson Lawen – the party which the Evans and the Hughes families always held to mark the start of the droving season. Usually William looked forward to it, but not this time. This time, he just felt depressed. All through the winter, he had imagined himself droving to London in the spring, but Dad was still refusing to take him. All William's efforts to persuade him had been useless and he felt bitterly disappointed.

However, in spite of his mood, he was enticed into the kitchen by the delicious smell of Mam's pies and puddings. The kitchen looked magical. Green boughs of pine wreathed the windows and the hearth. In the centre of the table, a bowl of primroses shone in the light of wax candles that Mam kept for special occasions. A side of pig sizzled and crackled on a spit over the fire, making William's mouth water.

The table was laid for eleven people and heaped with

chunks of ham, a lambs-tail pie and a pork and apple pudding. In between were piles of home-made butter, cheese, and barley bread. Mam's harp glinted in the firelight, waiting to be played.

The door swung open. "When can we start?" William's little sister, Anne, dashed in, skipped around and hugged Mam, who pushed her gently away.

"Calm down, Anne – can't you see I'm tired?" she said, wincing as she rubbed her back.

William's big sister, Margaret, turned from the sink. "Sit down, Mam." She steered her mother into her rocking chair by the fire and passed her a mug of mulled ale. "Drink this. You've been on your feet all day."

Soon Old Griff staggered in, stick first, a flagon of beer in his free hand. "Lovely decorations. How are you, Jane, my dear? You look a bit pale."

Lizzie came next, carrying a basket of oat cakes, jam and pickles, which she plonked on the table. She made straight for William, grabbed his hand and pulled him into the shadows under the stairs. "I've got a secret, William," she whispered.

"Have you?" asked William. Taking advantage of this welcome turn of events, he looked deep into Lizzie's eyes and squeezed her hand. "Tell me."

Lizzie snatched her hand away. "Stop fooling, William. This is real." She put her mouth close to his ear. "Me and my mam are going to London with the drove. But you mustn't say anything because my dad hasn't told your dad yet…"

"What! You're going to London too?" William couldn't believe what he was hearing.

Just then, Mr and Mrs Hughes arrived, and Lizzie backed away with a finger over her lips. William stayed under the stairs, overwhelmed with a sense of injustice and envy at Lizzie's good fortune. Miserably, he pictured her running free through the mountains, her fiery hair streaming behind her, whilst he stayed at home and fed the pigs. To make matters worse, the kitchen thrummed with gossip and laughter, now that all the guests had arrived, and no one seemed to notice he was missing. He slouched in the gloom, listening to pots chink and tankards clink. Mam was on her feet again, trading stories with Mrs Hughes about getting their husbands ready for the drove. Margaret sat by the fire with Old Griff, listening to tales of droving from his ancient past.

After a while, Evan and Mr Hughes, needing somewhere quieter to discuss business, moved near to where William was hiding, so that he couldn't help eavesdropping on their conversation. "I fear I've made an enemy of Mostyn Jones – he and that good-for-nothing son of his," said Evan. "I wouldn't trust him as far as a dog can whistle."

"And that's no distance at all," laughed Mr Hughes, swigging his beer.

"This is no laughing matter, Robert. Nobody's going to give him a job in his present state and I don't want him getting up to any mischief around here while we're away."

"Oh, come on, Evan. We both grew up with Mostyn. How many times have the three of us travelled together to London? He's a skilled drover. You know that."

"Indeed, he is," agreed Evan. "But when things don't go his way, he can get nasty, as we both know. You should have seen the look on his face when I refused to employ him. He meant it when he said he'd get his revenge."

"Well, give him a job then," said Mr Hughes. "Keep him sweet."

"Are you mad, Robert? You know what happened last time. He tried to make off with our cattle. He's a thief and a liar. I'll never employ him again." Evan swigged his beer and wiped his mouth with his shirtsleeve. "I'm minded to talk to Sir Edward about it, and ask him to keep an eye on the family."

"Mostyn won't harm your family," protested Mr Hughes. "What's more, you've got no proof that he's a thief. We should take him. Think of his children. They haven't had a decent meal in their bellies for weeks. Give him another chance, Evan. I am your deputy after all – surely I should have a say in the matter?"

"Not in this case," snapped Evan. The two men glared at each other.

"Come on, you two. We're ready to eat," called Mam.

Evan sighed and held out his hand. "Forget our differences for tonight, Robert. Shake hands for luck's sake, we've got a hard journey ahead of us." Robert Hughes shook hands unsmilingly and they took their seats at the table.

William didn't like Mostyn or Cade, but he didn't like the thought of the Jones family starving either. He stayed under the stairs, sulking, and wondering if Dad's decision was right. But eventually he was tempted out of his hiding place by the tantalising aroma of hot food. After all, there was no point in going hungry just because Lizzie was going on the drove and he wasn't. Starving himself wouldn't change Dad's mind, would it?

He squeezed on to the bench between Owain and Old Griff, who passed him a piece of pie. "Fill your belly, lad. Take what you can get in this life and don't fret about what you can't have. That's my motto."

When everyone had eaten their fill, Evan got to his feet for the traditional toast. "Here's to the health of the best drovers in Ynys Mon. May God keep us safe on our first journey of the season."

"Cheers!" Everyone clinked their mugs.

"And here's to Jane and her helpers for a delicious feast," continued Evan. "May God keep them safe while we're gone."

"Hear, hear!" Everyone clinked their mugs again.

Soon the table and chairs were moved aside to make room for dancing. Mr Hughes picked up his accordion and waited for Mam to fetch her harp.

"A tune, Jane, a tune!" the company clamoured.

But Mam shook her head. "I'm too tired," she said and collapsed into her fireside chair. William, for one, was disappointed. He loved to watch Mam's fingers rippling the harp strings and hear her sweet voice singing.

Old Griff came to the rescue. "Look what I found." He pulled an object that looked like the wide end of a cow horn out of his bag. "It's my grandfather's old pibgorn. He was well known as a pibgorn player, around these parts. Take a look." He handed the instrument to William. "You blow it here." He pointed to the narrow end of the horn. "To make different notes, you block these holes in the middle with your fingertips. Have a go," said Old Griff. William put his lips to the blowhole and filled his lungs with air. He blew as hard as he could, but the pibgorn didn't make a sound and he ended up spluttering all over it. Old Griff roared with laughter. "Not like that. Here, I'll give you a burst." He puffed out his cheeks and blew into the pibgorn with all his might. It screeched a note so loud that everyone shrieked and put their hands over their ears. Old Griff collapsed back into his chair with delight. "Well, I had a go, at least," he chortled. "No one can say I didn't try."

"Come on everyone, let's dance!" Mr Hughes seized his accordion and played the first notes of a jig before Old Griff could try again. Owain clattered out a clog dance while everyone clapped along. Then Mr Hughes played a polka, which got almost everyone on their feet. Owain seized Margaret and they galloped about like a couple of colts. Mrs Hughes grabbed Lizzie, who whirled her around and trod on her toes. Even William could not resist the fun. When the next tune started, he pulled Mam from her seat. "Come on, Mam, dance with me."

"No, William. I'm too tired. Let go!" she said.

"But you must have a dance," laughed William. He swept Mam into the polka, spinning her around the room. She tried to keep up, but after two turns, her hand slipped out of his and her head slumped against his shoulder.

"Mam! What's wrong? Help!" he shouted.

The music stopped. Evan dashed across the room and gathered Mam in his arms just in time to prevent her crashing to the floor. He carried her up to their bedroom, with Mrs Hughes hurrying after him, holding up a candle so that he didn't stumble on the stairs.

"Mam! What's happened?" called Anne, running after her in a panic.

But William caught her by the arm. "Stay here. Give Mam some peace. Mrs Hughes knows what to do." He steered Anne over to the hearth, where the rest of the party had gathered around the flickering fire. "This isn't like Jane. Whatever can be the matter?" said Old Griff. They shared their concerns about Mam and discussed possible remedies in subdued voices, while they listened to the thud of feet on the floorboards in the bedroom above and waited for news.

The fire was dying by the time Evan came back downstairs and all eyes turned on him. "She fainted. She's come around now," he said, sinking with a deep sigh into his chair. "She's with child. She hadn't told me because she didn't want to worry me before we left for London." He stared at the embers, head in hands. "I don't want to leave her like this. What am I going to do?"

William's heart was thumping. He remembered the two occasions after Anne was born, when Mam had miscarried a pregnancy and nearly died. But both times that had been in winter, when Dad was home, keeping them safe. Now both Dad and Owain were going away, leaving Mam in charge. What if the baby came too early and things went wrong again?

Dad turned gravely to Mr Hughes. "I have to go to London, Robert. We need the money – more than ever if there's to be another child. I can't afford to let Sir Edward down. Is there any chance that Gwen could help Jane out while we're away?"

William raised his eyebrows at Lizzie, knowing that Mrs Hughes wouldn't be there. Lizzie shrugged and made a face.

Mr Hughes cleared his throat. "Evan, there's something you need to know. Gwen and Lizzie are coming with us to London. Rhys Pryce, Gwen's brother, has offered Lizzie work in his cow-keeper's shop."

William let his jaw drop open and glared incredulously at Lizzie. Not only was she going to London, she'd also been offered a job when she got there. But Lizzie clearly didn't care about his feelings. She just stared him out.

Dad wasn't happy either. "This is my drove, Robert. I say who's coming on it or not."

"And I have to think of my family's future." said Mr Hughes. "The shop's not paying and my droving money alone is not enough. Lizzie can earn her own keep in London, working for Rhys as a milkmaid. It'll give her a better chance in life. It's all arranged. My brother, Dewi, is going to run the shop and farm while we're away. We'll buy a wagon at Rhuthun Market and load it with Welsh goods to sell. I'll share the profits with you."

"I don't want wagons – or women selling blankets – on my drove. Particularly not when my wife is in need of your wife's help," thundered Evan.

Mr Hughes shrugged. "I have no choice, Evan. If you won't let my family come with us, I'll find another drover who will. I didn't tell you before, because I knew how you'd react. I've been trying to find the right moment."

Evan got to his feet. "Well, you should have told me before. It's unforgivable, springing this on me at the last minute when there's no time to make other arrangements." He stalked across the room and grabbed the stair-rail. "I'm going up to Jane. I'll let you know what I've decided, in the morning."

The celebrations were over. Mrs Hughes and Lizzie collected up their dishes and drew their shawls around their shoulders and Anne and Margaret cleared away the remains of the food. William was stacking up dirty plates when Lizzie touched him on the shoulder.

"What?" he said crossly.

Lizzie looked upset. "I was just going to say that I'm sorry about your mam. And I had an idea, about you going on the drove, but if you're going to be like that, I won't bother to tell you."

William sighed and put down the dirty plates. "Thanks, about Mam," he said. "What's your idea?"

"Our dads will be meeting up with Sir Edward in a couple of days, to get their instructions for the drove. If you could go with them and talk to Sir Edward about going with them as a drover's boy, he might be able to help. After all, he is your dad's employer. Maybe he could get your dad to change his mind."

"There's no chance of Dad taking me to that meeting," said William gloomily.

"Don't be so sure about that, boy," said Old Griff, who had come up behind them. He looked at Lizzie. "I think you've hit on something there, lass. Now I'm going to see Sir Edward tomorrow, to give him some advice about a sick cow, so I'll mention your name to him, William. He likes to employ the young lads living on his estate." He poked William in the ribs with his stick. "So, stop sulking and cheer up. You never know what's around the corner."

5

16TH MARCH 1848

Dinas Farm, Ynys Mon, North Wales

On the day that Dad, Owain and Mr Hughes were due to have a business meeting with Sir Edward, William was shaken awake by Owain.

"Get up, William! We're wanted up at the big house."

"Not me," mumbled William, burying his face in the pillow.

"Yes, you. Come on! Sir Edward has sent word that he wants to see you."

William sat bolt upright, grinning. Old Griff's plan must have worked. He hadn't expected that.

Without any more persuasion he wriggled into his best breeches and shirt and charged down to the kitchen, where he devoured a hunk of bread and a mug of small beer.

"Ah, there you are, William." Dad appeared in the doorway, wearing a fresh smock, clean boots and the worried frown which hadn't left his face since he'd discovered Mam was pregnant. "I'm not sure why Sir Edward wants to see you this morning, but he does, so you need to be on your best behaviour. Be polite. Speak up when he talks to you and look him in the eye. He could be your employer one day, so it's important to make a good impression."

"Yes, Dad," said William, buttoning up his jacket.

On the way through the village, they called for Mr Hughes. He came out of his shop pointing across the Menai Straits. "There's that locomotive again," he said. William followed his gaze and caught a glimpse of black metal, moving through trees at the water's edge. White steam curled through the branches and a faint puffing sound echoed across the water.

"Is it one of those new steam locomotives?" he asked.

"That's right," said Owain. "They've been running in England for years, but they've only just started to be used here. They're carrying enormous stones to build a new bridge, I believe."

"I've heard that," said Evan. "Why do we need a new bridge when we've got a perfectly good one already? And why can't they use perfectly good horses to cart stone, like they've always done? Putting men out of work, for no good reason – ridiculous, if you ask me."

"We'd better get on." Owain, shook his head at William, who was about to ask more. Dad tended to have explosive views about change.

They set off again, with the two drovers and Owain making plans for their journey to London and William trailing behind, wondering how to make a good impression on Sir Edward. He set his cap at an angle, then straightened it; unbuttoned his jacket and did it up again. He spat on his hand and rubbed the back of his neck, wishing he'd washed more thoroughly that morning. He felt encouraged when they passed Old Griff sitting by his front door and the old man waved. Then, when he looked at the back views of Dad and Owain, deep in conversation and ignoring him completely, he felt depressed.

Plas-y-Bryn, Sir Edward's family home, nestled amongst trees on a hill about a mile from the Evans' farm. They crossed the back field and climbed along a path bordered with majestic beech trees, their branches gauzy with leaf buds. At the end of the path, they faced a great, square mansion. It towered over the countryside, a giant cube of grey and cream stone, surrounded by ornamental gardens and sloping lawns. Rising from its slate roof were turrets, gables and tall, decorated chimneys that reminded William of one of Old Griff's folk tales. Sir Edward was clearly rich.

They passed through enormous wrought-iron gates and scrunched up the long drive until they came to a giant oak door with a bell-rope hanging at one side, which Evan tugged. The door was opened by a manservant wearing a plum-coloured jacket and spotless white breeches. He waved them into a cavernous hallway and led them down a corridor into the library: a vast room lined on three sides with shelves of books. William was fascinated. He'd only handled three books in his whole life: Dad's farm diary, his school bible and Mam's collection of recipes.

On the fourth side of the library were four tall windows, through which he could see the Menai Straits and the mountains beyond. At one end of the room, several paces away, Sir Edward Ellis-Lloyd, a grey-haired and tweed-suited gentleman, was writing at a polished desk.

"Good to see you, Evans… and your sons." He leant across the desk to shake hands with each of them and Mr Hughes. "My word, William, you're almost a man now. Do you want to be a drover, too?"

William glanced at Dad dubiously, but this unexpected encouragement made him bold. Looking Sir Edward straight in the eye, as Dad had told him to, he said: "Oh yes, sir, I do – more than anything else in the world," and finished with his most disarming smile.

"Excellent. I'm glad you've come along," said Sir Edward.

"So am I," said William. His thoughts began to race.

While the men talked business, he worked out a plan. He'd heard that Sir Edward was passionate about steam locomotives – the ones that Dad disapproved of – and there was a painting of one here, hanging on a wall between two book-shelves. He sidled over to take a closer look, making sure that he stayed well within Sir Edward's line of vision. The locomotive had enormous wheels and steam billowed from its tall chimney. William spelt out with difficulty the caption beneath: 'Firefly-Class Locomotive.' As he examined the picture, he kept glancing at Sir Edward, and then looking back at the painting, until the gentleman noticed him and nodded in a friendly way.

Just then, however, Dad interfered with his plans by drawing Sir Edward into an argument. "I can't afford to buy your cattle at that price, sir. I won't be able to cover my costs."

"He's right," said Mr Hughes. "Living costs on the road have gone up. Then, if it's a dry spring, the grass will be poor quality, the cattle won't put on weight and they won't fetch enough at market for us to make a profit. You know that, sir."

"That's a gloomy outlook, Hughes. You and Evans always make a good profit. Besides, you know I'll do a deal if I'm wrong about the price. I won't let your families starve," said Sir Edward. He stood up. "Have a think about my offer, while I talk to William. He may have a question or two about my new painting of a 'Firefly.'" Sir Edward fitted seamlessly into William's plan as he strolled across the polished oak floor and joined him in front of the painting.

"This, young man, was one of the first steam locomotives to run on the Great Western Railway," he explained. "Locomotive design has moved on since then, of course. You may have seen the works' locomotives puffing up the line on the other side of the Menai Straits?"

"We saw the steam from one on the way up here, sir," said William. "I couldn't see much of the locomotive because it was hidden by the trees."

"Well, those trains are carrying the equipment to build the Britannia Bridge, which will be a feat of the finest engineering. It will allow steam trains to cross the straits and take goods to Holyhead quicker than ever before." Sir Edward flung out an arm and whistled, to indicate speed. "It's already happening in many parts of the country. We're behind the times, here on Ynys Mon, but we're catching up. Soon your father won't have to toil over the mountains to make his living. He'll be able to transport cattle to London by rail within a few days. What exciting times we live in, don't you think?"

"Oh yes, sir, I do. I can't wait to have a ride on a steam locomotive," said William.

Sir Edward appealed to Dad and Mr Hughes with a twinkle in his eye, but they were still standing by his desk, looking disgruntled.

"I don't agree with railway transport for cattle, sir," said Dad. "How much will it cost? More than the price of cattle, I'll be bound. And how will we fatten our beasts from the rich English pastures, if they're squashed into a truck on an iron road?"

"But this is progress, Evans. Steam locomotives will make our great Empire even greater. You need to get used to the idea," said Sir Edward. He winked at William as he returned to his desk. "Now, can we reach an agreement if I drop my price by a few pence an ox?" After a few more moments of haggling, a deal was agreed and the three men shook hands on it.

"Did you say you had another matter to discuss, Evans?" Sir Edward settled himself in his ebony chair.

"Yes, sir. I've refused to employ Mostyn and Cade Jones," said Dad.

"Oh yes? Why is that?"

"As you know I caught them trying to steal our cattle last season. I can't risk taking them on another drove."

"I agree. I'll back you on that one," said Sir Edward.

"Sir, I don't agree with Evan's view of Mostyn. There's no proof that he stole our cattle last year. I think we should give him another chance," said Mr Hughes.

Sir Edward looked at him thoughtfully. "Mostyn Jones may or may not be guilty of cattle theft, Hughes, but he can be unreliable and his son, Cade, is undisciplined, which is a great shame. That boy is not stupid and if he was given a chance, I believe he could make something of himself."

"I agree..." began Mr Hughes.

But Sir Edward silenced him with a wave of his hand. "We're not meeting today to decide Cade Jones' future," he said. "We're here to make sure you have a successful drove to London and with that in mind, I'll respect Evans' views, on this occasion. The journey to London is difficult enough, without employing drovers whom you don't trust."

"Thank you, sir, but I'm still worried," said Dad. "Mostyn threatened me when I sacked him. I'm afraid he might try to harm my family whilst I'm away."

"I doubt if he'd go that far," said Sir Edward. "But you needn't worry. I'm told that he and Cade have already left the island to look for work."

Dad shifted uncomfortably on his feet and twisted his hat in his hands. "That's as maybe, sir, but if they don't find work they'll come back here. Which brings me to another problem. My wife's with child. She miscarried our last baby, so I'm worried about her managing the farm without a man around. She's not the sort to spare herself from the lifting and carrying and then if Mostyn Jones starts bothering her she'll get really anxious. The truth is, I don't know what to do, to keep her safe, sir."

"Mm. Yes, I understand your concern. Unfortunate timing, at the start of the season. You'll be away for a fair few weeks. There must be something we can do to ease your mind," said Sir Edward. He thought about this, drumming his fingers on the desk.

William stood nearby, wondering if he dared voice the absurd idea that had just jumped into his head. But miraculously, he didn't have to. Sir Edward seemed to be a mind-reader.

"Here's a suggestion," said the gentleman, at last. "Why not leave Owain at home and take William on the drove instead? Old Griff thinks William's got the makings of a good drover. I asked the boy up here today to offer him a job working on my land, but this is a better opportunity for him."

William just couldn't keep quiet any longer, after that. "That's the solution, sir. Owain would be able to do so much more than me on the farm and although I'm not as experienced as him at droving, I'll soon learn. I learn really quickly, sir. I really do."

Sir Edward laughed and appealed to Dad. "William thinks it's a good idea."

Dad shot William a look of exasperation. "I'm not sure that William understands the seriousness and difficulties of long-distance droving, sir."

"Well, he's got to find out sometime. Owain started his training at William's age, didn't he? Besides, wouldn't it be good for Owain to run the farm for your wife while you're away? He's old enough to take on that responsibility, I would say."

Dad hesitated. "Mm, that's a possibility, I suppose. What do you think, Owain?"

William nodded vigorously at Owain, mouthing, "yes, say yes!"

Owain put a big-brotherly arm around his shoulders. "I like the idea," he said. "I'm sure I could run the farm for a few weeks and Mam will be safer with me, than with William."

"Cheek!" said William, pushing Owain's arm away.

"Excellent!" said Sir Edward. "You can call on me if you need advice." He held out his hand to Dad. "I think that's the best we can do for the moment, Evans. I'm sure you'll find William does better than you think."

Dad shook Sir Edward's hand gloomily. "I hope you're right," he said.

"Keep me informed of your progress. I have non-urgent

business to see to in London, so I'll time my trip down there with your arrival. Then, if there's a problem with your finances, I can sort it out."

"Thank you, sir," said Evan.

Sir Edward turned to William. "You look out for steam locomotives on your travels, young man. Come and tell me what you've seen when you get back."

William thanked Dad repeatedly on the way home. "I'll be the best drover's boy you've ever had."

"Well, that would be a wonderful thing," said Dad. "But I haven't decided for certain to take you. I need to talk to your mam first."

But William knew Mam would agree. She'd been trying to persuade Dad to take him droving all winter. "I just want to tell Lizzie – that you're thinking about taking me, I mean," he added as Dad frowned. "I won't be long. I'll soon be back to do my jobs."

"Go on then," sighed Dad. "But be back before noon. There's a lot to do."

Lizzie was washing her face at the village pump, her hair swept to one side of her swan-like neck.

"Dad's changed his mind. Old Griff and Sir Edward persuaded him. He's going to take me as a drover's boy and Owain's going to stay here and look after Mam. I'm going over the mountains and all the way to London, at last, at last, at last!" chanted William, prancing around the pump like a calf on its new legs.

Lizzie stood up, laughing. "That's great, William. We'll be travelling together." They linked arms and capered about, chanting, "We're going to London, we're going to London," only stopping when they were out of breath.

"It won't all be fun, though," panted Lizzie. "Look at the mountains now."

William looked. A dense cloud had obscured the crags and the Tal-y-Fan pass. "That's nothing," he said.

"You think? It'll feel like this under that cloud," said Lizzie, picking up her bucket and chucking a stream of water at him.

"Hey! Two can play that game." William grabbed the bucket handle and dragged Lizzie, still clutching it, towards the pump where he tried to refill the bucket with water. But it was impossible to pump up water and drag the bucket away from Lizzie at the same time, so they both ended up sliding down on the wet ground, laughing. "You wait – I'll get my own back when we're up in the mountains," said William.

"I won't be coming through the Snowdonia mountains," Lizzie told him. "Me and Mam are going by coach from Bangor to Rhuthun. We'll join you there."

"Hoity toity – listen to you – travelling the grand way," said William.

"Hardly! We'll get even wetter than you will, sitting on the outside of a coach."

"Easier than climbing up there, though," said William.

"I guess so," said Lizzie. Together, they watched the mist swirling around the jagged, peaks of Snowdonia, obscuring the path through the mountains and whatever unknown dangers awaited them.

"Sir Edward says Mostyn and Cade Jones are over there already, looking for work. They might find us," said William.

"What if they do?" said Lizzie. "Cade's harmless enough, if you don't annoy him. Mostyn's trouble, I agree, but your dad will take care of him."

But William still felt uneasy. Back at the farm, mucking out Seren's stable and feeding the pigs, he couldn't get Mostyn and Cade out of his mind. And why did Lizzie have to take Cade's part?

6

16TH – 19TH MARCH 1848

Dinas Farm and Pontarcarrog, Ynys Mon, North Wales

Over the next few days, William forgot his fears and pictured himself as a hero: swaggering through the mountains with Mab leaping at his side, driving cattle expertly through London, making a fortune in Smithfield Market. There were moments when he felt as if he was going to explode with excitement.

Meanwhile, Evan kept him busy filling saddle bags with supplies: hemp leaves, oils and potions to keep men and cattle healthy, emergency rations of onions and oats, plugs of tobacco and blankets for the night watch. When he'd packed the bags, he rubbed soft soap into the brown paper that he and Dad would tie around their legs with leather thongs, to keep out the rain.

His excitement was dampened when Owain filled the tin bath with hot water and insisted he get in. He washed himself, and got out as soon as he could, but failed to prevent Owain from slapping pig fat all over his body. "Ugh! It stinks!" he protested, pulling a face.

"It'll keep you warm, William. You'll be grateful to me once you get up in the mountains and find yourself sleeping rough," said Owain. "You may even have a snow blanket. So, unless you want to die of exposure, which is quite common, for drovers' boys... there was Old Jonathan's son—"

"Yes, I know," interrupted William, who'd heard all this before. "I'll be fighting my way through blizzards, chilled to the bone, while the cattle fall over cliffs to their death." He wiped a glob of pig grease off his chin. "Watch where you're putting that stuff."

"I'm serious, little brother. It's a dangerous journey. Just because you've heard all the stories before, doesn't mean they're not true," said Owain, handing William a newly mended button-up vest and a pair of woollen long johns. William pulled a pair of breeches over these, then put on a smock. Next, he pulled on thick, Bala-knitted socks and slipped his feet into a pair of old clogs, worn down from years of droving, but still usable. Finally, he wriggled into a cut-down greatcoat with an enormous collar that swallowed his ears.

"And another thing," said Owain, when he'd finished laughing. "Don't expect any favours from Dad, because once he's on the road, all he can think about is getting to London and making money. If anyone gets in his way when he's busy, they're in for it – and that includes you... William! Are you listening?"

"Yes, yes," lied William. Free at last from bossy Owain, he ran into the yard to find Mab. Dad was kneeling by the kennels, brushing down his own dog, Rhett.

"I'm going to take Mab up on the field, for a bit more practice, Dad." William released Mab's chain and she jumped up at him excitedly.

"Practice? What for?" asked Dad.

"For the journey. I want to go over the commands."

Dad looked stern. "William – you're surely not expecting to bring that idiotic dog to London with us? She'd frighten half the cattle before we'd even crossed the Tal-y-Fan Pass."

"But she comes everywhere with me," said William. "She'll pine for me if I leave her behind."

"For goodness' sake boy!" thundered Evan. "This isn't a Sunday School outing. I'll have enough to worry about, without having to deal with a rogue dog. She's not coming. Understand?"

For once, William couldn't speak. He just had to get away. He dashed down the lane with Mab on her leash, not caring where he was going. He tore across the bridge with Mab yapping at his heels. He would have run up the hill and down to the sea, but as he turned the corner, he bumped smack into Old Griff.

"Hey! What's going on, boy? You look as if you're being chased by a dragon." Mab bounced around Old Griff, winding her leash around his ankles until William untangled her, muttering apologies.

"Come and sit down." Old Griff opened his garden gate and pointed at the bench by his front door. "The outfit's grand, by the by. That collar should keep your ears warm. Now, what's the matter?"

William was close to tears. "Dad says I can't take Mab on the drove 'cos she's an idiot dog – but he's wrong. I've been working so hard, training her up. I know she won't be a nuisance. I don't want to go if she can't come."

"Now, now, now, don't be so hasty," said Old Griff. "Your dad needs you. Do you think he wants to leave your mam in her present state? You're the only person going with him who'll understand his worries. You can't back out now, just because of a dog. Grow up, William. This is the chance you've been waiting for. Take it." Old Griff pulled a lump of tobacco out of his pocket and broke off a chunk. "And learn to do what you're told while you're at it, or you'll be no good to Evan at all."

Old Griff usually stood up for William, so the old drover's criticism shocked him. He still felt angry with Dad, but maybe Old Griff was right? Maybe he was being a bit selfish? A great adventure lay before him. It would be daft to back out now, even for Mab. And besides, he still wanted to go droving more than anything. "P'raps I am being a bit hasty," he said at last. "You and Dad know a lot more about droving than I do."

"Indeed, we do. And that's the first sensible thing I've heard you say today." Old Griff spat out a gob of tobacco and straightened up. "Forget about Mab. Being without her will be the least of your worries." He thought for a minute, before giving William a one-toothed grin. "Besides, all sorts of unexpected things can happen with drovers' dogs."

"What do you mean?"

"My father was a drover for thirty years and he trained many dogs in his time. Drovers' dogs have a tough life, you know. They get worked hard, and they either survive or they don't. When they die, and they often die young, their masters shed few tears. They're too busy surviving themselves to mourn a dog's passing. Now, my father had one dog that was different. Dylan was his name. Your Mab reminds me of him.

47

He adored my father – followed him everywhere. Sometimes father would leave him behind, because he wasn't the best cow-dog in the world. But Dylan would soon break free, and he always tracked Father down, even if he had to travel a hundred miles. He knew the inns where father stayed, you see. When he did take Dylan with him, father would send the dog home on his own at the end of the journey while he travelled back by coach. More often than not, the dog would get home first. I've known other dogs do that as well, but they don't all make it. Dylan always did though and he lived to a ripe old age."

"Do you think Mab might follow me, like Dylan followed your father?" asked William.

Old Griff laughed. "Oh, I couldn't say, boy. I couldn't say." He scratched Mab's ears so that she plopped her chin on his knees and gazed up at him adoringly. "We'll look after each other while you're away, won't we, girl?" Mab thumped her tail happily against William while Old Griff gazed at the distant mountains. "I'll have to make sure to tie her up when I take her home, though. Your dad would never forgive me if she escaped and tried to come after you." He winked at William and chuckled to himself.

PART TWO

OVER THE
MOUNTAINS
TO ENGLAND

7

20TH MARCH 1848

Ynys Mon, North Wales

When at last the time came for them to leave, William felt as if he'd been turned inside out. He'd grown up waving goodbye to Dad and Owain and now he was the one receiving fond farewells. He was delayed by Mam, who clutched him in a bear hug, while his sisters, Anne and Margaret, both kissed him – one on each cheek. William wriggled free with a lump in his throat.

"Keep safe, Mam – you and the baby," he said. Then he dashed over to Mab's kennel, where she was whining and straining on the end of her leash and flung his arms around her neck. "I'll miss you, Mab. I'll be thinking of you every single day."

"Just go, William. Don't keep your father waiting," sobbed Mam.

Tears stung William's eyes as, with a backward wave, he sprinted down the lane and through the village. His stomach had been churning all morning – he'd thought he was going bring up his porridge at breakfast time – but he knew it was just excitement.

When he reached the Hughes' shop, Lizzie leapt into the road, barring his way with outstretched arms. "Well look at you, Drover Boy – hat and all!" she declared. Before he could stop her, she grabbed his hat brim and pulled it over his eyes, yanking his face so close to hers that he thought she was going to kiss him.

"Lizzie – behave yourself!" said Mrs Hughes, pulling her daughter away. "Don't mind her, William, she's dizzy. We'll be setting off ourselves in a few days. We'll take the mail coach from Bangor and meet you at Rhuthun Market."

"Over the mountains and far away," sang out dizzy Lizzie, twirling around.

"I'll see you there, then," muttered William and carried on up the hill, his face glowing like the rising sun.

Mr Hughes and Old Griff were at the top, directing a stream of bellowing cattle. Old Griff thrust a stick into William's hand. "Take this boy. It belonged to my old dad and I want you to have it. It's cut from elder. Wards off evil spirits and keeps you safe."

"Thanks," said William. He cut the air with the ancient elder stick, half expecting sparks to fly from its tip.

Mr Hughes herded the last of the animals on to the road. "Stay with me, William, and you'll be fine."

Once on the road, William got to work. He smacked a stray ox firmly on the rump, bringing it back in line, then jogged along at the back, encouraging stragglers. Further up the line he could see Tom Morris, assistant drover and travelling blacksmith, and Owain, who was coming with them as far as Menai. Beyond them, the heads of Cefyn Haf, another hired drover and two hired boys, Morgan Parry and John Penn, were bobbing about amongst the herd.

Just before they reached Beaumaris, Dad trotted up on Seren. The Welsh cob picked her way neatly along the side of the drove, her black mane tinted chestnut by the morning sun.

"Wonderful day. We'll stay dry by the looks of it. Ride with me, William. I want to show you a thing or two."

This was a glorious moment for William – Dad inviting him to ride pillion at the head of the drove – an experience he had dreamed of for years. He vaulted on to Seren's back, wrapping his arms around Dad's thick waist. Dad 'hallooed', to clear a path through to the head of the drove, and they were soon cantering past the grey-stone walls of Beaumaris Castle. The town was busy and customers at the George and Dragon cheered them on. William posed like a king in the saddle, waving his hat at these admirers of his very own dad, Evan Evans, the most respected drover in Ynys Mon.

Behind them, the cattle surged through the main street like a black river, bawling and jostling each other between the houses that hemmed them in. Looking back, William spotted Big Beast tossing his magnificent white horns. Villagers hastily retreated behind their front doors, for it was not unusual for a bystander to get kicked or even gored by a frightened ox when a drove passed through.

"We'll soon be at Menai," said Dad. He spurred Seren into a canter and they soared along beside the sparkling sea. They trotted through Menai, with Dad yelling out, "Heiptrw ho!" the ancient, warning cry of drovers. When they reached the Menai suspension bridge, he pulled up, patting Seren's neck as she came to a halt, her flanks beaded with sweat and her nostrils flared.

The Menai suspension bridge dominated the shoreline, dwarfing the cottages along the coast. On either side of the straits, a line of four gigantic limestone arches rose from the sea, supporting the iron suspension cables that held the road above the water.

"Incredible feat of engineering – the road's suspended over the straits like a washing line," shouted Dad into William's ear. "Built by Thomas Telford. I remember when it opened, twenty-two years ago. It changed our lives forever. Did I ever tell you how we got the cattle over the straits before it was built?"

William had many memories of being told this tale as the family sat around their glowing kitchen fire on cold winter nights, but he humoured Dad by saying, "Tell me again."

Dad pointed across the straits. "See that fast-running water between the sands and our island? When I learned to be a drover's boy, there was no bridge for us to cross. We had to drive the cattle into the water and make them swim to the sands on the other side. My father would take a calf in a boat, so that its mother would plunge into the water after it and the rest of the herd would follow. Us boys and the drovers would row alongside them."

"Did any of them ever get washed out to sea?" asked William, in time-honoured fashion. "Rarely. And if they did, they often managed to swim to shore further down. Timing had to be perfect. We had to reach the sands before the tide came in. My father was an expert, as was his father and grandfather before him, going back for generations. They were fearless, brave men, all of them and you should be proud to be their descendent."

The mountains of Snowdonia loomed over them as they approached the bridge, reminding William that he would soon be passing beneath their mighty peaks. As they rode on to the bridge, foaming waves crashed against the arches and slopped against the shore. An icy wind savaged them, rattling the iron suspension cables, numbing William's ears, in spite of his enormous collar, and making his jaw ache. He could feel Seren bracing herself as the blast forced her sideways, but she battled on, leaving the island of Ynys Mon behind and prancing on to the mainland of North Wales.

"Here begins your journey to London, William," shouted Dad. "You'll remember this day for the rest of your life—"

He was interrupted by a deafening scream, louder than the wind. This was followed by a clanking and shushing and a flash of fire, as a steam locomotive rushed past on the bank above them. It was travelling at tremendous speed – faster than a galloping horse – and pulling a line of trucks filled with massive blocks of stone.

"A steam locomotive, Dad. A steam locomotive! It's carrying stones to build the new bridge, like Sir Edward said." William jumped up and down in the saddle with excitement.

"What are you looking so pleased about?" Dad snarled, as soon as they could hear each other again. "That heap of metal will ruin our lives. When that railway bridge is built, trains will be able to carry goods, including livestock, all the way from Ynys Mon to London. How will long-distance drovers, like us, make a living then?"

But William hardly heard. He watched the locomotive until it was out of sight. "What makes it move, Dad? Nothing's pulling or pushing it. What makes it go?"

"What makes it go?" yelled Dad, making Seren skitter as he thumped her saddle with rage. "Is that all you're interested in? What makes it go? It's the devil that makes it go, as far as I'm concerned." He steered Seren on to the sands, from where they watched the stream of cattle behind them clattering over the wooden planks on the bridge. "Down you get, William. You won't ride with me again before we get to London – you'll be treated like the other boys. I'll head these animals off towards the sands and you do the same with the rest as they come off the bridge. When they've all gone through, join Mr Hughes and Tom at the back. I'll go on ahead as soon as Tom gets here."

"All right, Dad. See you in Aber." William slid off Seren and faced the black, heaving mass of cattle. They surged off the bridge lamenting and jostling each other, their eyes rolling with fear. William's instinct was to run, but he stood his ground. The last thing he wanted was to look a fool in front of John, Morgan and Cefyn, who were driving the oxen towards him – and Dad was still watching him as well. This was his chance to show he could do the job.

"I'm sending them your way!" he yelled to John and Morgan as the black stream of oxen headed on to the sand.

"Keep them coming!" John yelled back.

The three boys worked as a team and by the time Mr Hughes and Tom Morris appeared with the stragglers, the rest of the herd was ambling along the shore.

William idolised Tom Morris, the blacksmith. He was as strong as a bull and a fearless fighter. But he was also fair-minded and funny. He had a habit of cracking jokes whilst running his hands through his mass of black hair with an infectious laugh. He rode an old brown horse, slung with blacksmith's tools, and specialised in shoeing both cattle and horses, which made him essential to long-distance drovers like William's dad. Not only that; he was old enough to have a drovers' licence and spoke English fluently, which made him a formidable haggler in the English markets.

William was looking forward to working with Tom, but Mr Hughes had other ideas. "You go on ahead, Tom," he called. "Cefyn and the boys can help me here."

"Right you are. Hurry the beasts along or we won't get them off the sands before the tide turns." Tom's blacksmith's tools rattled as he kicked his horse into action and set off. Soon he had become a distant blot between the dark column of cattle and the grey sea.

They drove the last of the cattle up the winding road to Aber just before sunset. They would stay here for two nights so that the cattle could be shod, in preparation for the long journey ahead. There were rich pastures here and the local blacksmith, Alun Bran, would help with the cattle-shoeing. William cheered as a square of whitewashed houses, the smithy and the Black Bull inn came into view, but before he could rest, the cattle had to be driven into the pastures. This took time, because the animals were confused by their new surroundings and kept blundering off in different directions.

"They're all mixed up so they're trying to find their friends," Mr Hughes explained. "Boys, you help Tom, while I give Evan a hand."

Evan was still on horseback at the front of the herd, turning cattle off the village road and into the field. Once the herd was settled, he dismounted and handed Seren to a stable lad. "Come on, Robert, time for supper," he said.

William had eaten nothing but a hunk of bread since breakfast and the mention of food made him ravenous. He chased after Dad and Mr Hughes as they walked over to the Black Bull, but when he caught them up, he got a surprise. Dad looked down at him as if he were a stranger, blocking the doorway with his great bulk.

"Where do you think you're going, William?"

"To get something to eat, Dad."

"Not with us, you're not. You're a drover's boy now and you'll be treated like the rest. Now get back out there and finish the job." Dad turned his back and disappeared into the bar, leaving William in shock. He hadn't expected to be treated like this by his own father.

"Oh dear, daddy's boy has got to go hungry. What a shame." William looked around to see Morgan and John, leaning against a wall, sniggering.

"That's enough, lads," said Tom. "I need the three of you to work as a team tonight. So, no messing, if you want your pay – understand?"

"Yes, Tom."

The three of them followed Tom into the pastures, where the cattle were grazing peacefully. "Sleep with one eye open. There's nothing to stop these beasts wandering off, apart from you three and Cefyn. Bed down at intervals around the edge of the field –there, there and there. Cefyn will sleep by the road." Tom pointed to four separate locations.

"It's warmer sleeping together," grumbled Morgan. He looked up at the clear sky. "There might be a frost."

"You're being paid to be lookouts, not to keep warm. I'm off to the inn and I'll be back out soon with blankets and food. In the meantime, sort out your beds," said Tom, walking off.

Morgan and John took knives out of their pockets and began to cut handfuls of long grass from the edge of the field.

"What are you doing?" William asked.

"Making our beds," replied Morgan. "Why? Are you expecting daddy to bring you a mattress?" He and John smirked at each other again.

"No," said William. He stomped over to his sleeping spot, feeling stupid. There, he took out his own knife and slashed angrily at the undergrowth. When he'd got a big enough pile, he flung himself on to it and then leapt up again clutching his legs and sucking one hand. "Ow!"

Morgan and John came running over, laughing. "Did you forget to check for thorns? Oh dear. Let's have a look. Here's the culprit." Morgan yanked at a dead bramble stalk that had got caught amongst the grass. "Hidden in those bushes you'll find some old hay. Help yourself," said Morgan.

"Thanks," mumbled William. Soon he had gathered an armful of damp, rotting hay and heaped it on to his bed.

Presently Tom returned with supplies. "You won't get food like this every night," he said. "Make the most of it."

He handed each of them a mug of beer and a slice of lambs-tail pie, which they ate greedily, gulping down beer between mouthfuls. William couldn't remember ever feeling so hungry. He savoured every mouthful of pie and every swig of beer and could have eaten the same again, but Tom didn't offer second helpings. Instead, he tossed them some tatty blankets. "Make yourselves comfortable. Any problems with the cattle, wake Cefyn. He'll be out soon. It's my turn to sleep at the inn tonight. Sweet dreams."

William collapsed on to his heap of grass, overcome with exhaustion. It was a long time since he'd walked so far in a day and his legs ached. It was almost dark and candlelight flickered dimly through the windows of the Black Bull. A stone dug into his back and cold seeped up from the ground. The air felt close to freezing. He drew the blanket tightly around his body, but the cold penetrated his boots and stung his earlobes. He understood now why Owain had insisted on smearing pig fat all over him and was glad of the itchy, knitted vest that Mam had made him wear.

He thought of Mab, snug in her kennel. If she'd been with him, she could have cuddled up and kept him warm in his cold, prickly bed. It was mean of Dad not to let him bring her – but then look at the way Dad had refused to let him, or John or Morgan eat in the Black Bull. What other refusals lay ahead? He felt homesick already. He worried about Mam and the unborn baby; missed Old Griff, who always helped him; and smiled at the memory of Lizzie hanging on to his hat when she'd said goodbye in Pontarcarrog. A jutting stone tormented his hip and when he turned over, six more dug into his side. The craggy outlines of the mountains seemed so near that when he craned his neck to see their peaks, he felt as though they were bending over him. But gradually the darkness swallowed them and the gentle breathing of the cattle soothed him into a restless sleep.

8

21ST MARCH 1848

Aber: the village at the foot of the mountains, North Wales

Alun Bran, the village blacksmith, staggered out of the smithy early next morning, weighed down with boxes of cattle shoes and nails. When he saw William, he did a double take. "You must be Evan Evan's son and no mistake," he said. William, who was still waking up after a restless night on the cold, lumpy ground, managed a nod.

"Good to see you, Alun," said Evan. The two men exchanged news, with much joking and laughter, before planning the day. Evan organised his men into two teams. William, Cefyn and Tom would work in the pen up the hill, while he, Alun and Robert would work in the smithy. Morgan and John would bring the cattle to each team and drive them back to pasture when they were done.

"Why aren't Mostyn and Cade Jones with you?" asked Alun, when Evan had finished giving instructions. "What's going on between you? They came through here last week.

Fed up they were – can't find work. Flew into a rage when I mentioned your name."

William's heart sank. So, Mostyn Jones was still angry with Dad – bad news. He scanned the mountainside, half expecting to see Mostyn and Cade up there, spying on them.

"That's my business." Evan clenched his fists. "One thing's for sure: that man will never work for me again."

Mr Hughes, who was just coming out of the inn, heard the conversation and joined them. "In my opinion, Evan should have given them a second chance," he said. "It's a cruel thing, to deny a family man a chance to earn his living."

"Who asked you?" growled Evan.

But Alun Bran interrupted. "It's a shame, in one way," he said. "Mostyn's a skilled cattle handler – could have done with him here today. But from the look on your face, Evan, I can see the matter's serious. I wouldn't like to get on the wrong side of Mostyn or his son, I must say."

He put a peace-making hand on Mr Hughes' arm and steered him towards the smithy. "Now, Robert, let me show you my new furnace. You'll be impressed."

"I wouldn't like to get on the wrong side of the Joneses either," Morgan whispered into William's ear. "The last time I saw Cade Jones, he said he's going to really show you what he can do with a stone next time he sees you."

So, now Cade was boasting about his stone-throwing skills. "Let him try!" said William.

Evan slung a coil of rope over his shoulder. "Right, everyone, let's get started!"

William, Tom and Cefyn staggered up the hill to the cattle pen with the heavy boxes of nails and cattle shoes that Alun Bran had spent the winter months forging. The shoes were half-moons of iron, designed to fit on to each side of an ox's cloven hoof. Each hoof needed two shoes – eight shoes per ox – which for a whole herd was a lot of shoes to be carried up a hill. A big pot of pig fat was needed as well, so that William could grease the shoes and nails. There were strong ropes that would hold the oxen still whilst the shoeing was being done. When they had the equipment set out, Morgan drove six oxen into the stone pen and William picked out one ox for Tom to shoe.

"Good start," said Tom as he threw a noose over the animal's head. "Let's do this fella, then."

William and Cefyn each grabbed one horn whilst Tom tied the ox to a post. It tossed its head with a force that almost wrenched William's arms from their sockets. That done, Tom flicked a second rope into the air with precision, so that a loop formed and lassoed the ox's body. As Tom jerked the rope tight around its legs, Cefyn slapped its rump and it thumped to the ground. Cefyn then tied its front legs together and stuck a v-shaped stick between them to keep the ox still while Tom did the same with its back legs. Once the ox was secured, Cefyn grabbed a scraper and trimmed its front hooves, checking they were healthy as he worked.

"Nails, William," called Tom, positioning a half-moon-shaped shoe on one side of a cloven hoof. William handed Tom the nails and watched him hammer them into the hoof through ready-made holes in the shoe. When this was done, Tom attached another shoe to the opposite side of the hoof in the same way. Kerchink, kerchink, kerchink! The sound of hammering echoed around the mountains. Meanwhile Cefyn cleaned the ox's back hooves ready for Tom to repeat the process. William's job was to feed a constant supply of nails to Tom, and to check that each nail was smoothed off when a hoof was finished. Tom worked efficiently, so that each animal was speedily shod, released, and pushed out to Morgan, while William fetched the next one. It was exhausting work and by the time the sun was high in the sky, he was aching all over.

"We'll break now," said Tom, at last. He flung himself on to the spongy grass, uncorked a flask of beer and passed it round with a loaf of barley bread. "Have you done this before?"

William shook his head as he broke off a lump of bread and stuffed it into his mouth.

"Well, you're a natural, it seems to me," said Tom. "You work well with the cattle. Some lads get them all wound up, but you know how to keep them calm."

"Dad taught me that," said William. "He says if an animal trusts you, it'll do what you want. Mind you, I'd never trust a man again if I was one of these oxen. Being shod must be terrifying."

"They get over it," said Tom. "Got short memories. If you didn't shoe them, their hooves would get wrecked on the hard, English roads. Most of them wouldn't make it to London."

William lay on his back, watching wispy clouds scud across the sky above the jagged, grey rocks of the mountain pass and wondered if he would enjoy being a blacksmith. Down the hill, Dad's team was still shoeing and men's shouts, the braying of cattle and the clink of hammers filled his ears.

"Right lads. Let's get on. We've done twenty-eight so far. We'll have sixty done by sunset – easy," said Tom, jumping to his feet.

"Easy? Where've you been all morning?" laughed Cefyn. "I'll show you 'easy' when I put a jug to my lips tonight!"

William struggled to his feet, feeling as though his body had been trampled by a giant. Tom laughed. "You'll be fine when you've warmed up, lad. I'd lend you these, but I need them myself today." He rolled up his sleeves to show muscles the size of rams' horns.

"Do you ever get a nail in the wrong place?" William asked, as Tom hammered along the hoof-edge of the next bellowing animal.

"Not often." Tom took another nail. "You soon learn to be careful. An upside-down ox in pain is no fun. I nearly had all my teeth kicked out once. Right, this one's done. Bring us the next."

William found a new confidence as they worked, swinging into a rhythm, so that by late afternoon they were nearing Tom's target of sixty cattle. It was then that Big Beast appeared. William recognised his bellowing as Morgan drove him across the field.

"Here comes trouble," said Cefyn. "This one's half a head higher than the others and he's in a state."

"Leave him to me. He knows my voice," said William. He turned to Big Beast. "Come boy, steady now." He spoke low, as Dad had taught him and Big Beast responded, allowing him to approach and slip the noose over his head. Big Beast also allowed Cefyn to tie the rope to the post. He obediently stayed still while Tom curled the lasso in the air. But the moment he felt the rope around his legs, he knew he had been betrayed. He let out a cry like the lament of the dead and flung himself away from the post, diving headfirst to the ground. As he fell, he cracked one horn on a rock and the top half snapped off.

"Help!" yelled William as he, Tom and Cefyn flung themselves at the bucking animal. Morgan and John rushed to the rescue. Even with the five of them, it was a gargantuan effort to get the terrified Big Beast calmed down, shod and driven up to the top field, with the rest of the cattle.

"What'll Dad say? Big Beast's his favourite. He was expected to fetch a good price," said William, picking up the discarded section of horn and running his finger along the jagged edge.

"The state of an ox's horns doesn't affect the value of its meat." Tom put an arm around William's shoulders. "This wasn't your fault, William. You're doing a great job and I'll make sure Evan knows it." But William doubted if Tom's praise would make any difference to Dad's views.

They finished shoeing at sunset, beneath a crimson sky. As soon as they'd cleared up, William dragged himself up to the top field with Tom, to check on Big Beast. John and Morgan followed them, so they could gloat about the accident, William thought. Dad was already there, watching the oxen tear up mouthfuls of grass, their feet twitching with the unfamiliar feel of their shoes. Big Beast lifted his head, his damaged horn poking up like a broken branch.

"What happened to him?" asked Dad.

"He had one of his panics and bashed his horn on a rock," said William. The look Dad gave him made him feel guilty, even though Tom had said the broken horn wasn't his fault.

"Shame. We haven't had an accident like that in years. Look at the state of him. It might knock something off his value," said Dad.

"You know that's unlikely, Evan," said Tom. "I've told William, broken horns don't affect the value of the meat.

These things happen from time to time. None of us are to blame. William's worked hard and done a good job today. He deserves your praise."

Evan glared at Tom. "I'll decide when to praise my own son, thank you," he said.

Tom sighed, and pushed John and Morgan forward. "These boys want paying, Evan."

Evan delved into his pocket, counted out two sets of coins and handed them over. "Well done, lads. Good day's work. If you do as well tomorrow morning, I'll be asking for you on my next drove."

Why was Dad happy to praise Morgan and John, but not him? Resentfully, William stepped in front of Dad and held out his hand, palm upwards.

Evan shook his head. "You're not casual labour, William. You're family and you're my apprentice. You get free food and free training. That's all."

Tom put a hand on William's shoulder. "Surely William should be paid for today, Evan? He's been working alongside John and Morgan and he's worked just as hard as they have."

Evan frowned. "So, you think you can tell me when I should pay my son, as well as when I should praise him, do you?"

But Tom remained unmoved. "Not at all. I just like to see fairness. After all, you always treat Owain to extra pay if he's done well – and he's family."

William bit his lips, to hide a smile. Clearly, Tom wasn't afraid of standing up to Dad. And by the look on Dad's face, he was beginning to waver. William thrust his hand further forward, hopefully.

"All right, all right! I'll say this for you, Tom Morris, you don't give up – but then, maybe that's why I employ you."

Dad dropped some coins into William's hand. "That's a special payment, William. If you think today was hard, wait until you've driven one hundred and fifty cattle through the pass tomorrow – in bad weather, by the looks of it." He waved at the darkening sky. "I'll think about paying you a regular wage when we get to Rhuthun and I've seen how you cope in the days ahead. Now go and get supper, the three of you."

"I wish my dad wasn't so harsh," William complained to Morgan as they raced down the hill to the Black Bull.

"You think that's harsh?" said Morgan. "At least you've got a dad – and he feeds you. My dad's dead. If I don't get paid, I don't eat and neither do my mam or my sister."

9

22ND MARCH 1848

The Tal-y-Fan pass, North Wales

They finished shoeing the cattle around noon the next day.

"Ugh! Here we go. Back to stone picking. I wish I were coming with you, William Evans," said Morgan. William watched him and John set off for home, leaping from rock to rock down the hill towards the white-flecked waves of the Menai Straits.

"No time to dawdle, William," called Dad. "We need to get the cattle into the pens at the head of the Tal-y-Fan pass before nightfall."

"Coming!" William ran excitedly towards the craggy mountains that loomed above him. He had been longing to travel through the Tal-y-Fan pass since he was a small boy and now at last his time had come.

"Looks like hail. Let's hope we get the cattle settled before a storm comes," said Dad as they drove the cattle on to the road. Up ahead, iron-grey clouds blotted out the mountain tops and freezing air stung William's cheeks. He turned up his coat collar and pulled the brim of his hat over his ears, surprised by the force of the howling wind.

The road rose gently at first, through woodland bounded on one side by a stream and on the other by a wall. This kept the oxen going forward, stumbling on their new metal shoes. As before, William and Mr Hughes brought up the rear. Soon, the road got steeper so that the cattle, unused to climbing hills, slowed right down or stopped altogether. "Keep them going, William," shouted Mr Hughes. "Use your stick if you have to."

William did his best. He sympathised with the cattle, for there were no hills this steep on Ynys Mon and his legs were soon aching torturously. Then they came out into open country to find themselves enveloped by a wild storm. Up ahead, William saw Tom dismount and lead his horse, using his dog, Kyn, to keep his group of cattle together. An icy wind tore at William's clothes and flung hailstones in his face. Panic broke out amongst the beasts that he and Mr Hughes were driving. No longer restrained by streams or walls, they fled in all directions, seeking shelter where none was to be found. Mr Hughes stayed at the back, trying to keep the animals going forward, but William found himself surrounded by swaying horns and flailing hooves and didn't know which way to turn.

Tom came back to help, clambering alongside them through the mist. "Get that one, William. Call Kyn," he yelled.

William whistled for Kyn and sent him scrambling after an ox that had left the path and was in danger of laming itself on hidden boulders. The dog snaked expertly around the tussocks of grass and stone, capering around the ox and driving it back to the herd. Once it was safe, William and Tom went after another beast and another, whilst hail, rain and buffeting wind attacked them mercilessly. William began to despair that they would ever reach the head of the pass. It was easy to imagine how you could get lost in the mist and die of exposure. But at last they stopped climbing, and reached a plateau. He could just see Tom, shouting and pointing, but his words were lost on the shrieking wind. Peering into the mist, William made out the dark shapes of cattle that had reached the stone enclosures and were being driven into them by Dad and Cefyn, only a couple of hundred yards away.

"William – round up those stragglers!" yelled Mr Hughes.

William mustered a final burst of energy and chased after a small group of oxen heading into the gloom. He had to spring across ankle-twisting humps of grass to cut them off, but he succeeded and before long, he was driving them triumphantly into the pens. Once all the cattle they could find were secured, he, Tom and Mr Hughes struggled over to the meagre shelter of an over-hanging rock. Here they huddled together with Dad and Cefyn, soaked to the skin and numb with cold, while rain pelted down.

Eventually, but not before William had lost all sensation in his hands and feet, the mist lifted, the wind subsided, and the rain stopped.

"We'll be off now, Tom," said Evan, climbing into Seren's saddle. "Do you want a lift, Robert, or would you rather walk?"

Mr Hughes patted Seren's flank. "I think I can bury our differences for a while, if it means a jug of beer and a hot meal," he said, swinging himself on to Seren's back, behind Evan. The horse shifted under his weight, and Evan steadied her.

William's stomach rumbled at the thought of beer and a hot meal. "Where are you going, Dad?" he asked.

"He's off to a nice warm bed at Farmer Moss's place," said Tom, pointing up the track. "It's all right for some."

Evan laughed. "Away with you! What do you think I pay for you for? Many's the time I've slept out in rough weather. I deserve a bit of comfort, these days." He looked down at his son. "William, tomorrow at first light I need you to count all the cattle. If there are any beasts still missing, they'll have to be found. We can't afford to lose a single ox. Don't forget, it's the sale of each one that puts the food on your plate. We're making them walk two hundred and fifty miles through unfamiliar lands. That's not a natural thing for them and they need to be well looked after. We don't want to end up with a load of skinny, sick beasts that fetch nothing in Smithfield Market. Do you understand?"

"Yes, Dad," said William, blowing on his freezing hands.

"Good. We won't be far away. The farmhouse we're going to is just around that bend. See you in the morning."

Wearily, William watched Seren fade into the mist, as she picked her way along the track. His stomach felt hollow as a dead tree and he still couldn't feel his feet. Water had run inside his coat and soaked his woollen vests, so they were damp and heavy. His thighs ached, his cheeks smarted from the hail attack – and Dad's only concern was a warm bed and the welfare of his cattle.

"Cold supper tonight. It's too wet for a fire," said Tom, rummaging in his supplies. He passed around chunks of dry bread and cheese and handed William a flask. "Drink this, it'll warm you up."

"Thanks." William poured the liquid generously down his throat. "Aaah… I'm on fire!" He danced around clutching his neck.

"Never mind fire. Stand still. You're splashing mud on my supper," said Cefyn.

"I told you it would warm you up," laughed Tom.

William was so hungry that he would have eaten rats without complaint, so he swallowed his bread and cheese in a few mouthfuls. The food gave him enough energy to help Cefyn and Tom gather dead heather and soggy bracken to make a bed under the over-hanging rock.

"Bit damp, but you'll soon get warm," said Tom.

William pulled the brim of his hat closely around his ears, wrapped himself up to his chin in his blanket and snuggled down between the two drovers. He lay listening to their feeble jokes as they shared what was left in Tom's flask and felt safe for the first time that day. But the feeling didn't last long. Just as he was drifting into sleep, Cefyn dug him in the ribs with a chuckle.

"Hey, William, listen. Can you hear the tomb ghosts?"

William's eyes snapped open. "Tomb ghosts? Where?" He sat up and looked around, but it was far too dark to see anything. He couldn't even see Tom or Cefyn in the absolute blackness and they were right next to him.

"Oh, you won't see them, but you may hear them wail – 'oooohaaa'. On wet, moonless nights they get lonely and wander the mountains, looking for a victim to take back to their tomb… 'oooohaaa.'"

"Shush, Cefyn. You'll scare the boy. Let him sleep," said Tom.

But William guessed Cefyn was fooling. "Fear not!" he said. "I have Old Griff's ancient elder wand, to protect me from evil spirits." He whipped the stick out from his blanket and slashed it in Cefyn's direction.

"Ow! Get off. That's my nose," shouted Cefyn, fending off William, but failing to grab the stick. They grappled with each other, snorting with laughter, until Tom complained about the noise. A few minutes after that, Cefyn began to snore.

William tucked the stick back into his blanket and shut his eyes, but the image of a tomb seemed to be imprinted on his eyelids. "Is there really a tomb, Tom?"

Tom sighed. "Am I never to be allowed to go to sleep? Yes. There are a few ancient stone tombs in these mountains. There's one near this path. You'll see it in the morning, if the weather clears. All the tombs are empty now, so there's nothing to fear."

But William's thoughts were on a different track. "Could grown-up men shelter in them?"

"Of course; they were built to house the dead. Why are you bothering with this now?" said Tom.

"I just wondered where Mostyn and Cade Jones had got to. I wondered if they might be sheltering in one."

"Oh, William – forget about Mostyn and Cade Jones. They're at least two days ahead of us. I doubt if we'll come across them at all on this trip. And you certainly wouldn't find Mostyn sleeping in a tomb. He's too fond of his drink. He'll always kip down near an inn – and the nearest inn from here is ten miles away. Now get some sleep."

10

23RD MARCH 1848

The Tal-y-Fan pass, North Wales

William woke up thinking about tombs. The mist had lifted and the mountains glowed pink from the rising sun. He looked around for Cefyn and Tom who were over in the pens, checking the cattle. Then he scanned the hillside for the tomb and saw what he might be looking for – a pile of enormous stones, a few yards above the path. He was pretty sure that Tom was right: Mostyn and Cade would be miles away by now, but he still wanted to make sure.

His body felt like a lump of damp clay as he pushed off his blankets and stood up, shivering. He stumbled over hummocks of grass and climbed up until he was standing in front of a black hole the width of his arm-span. Two giant slabs of white stone formed the sides of the tomb and a third slab was balanced across the top of them to form the roof. William crouched down and peered inside, his heart thumping. The tomb appeared to have been dug into the hillside, but it was too dark inside to see how far in it went. He picked up a small stone and skimmed it into the blackness. It hit what sounded like a bigger stone and then there was silence. He could smell damp and stale air; but no bodies, either alive or rotting. He crawled into the darkness, feeling the earth floor for bits of food or other signs of habitation, but all he found was sheep droppings. There was no evidence that Mostyn and Cade had spent the night there – not that he was afraid of them, of course.

Tom's voice broke into the black silence. "What are you doing, William? You're meant to be counting cattle."

With great relief, William shuffled backwards into the light and ran back to his job. The oxen were hard to count – shifting about and waving their horns, but as far as he could tell, none were missing. Across the sea, William could just see the hump of Ynys Mon and he prayed that Mam was well. Would Mab be pining for him? He missed the scent of her soft fur when he buried his face in her neck. Back at the camp he gulped down mouthfuls of cold, lumpy porridge and boiled onions.

"Ugh! The cattle get fed better than this," he complained.

"You know why?" said Tom. "Because they'll make more money for us than you will. Stop moaning and pack up your bedding."

Soon, Dad and Mr Hughes arrived, riding Seren and looking as if they'd had a comfortable night.

"We'll get down to the river while the weather's still good," Evan told Tom. "There's another storm coming by my reckoning and I want to get at least half the herd across before nightfall."

"Which river?" William asked as he and Tom drove the cattle on to the path.

"The Conwy. We have to take the cattle over on the Tal-y-Cafn ferry. It's not a problem unless there's a storm. Then the river turns into a torrent and the ferry crossing gets dangerous."

Further on, the pass was narrower and overhung with jagged rocks. By the time they reached the Conwy Valley, rain clouds were starting to build again. Craggy mountains and rounded hills stretched as far as William could see, their peaks granite-grey and purple against the thundery sky. Down in the valley, the River Conwy gleamed and swirled between dark trees and lime-green mosses.

"Take it easy, William," said Mr Hughes as they prepared to follow the rest of the herd down the steep slope to the river. "The ground's slippery and we don't want oxen getting injured. See how Tom and Cefyn are holding back and letting each ox find its feet?" William did his best to guide the poor oxen as they slithered on the slippery stones and mud, some bellowing with fear. To his relief, they managed to get the whole herd safely down to the riverbank, where Dad was waiting for them.

"Well done. We've made good time. I'm going to bargain with the ferryman. Join me when the cattle are in the pens," he said.

The ferry consisted of a wide, wooden raft with rails down each side. It see-sawed about on the river as the choppy waters nudged it against the bank. A wooden platform with wheels was positioned nearby, so that men and animals could board easily. The stout old ferryman and his young assistant were leaning on their poles, haggling with Evan when William, Mr Hughes, Tom and Cefyn arrived.

"Costs more when the river's rising. More risk, more time," the ferryman was saying.

"Looks dangerous to me, Evan. We should wait until tomorrow," said Mr Hughes.

"We could wait all week for the weather to improve; just think of the cost!" snapped Evan. He turned to the ferryman. "You think it's safe?"

"I'll risk it," said the ferryman.

"Of course, you will, for what we're paying," said Mr Hughes.

The ferryman shrugged. "We'll be all right if you keep your cattle calm. If they take fright, they could have us over."

"We know how to handle our cattle," said Evan. He turned to his team. "You heard him? Calm and steady. If we're careful, we should be able to get a good number over before dusk. Ten at a time, except when there's a horse on as well. I'll take Seren on the first trip. You come over on the next one with your horse and equipment, Tom. Cefyn, you travel back and forth on the ferry. William and Robert will bring groups of cattle to the ferry and come over with the last load. I'll get some boys from the village to mind the beasts left on this side tonight."

Tom and Mr Hughes exchanged worried looks. The mountaintops were now blotted out by malevolent, charcoal-coloured clouds. "Those look like storm clouds to me. I can hear distant thunder," said Mr Hughes. William thought he'd seen lightning, but it was too far away to be sure.

"Maybe Robert's right – we should wait until the morning," said Tom.

"No," said Evan. "I don't want the expense of an extra night at the Tal-y-Cafn inn. The ferryman knows what he's doing."

"Don't you worry, I'll call a halt if conditions get dangerous," said the ferryman.

"Well, I think you're making a bad decision, Evan," said Mr Hughes.

But Evan ignored him, coaxing Seren on to the ferry and tethering her to the railing. "Bring on the oxen!" he commanded.

Tom and Mr Hughes shared a look of exasperation. "What's the point of me being his deputy, when he never listens to my advice?" said Mr Hughes.

"He's that stubborn when he's set his mind on something, nothing can shift him," agreed Tom.

William was glad to learn that Tom and Mr Hughes found Dad as stubborn as he did. However, the task of driving the first load of cattle on to the ferry soon put everything else out of his mind. The combined weight of the cattle had to be distributed evenly across the wooden boards because an uneven load could cause the ferry to capsize. The oxen were hungry, wet, and frightened and could see no possible advantage in going on to the ferry at all, let alone in any particular order. William and Cefyn would just get one ox settled, when another would shift around and unsettle the others. Mr Hughes, who was having just as much trouble as William, shouted conflicting instructions across their black, heaving backs. By the time the oxen were all safely on board and the ferryman had pushed off from the bank with his pole, William was covered in bruises.

"Well, at least that's the first lot over," he said, as he squelched back up the riverbank.

But Mr Hughes was staring up at the mountains. "There's another rumble of thunder. I just hope Evan knows what he's doing."

Down on the river, the ferrymen were forcing their poles against the current to keep the ferry on course. But

Dad wasn't going to give up. As soon as one load of oxen reached the far bank, he signalled across the water to keep them coming.

Tom went over next, with his horse and equipment and another six oxen. Cefyn stayed by the landing stage while William and Mr Hughes drove the cattle down to him in groups of ten. "Pack them tight and keep them bunched in the middle," the ferryman shouted.

Foaming white streams, fed by the storm, cascaded down the mountainsides into the River Conwy, so that on each new trip, the river was more turbulent and the oxen became more frightened. William could see Tom and Dad struggling to unload them as the water eddied and swirled. Nevertheless, nearly half the cattle had crossed over by the time the ferryman yelled out the words that William longed to hear: "It's getting too dangerous. We'll make this the last trip."

A wall of rain was now marching up the valley. Driven by a howling wind, it lashed William's face and ran in rivulets down his neck. Mr Hughes seemed to be having problems gathering the last group of oxen and William soon saw why. At the back of the group was Big Beast, bawling, swinging his head and unsettling the rest of the group as they slithered down to the river.

William bounded up the bank. "I'll see to him," he shouted, flinging one arm across Big Beast's neck and grabbing his damaged horn with the other. "All right, boy, calm down, calm down…" He spoke soothingly into Big Beast's ear, just as he had seen Dad do when an ox took fright. To his relief, it worked. Big Beast stopped moaning and began to follow the other oxen, but now he was travelling far too fast. William bounced along with him, still hanging on to his horns and trying to avoid being kicked. "Steady, boy, steady," he kept saying, but Big Beast raced on. At the water's edge, the front oxen skittered and skidded on the sodden wooden planks as Mr Hughes drove them on to the rocking ferry. The rumbles of thunder were louder now, and the river was flowing at a horrifying speed.

William had just got Big Beast pointed at the raft, when prongs of white lightning pierced the clouds and there was a deafening crack of thunder right overhead. This spooked Big Beast, who leapt on to the ferry, roaring louder than the wind, and charged straight at the down-river railing with William still clinging to his horns.

"Get that animal off before we tip sideways!" shouted the ferryman.

But Big Beast did that for himself. He careered into the railing, crashed through it and plunged into the river, with William still clinging to his horns. William hit the water with a force that knocked the air out of his lungs. The ferry lunged sideways, then righted itself, so that the water sucked him under and threw him out again, swamping his head and dislodging one hand from Big Beast's good horn. Somehow, he hung on to the damaged horn with the other as he rose to the surface, gasping and kicking. The river was sweeping them away from the ferry. If he let go of Big Beast now, he would certainly drown.

He lunged for Big Beast's good horn with all his might and brought himself up against the ox's flank. His fingers brushed the base of the horn, but couldn't get a grip. He slipped back, spluttering as water shot up his nostrils and down his throat. He was just about hanging on with one hand, his arm burning with pain, and he knew he mustn't give up.

A rock jutting out of the water gave him his chance. As they rushed past, he levered his foot against it and with a gigantic effort, hurled himself on to Big Beast's back, clutching the good horn with his free hand. Then, somehow, he managed to position himself so that he was lying along Big Beast's back with his head wedged against the ox's neck. As he lay there, coughing and spluttering, the rhythm of four powerful legs throbbed through his body as Big Beast swam his way across the current.

Gratefully, William hung on, but his limbs were so cold now that he could hardly manage to grip. As Big Beast battled on, he began to feel drowsy and wanted to slip into the water and go to sleep. But then they came to a bend in the river, where the water slowed as it hit the bank and William heard shouting. The voice was familiar – it wanted him to do something, but he wasn't sure what. He was icy cold now and could barely move, but he managed to turn his head in time to see a rope flying through the air. It slapped him across the face and sank into the water.

"William! Wake up. Put this over his head. William! William! William!"

Was that Tom's voice? Somehow, William forced himself upright as the lasso flew at him again. This time it dropped on to Big Beast's horns and William managed to push it over the ox's head. "Pull! Pull!" came the shouts from the bank as a line of men tried to haul them in. Tom was at the front with Evan behind. Big Beast moaned with pain as the rope tightened around his neck, but he kept on going.

And they made it. Big Beast's strength and the force of the rope got them through the current and into calmer waters. Soon, Big Beast was stumbling on shingle in the shallows.

"One more push, boy," gasped William, squeezing the ox's sides as if he were riding a horse. This annoyed Big Beast so much that he tossed William off his back. William landed face down, banging his head on a stone, but strong arms immediately yanked him out of the water.

Sometime later, he awoke from a deep sleep to find himself wrapped in blankets and surrounded by a babble of voices. For a long time he just lay there, feeling confused. He vaguely remembered being thumped on the back a lot and then carried quickly across a bumpy field. Now, he seemed to be in a tavern. His own damp clothes were steaming in front of a fire, which meant that he must be naked. He pulled the blankets around him more tightly as he listened to bursts of laughter and the clink of glasses. The talk was about him…

"William's a brave lad, Evan…" said someone who sounded like Tom.

"Clever too – there's not many who'd be able to steer an ox to the bank in that torrent."

"Why on earth were you running the ferry in this weather? That's what I'd like to know…"

"I didn't know they were going to drive on that nervous beast at the last minute."

"Yes, Robert." William recognised Dad's voice. "What were you thinking of? You know what Big Beast's like."

"It wasn't my fault," said Mr Hughes' voice. "It was William. He pushed the animal on to the ferry—"

William sat up instantly. "No, I didn't. You got Big Beast into such a state that I couldn't stop him!" he shouted, but his words came out as a wheeze and ended in a fit of coughing.

In a second, Dad was at his side. "William! You're awake." William tried to repeat that Mr Hughes was wrong, but Evan didn't seem to understand. "Don't try to talk now. We'll get you upstairs to bed and bring you some soup."

Soon William found himself in bed, with Dad sitting beside him, feeding him soup and talking to him kindly. After he'd gone, William felt happy. It had taken a near drowning experience, but at last Dad was proud of him. Not only that – he was lying in a proper bed for the first time since he'd left home. However, he slept little. His head throbbed and the slightest movement sent shots of pain through his bruised body. Every time he dozed off, he was visited by terrifying memories: the penetrating cold of the river, his struggle to breathe under water, riding Big Beast through the raging torrent. He had survived against all odds. What a start to his journey – he hardly dared to think about what else might happen before they reached London.

11

24TH – 26TH MARCH 1848

Tal-y-Cafn to Rhuthun, North Wales

They had to wait a whole day before it was safe to ferry the rest of the cattle across the swollen river. William was pleased to have this chance to recover, but Dad saw it as a costly delay. Their next big stop would be Rhuthun Market, where they would stock up with supplies before crossing the border into England. Now they would have less time there, because they were a day behind schedule.

So, Dad was not in the best of moods when, on the morning of their departure, the ferryman demanded the price of the railing that Big Beast had broken. "You were in charge of Big Beast, Robert. That should come out of your wages," Dad told Mr Hughes, who was lingering in the doorway of the tavern with a mug of beer in his hand.

"It wasn't my fault." Mr Hughes poked his tankard at Evan, sprinkling him with drops of beer. "It was the storm that spooked Big Beast. I seem to remember advising you to wait until it was over before crossing – but you always know best. I'll wager that ferryman only agreed to cross because you offered him extra pay. If anyone's going to pay for his railing, it should be you. You made a bad decision, Evan. You're damned lucky William didn't drown, never mind who's paying for the railing. What's more, if you'd agreed to employ Mostyn and Cade Jones on this drove, as I thought you should, we wouldn't have had to rely on the skills of an inexperienced boy."

William was adjusting Seren's saddle when he heard this annoying remark. So, that was what Mr Hughes thought about him, was it? How dare he talk about him as if he were helpless! It wasn't luck that he hadn't drowned – it was down to sheer bravery, skill and strength. He puffed out his chest and pictured himself riding Big Beast through the current and reaching the riverbank. If Lizzie had been watching, she'd have thought him a hero! Never mind the cost of the railing – if William hadn't steered Big Beast through it, the whole ferry would have capsized. He might be inexperienced, but he'd done the right thing. He left Seren and marched across the forecourt to Dad. "Dad, let me say something…" But Dad ignored him and took a step towards Mr Hughes.

"Don't you criticise me, or my son. I know what's best for my own drove."

Fortunately, Tom overheard. "Hey! This isn't worth an argument, Evan. What's done is done," he said, touching Evan's arm. "Pay off the ferryman and let's go. If we don't move on soon, we'll miss Rhuthun Market."

Evan continued to glare at Mr Hughes for an uneasy moment, clenching and unclenching his fists. But at last, he nodded to Tom and turned away. "Let's get these cattle on the road."

For the next two days, the weather was kind: sharp showers in between watery sunshine and light winds. They were able to drive the cattle over the moors at a good pace, making up for the day they had lost.

Big Beast quickly recovered from his ordeal and trundled happily along with his group, but for William, who was covered in purple bruises, walking was torture. At night, he dreamed he was drowning and would wake sweating and gasping for breath, mistaking the stony moorland where he lay for the stony riverbed. At these times he often thought of Lizzie. He was longing to tell her his story. He knew she would tease him, but he quite missed that – no one else made him laugh like she did. He would imagine her bringing him tasty food, like she had done at home in the barn, and admiring him for his bravery.

He was still bothered about the whereabouts of Mostyn and Cade Jones. According to the landlord of the Tal-y-Cafn inn, they had stayed there a few days ago and were complaining bitterly about Evan. He thought they intended to hire themselves out at Rhuthun Market. William could only hope he was wrong.

As they crossed the moor, which was yellowed by winter frosts and peppered with grey boulders, William scanned the landscape for a sight of them. Several times he spotted two people walking together, but they were always too far away to be recognisable. Sometimes, he thought he saw a stray dog weaving between trees or heard distant barking. There was nothing unusual about this. They were at the start of the droving season, on the main route out of North Wales, so other drovers and dogs were everywhere. But this particular bark stuck in his head because it reminded him of Mab. The second time he heard it, he noticed that Rhett had his ears pricked and was sniffing the air.

"Does that sound like Mab's bark to you?" he asked Tom.

But Tom just laughed. "Don't be daft, William. Mab's safe at home with Old Griff."

But was she? William remembered how Old Griff had winked at him when he'd talked about cattle dogs that find their owners. What had he said? "Your dad would never forgive me if Mab escaped and tried to come after you."

They came down a hillside into Rhuthun, early one evening. The town nestled in the flat-bottomed Clwyd valley, where two rivers flowed, and lush green grass offered a treat to the weary cattle. William flopped on to the spongy ground to rub his sore legs and admired the outline of the Clwyd hills, undulating along one side of the valley like the back of a dozing dragon. He was just dozing off when he heard a shout.

"William! Where are you?" William leapt to his feet in time to see Dad striding towards him, parting the cattle as he called. "I need you on watch. Robert and I are going into town. I want you over there, on the river side of the herd. Cefyn's over by the road and I've hired the innkeeper's lads to keep watch in between. Tom will be in the Drovers Arms, in case you need him. He'll bring you food when he's had his supper."

William's mouth watered at the thought of a decent meal. Maybe rabbit pie?

"Pay attention, William," said Dad. "The first drovers' market of the season starts tomorrow. There could be thieves about tonight who think we won't miss an ox or two. If you suspect anything, call the others. Don't try anything on your own. Take this cudgel. You shouldn't need to use it, but it helps to scare off intruders." William slapped the rounded head of the heavy wooden cudgel into the palm of his other hand, wincing when it hurt. Dad laughed. "There's no need to look like that, boy. You'll be fine. Just use your common sense and stay alert. I'll see you in the morning." He tousled William's hair affectionately before strolling off.

William positioned himself near the river, as Dad had directed, with his stomach rumbling. It wasn't long before Tom arrived with beer and the much-needed pie – it was lambs-tail, not rabbit – but William was too hungry to care. When he had devoured it, they took a walk to check the quietly grazing herd. All seemed well. Cefyn and the two boys from the inn seemed relaxed at their posts, but William was glad he had the cudgel.

"You don't need that," said Tom. "There won't be any trouble tonight. All drovers want is a few pints of beer with their mates before the market tomorrow."

When Tom went back to the inn, William wrapped himself tightly in a rug and leant against an oak tree, sitting up in case he fell asleep. A brisk wind chased dark clouds across the sky, occasionally unveiling a sliver of moon. When there was no moonlight, it was so dark that he could hardly make out the shapes of the cattle. He could hear them munching though, and smell the wild thyme and clover crushed beneath their feet. He was soothed by the gurgling rivers, muffled laughter from the inn, distant barking...

Barking? William opened his eyes. It was that high-pitched bark again – the one like Mab's. He strained to listen but heard nothing more. It must have been a fox. He was missing Mab – that's why he'd thought it was her. She was more likely to be whining than barking right now: chained in her kennel back home, pining for him…

"Pssst – William." William jumped and grabbed his cudgel as Cefyn's furrowed face loomed dimly in the moonlight. "It's all right. It's only me."

"You scared me."

Cefyn grinned. "Sorry. Look – I've brought you another beer." He passed William a mug. "I'm going off with the boys for a bit of cockfighting – our little secret. No need to tell your dad." Cefyn tapped the tankard.

"But you're on watch," said William.

"It's taken care of. The boys are over there and Tom's at the inn. That's more than enough to keep watch on a quiet night like this."

"But…"

Cefyn put a hand over William's mouth. "Shhh! Don't worry. Your Dad's a fusspot. All will be well. I won't be long, but the cock-pit here is the best in Wales – too good to miss." He winked, before melting away into the blackness.

Should William tell Tom? Not yet. He didn't want to get Cefyn into trouble. He decided to stay where he was and drink his beer, which tasted delicious. When he'd finished it, he picked up the cudgel and walked through his and Cefyn's sections of the herd. Everything was quiet. The animals shifted as he passed, filling his nostrils with the comforting scent of dung and cattle breath.

On his way back, he met Dad's dog, Rhett and squatted down to ruffle his ears. "There's nothing out there boy, is there? You've checked, haven't you?" Rhett nuzzled his hand and thumped the ground with his tail. "That's good then," said William. "Come on."

But back at the oak tree, Rhett became restless, pricking up his ears and emitting low growls like he'd done that day when they were up on the moors. "What's up, boy?" asked William, rubbing the dog's back. The moment passed and Rhett settled down with his head between his paws. William wrapped himself up in his blankets and slumped drowsily beside him, one arm flung across the dog's back.

He was awoken by cattle jostling each other. Something was wrong. He sat up quickly. Rhett had gone. It was too dark to see anything, but he thought he could hear men's voices. He lay on his belly and slid towards the sound, dragging the cudgel. When he got near enough, he lay still, praying that he wouldn't be trampled on by oxen and straining to make out the words.

"Steady, boy, steady. Go gently, son. Feel for the letters on its rump. Found any?"

"Think so."

"Good. Trace them with your finger. You're looking for EE or EL."

"Found something. Ow! That's my knee! Keep the beast still, Dad."

"Hurry. Before we get caught."

William's heart missed a beat. Son? Dad? Whose dad? He knew those voices.

"Here we are: EE."

"It's his mark. Evan Evans."

"Not necessarily, Dad. It could be some other EE. This is foolish. How are we going to get the beasts away without them bellowing?"

"We'll be quick. Just take two. Evan owes me two, at least."

Mostyn and Cade Jones – it must be. At that moment, the clouds parted and in the moonlight William could clearly see them. What's more, they were stealing his dad's cattle. He had to get help, but he'd be too slow on his belly. Cautiously, he raised himself on to his hands and knees, but as he did so, the ox nearest to him shifted and knocked a hoof against the cudgel.

"Who's there?" Cade picked up a stone. "Run, Dad!"

The sight of the stone filled William with rage. Cade had his back to him, so he probably could have got away unseen, but he chose not to. Instead, he jumped clear of the ox and landed his boot in the middle of Cade Jones' back, knocking him to the ground and shoving his face in the mud. Out of the corner of his eye, he saw Mostyn running towards the river. Then clouds curtained the moon, leaving him and Cade locked together in the dark.

William anchored his fists in Cade's hair, using all his strength to keep the boy down as he bucked and twisted and swore. William knew he had to keep him on the ground. He was no match for an upright Cade. If the bully got back on his feet, he would use his bulk and height to smash William to pieces. A wave of fury surged through William's fists. "You think you can steal our cattle?" Wham! He landed a blow on Cade's ear. Thwack! "You and your good-for-nothing dad." Crack! "Here's one for the stone you threw at Big Beast. And one for the beating I got. And another!" A white-hot anger fuelled William's strength as he pummelled Cade's head until his enemy had stopped moving. He paused, gasping for breath. Another shaft of moonlight lit up Cade's body, lying still as a dead rat. Restless cattle surrounded them, snorting, and tossing their heads.

What had he done? Keeping his legs tight around Cade's back, William leaned forward. The boy was still breathing;

just stunned. William would have to get help now. He stood up, rubbing his throbbing fists, and started to creep towards the Drovers Arms, keeping low, just in case Mostyn was still around.

He had taken just six steps when a stone thumped between his shoulder blades. As he whipped around, Cade Jones seized him by his coat collar, belching rancid breath in his face.

"You thought you'd finished me off, didn't you? Well, I don't go down that easy!" Cade's fist thudded into William's head, jarring his neck sideways. Blow upon blow rained down until William lost his balance and fell to the ground, tasting blood.

"Ha! Look what I've found!"

William opened one eye long enough to see Cade towering over him, swinging the cudgel. He braced himself for the blow, but it never came. Instead, the night air erupted with barking as two dogs emerged from the darkness and leapt at Cade. They sank their teeth into his legs and arms, snarling. He yelled with pain and lashed out with the cudgel, but the dogs worked as a team, writhing and twisting, so that when their victim turned towards one, the other attacked him from behind.

Groggily, William wiped snot and blood from his face with his sleeve and propped himself up on his elbows. He knew one dog was Rhett, but he couldn't make out the other. Then the moon emerged once more from behind a cloud, revealing a flash of white and fox-brown.

The commotion brought Tom running from the inn. He called off the dogs and flung himself at the intruder, but Cade, slick as a ferret, wriggled free and limped off after Mostyn in the direction of the river. William tried again to get up, but this time he was knocked back and smothered with love by an ecstatic brown and white Welsh cow-dog who slobbered all over his stinging face and thumped him with her tail.

Mab!

12

27TH MARCH 1848

Rhuthun, North Wales

William could only open one eye when he woke up the next morning. He sat up, clutching his head, which felt as if it was going to fall off his neck, then somehow staggered to his feet. He could have been climbing a rock face, for the amount of effort this took. Through an open door he saw an inn sign swinging in the wind: THE DROVERS ARMS. Of course, he was in Rhuthun now – here for the market. He shut his good eye and began to remember: a fight with Cade Jones… cattle… Mostyn…

He ran a hand over his jaw, which was swollen on both sides, and explored his gums with his tongue. He didn't seem to have any teeth missing. His body had barely recovered from its near-drowning experience in the River Conwy and now it was covered in lumps and bruises inflicted by Cade Jones. Worse still, some of the damage was on top of old wounds.

Outside, Dad was shouting at Cefyn. "William's only fourteen. It's his first drove – and you leave him alone to go cockfighting? I didn't hire you to get drunk watching a cockfight. My boy got beaten to a pulp last night while you were enjoying yourself. There he is – look at him! Proud of yourself, are you?"

When Cefyn saw William, he gasped. "That eye looks bad, sorry lad. I'd have stayed if I'd known you'd get in a brawl." He glanced warily at Dad's stick.

"It wasn't a brawl, man. William was protecting our cattle, like you should've been. And you will be sorry now. I'm docking you a day's pay. If I wasn't short of drovers, I'd sack you."

Cefyn opened his mouth to speak but shut it again when he saw the look on Evan's face. Even though Cefyn was in the wrong, William felt a bit sorry for him. It was no fun, being the target of Dad's anger.

The sound of barking distracted him. Mab! There she was, tethered to a tree, alternately barking and whimpering. William limped over to her. He was sore, but all his limbs seemed to be working. "How did you get here, you impossible dog?" He slid down with his back against the tree trunk, letting Mab lovingly lick his wounds and bounce up and down on his tender legs.

"Keep her licking, it'll help your cuts to heal. Let's have a look at you." Dad cupped William's chin in one calloused hand and ran the fingers of the other over his face. "No bones broken," he said as William winced. "Tom got to you just in time. You were brave last night. I'm proud of you, son."

William's heart leapt. "Thanks, Dad," he muttered through his throbbing teeth.

"So how on earth did this damn dog get here?"

"I don't know, Dad. When we left home, she was tied up in the yard," William mumbled through his battered lips, sounding as if he were speaking through a mouthful of soggy bread.

"Well, it's not like Owain to lose a dog."

"I know. Besides, Old Griff was looking after her as well," said William.

"Old Griff? That wily old devil? That explains a lot. Did you tell him you wanted Mab to come with us?"

William looked at Dad sheepishly.

"Mm… I know him only too well!" said Dad. "I bet he gave her a chance and she took it. She must have followed Rhett's scent. Not many dogs could do that for such a distance, but I've known one or two." He bent down and scratched the delighted Mab behind the ears.

William rested his cheek on her warm fur. "Can I keep her with me, Dad… please?"

"Well…" Dad looked up at the hills. "She did save you from a cattle thief, I suppose." "Two cattle thieves," interrupted William.

"Two? Tom didn't say there were two!"

"He didn't see them both. Mostyn ran off when I hit Cade. Didn't you realise it was Mostyn and Cade Jones, Dad?"

"What? Are you sure?"

"Yes, of course. I couldn't have got any closer!"

"That's disgraceful! And it proves that Mostyn Jones is a cattle thief. I was right not to employ him. Wait till I tell Robert." Dad took a few paces in the direction of the Drovers Arms, then stopped to think, tapping his stick against his leg before coming back to William. "It was unlucky that they picked our herd."

William struggled to his feet. "It wasn't unlucky, Dad. I think they've been tracking us."

"Do you? Why?"

William related the conversation that he'd overheard between Mostyn and Cade. "They were looking for your mark, Dad. Mostyn said you owed him two oxen."

"Did he indeed?" Dad folded his arms across his chest. "So Mostyn meant it when he threatened me. This must be his idea of revenge." He gave William a friendly slap on the shoulder. "Well, Mostyn Jones won't get the better of us, son. We Evanses know how to look after ourselves."

William winced and rubbed his shoulder. "So, can I keep Mab?"

"You never miss a chance, boy, do you? Yes, I suppose so," said Evan, looking amused.

"Hurrah! Aargh!" William punched the air and ended up nursing his injured arm.

"But that dog stays on a leash when we're travelling, at least until I think she can be trusted to follow commands. And she's not coming to market with us this morning. Is that clear?"

"Yes, Dad." William looked towards the road. "Is it a long walk to the market?"

"About ten minutes. Why? Are you in a lot of pain?"

"A bit – I won't be able to go fast," said William.

Dad looked down at him with a twinkle in his eye. "That's a shame. The Traveller's Rest, where the Bangor coach comes in, is quite a lot further."

William felt himself blushing. "You mean the one that Lizzie and her mam are coming on?"

"Yes. They're due in about noon."

William's spirits soared. He could hardly wait to see Lizzie again – but then he had doubts. Would she want to see him? He must look an awful sight – all battered and bruised. But he had so much to tell her, he couldn't stay away. "I think I can walk that far," he said.

"Right then," said Dad with a grin. "Let's get going."

13

27TH MARCH 1848

Rhuthun, North Wales

The hustle and bustle of Rhuthun Market took William's mind off his aches and pains. Everywhere he looked, farmers were competing with each other for space, like chickens jostling for grain. All kinds of animals were being driven into pens: horses, ponies, cows with calves, oxen, bulls, pigs, sheep, geese, hens. Stout women in patterned shawls were unpacking their goods by the roadside, snapping at dogs and children who got in the way. Drovers from all over North Wales, their faces wind-blown and red-cheeked, were arguing in groups or bargaining over cattle.

Mr Hughes met up with them at the cattle pens.

"I need to talk to you about Mostyn and Cade Jones, Robert," said Evan.

"Not now, I haven't got time. I want to buy a strong horse and a Denbigh wagon before the coach gets in," Mr Hughes said. "Gwen's sister's coming over with socks and blankets from Bala, for us to sell in the London markets. We need a wagon to carry them there and it'll provide some shelter for the women as well."

Evan looked annoyed. "This isn't a pleasure trip. Robert. A loaded wagon will slow us down, particularly if it's got women riding in it."

"No, it won't. Gwen and Lizzie know what they're doing. They'll keep up with the herd."

"I'll help," said William. He imagined himself driving the wagon with the horse's reins in one hand and his spare arm flung around Lizzie's shoulders while she cuddled up to him.

"You, William, will be needed to herd cattle," said Dad. He turned to Mr Hughes, impatiently. "I can see you've made your mind up, Robert, and I need you on the drove, so there's not much I can do about it, I suppose. You'd better get on with your purchases. We can have that talk later. William and I are going to buy a few more oxen to sell in London. We'll meet you when the coach comes in."

There were some high-quality Welsh Blacks for sale in Rhuthun Market and Evan bought a dozen ready-shod animals, fit for the journey to London. He and William drove them to a holding pen and paid a boy to look after them, before walking into Rhuthun centre.

The coach from Bangor pulled up outside the Travellers Rest just after noon, with a blast of the coachman's horn. The four horses, two browns, a grey and a chestnut, tossed their heads and snorted, their steaming flanks heaving and running with sweat. The wheels of the coach were caked with mud, and mud was splattered all over the red and cream doors.

William ran over to the coach driver. "Have you got Mrs Hughes and Lizzie on board?"

The coach driver eased himself out of his seat with a groan. "That road from Bangor's a disgrace. All potholes and mire. Who do you want, boy?"

"Mrs Hughes and her daughter," said William.

"Inside or outside?" asked the coach driver.

At that moment, an elegantly clothed gentleman emerged from the inside of the coach and helped down a squealing lady, wearing a green velvet dress and bonnet.

"Outside," said William, looking up at the carriage roof, where people were falling over each other, trying to grab their luggage. He saw Mr Hughes lift his wife off the ladder and give her a hearty kiss on the mouth. Behind her, Lizzie was climbing down backwards, swinging a bundle of possessions. William reached up to take it from her and put it on the ground.

"William! Thanks."

William felt suddenly shy. "Err… good journey?" he asked.

"Exciting –– I've never been this far on a coach before. But it was cold and wet and muddy. Feel my hands – they're freezing." William wrapped his warm hands around Lizzie's, and they laughed as he rubbed them back to life.

"What happened to you?" Lizzie reached up and touched his half-closed eye, making him wince.

"Cade Jones…"

"Cade Jones is here?"

William felt a pang of jealousy at the kindly way in which Lizzie said Cade's name. "Never mind Cade, what happened to you?" he said, hastily. "You look as though someone threw you into a bog!" He licked his finger and scrubbed a spot of dirt from her cheek.

"Our coach got stuck in stinking mud. All the outside passengers had to get off and push. We went in up to our knees. It was disgusting," said Lizzie.

"It certainly was," agreed Mrs Hughes, coming around the back of the carriage. "Why on earth did I put on my Sunday dress? It's ruined." She flapped her skirts and flakes of mud flew off in all directions.

"Gwen! Glad to see you safe. How's my Jane?" asked Evan, joining them.

"She's doing fine," said Mrs Hughes. "Owain and Margaret are treating her like a queen. She's not allowed do to anything she shouldn't. She felt the baby kick for the first time just before we left." Mrs Hughes fished in her apron and brought out a letter. "Here you are, Evan. She sent her love."

Evan kissed the letter and put it in his pocket. William felt so relieved to hear that Mam was well. He'd clearly been more worried about her than he'd realised.

They were interrupted by the shouts and laughter of young children running towards them. "These are my cousins from Bala. They've brought goods for Mam to sell in London," said Lizzie, as the children clamoured for hugs.

Lizzie's aunt and uncle came close behind, pulling a donkey cart laden with home-spun socks, blankets and other woollen goods. Mrs Hughes hugged her sister with such enthusiasm that she almost got tangled up with the donkey.

William had heard about the Bala knitters. Their goods were highly prized in London. There were even rumours that kings had worn them. The Bala women spun the wool and wove it into blankets whilst their menfolk knitted stockings as they went about their daily business. They had brought their goods to Rhuthun to sell in the market and Mrs Hughes was likely to be one of their best customers.

"William, I need you to do something for me," said Dad. "I'm going to look over Robert's new horse and wagon and have a word with him about Mostyn Jones. Can you pay off the boy minding our new cattle and wait by the pen until I get there? Then we can drive them back to camp for Tom to check over." He handed William some coins.

William and Lizzie exchanged looks. "Can Lizzie come?" asked William.

"I don't see why not," said Dad. "I'm not used to girls travelling on my droves, but if she's going to be with us, she might as well learn to be useful."

"Huh! *Learn* to be useful," muttered Lizzie to William as they set off. "I already know how to handle cattle. I don't need to *learn*."

Shouting, whistling, neighing, braying and a general cacophony of human and animal noises surrounded the pens, as buyers moved off with their purchases and sellers packed up their stalls. Nearby was the hiring bay, where a small crowd had gathered. There were about two dozen men and some boys standing in a line while farmers and drovers, looking for workers, wandered up and down scrutinising and questioning them.

William paid off the boy minding Dad's new Welsh Blacks. While he and Lizzie were waiting for Dad, he thought he would point out their saleable features: strong legs, glossy coat... But Lizzie wasn't to be distracted. She sat on a large stone near the pen and patted the space beside her.

"So, William, tell me what happened between you and Cade last night?"

William sat down with a sigh. "What's it to you? It's best forgotten."

"Because you're both my friends and I care about you being hurt," said Lizzie.

"He didn't hurt me as much as I hurt him," boasted William. Then he realised what Lizzie had just said. "What do you mean – you're his friend? Why would you want to be friends with that idiot?"

Lizzie shook her head in exasperation. "Why shouldn't I be friends with Cade? I've known him all my life, just like you. Our mams were friends and he used to come and stay, sometimes. It was around the time my sister died and I think looking after Cade helped Mam to get over it. We were almost like brother and sister for a while, so even though we hardly see each other now, I still have a soft spot for him." She glared at William. "He doesn't fight all the time. He does have a good side to him, you know."

"Not one that I've ever seen," said William.

Lizzie scoffed. "Don't be silly, William. I don't think you've even tried to like him. I know he's rough, but so would you be if you'd been brought up by Mostyn Jones." William glared at her. "Don't sulk. Tell me what happened… please…" she stroked the back of his hand and smiled persuasively.

"Oh, all right," said William. He began a shortened version of his story. He didn't tell Lizzie that he'd started the fight even though Cade was about to run off, and he played down the damage they'd done to each other. He made himself out to be the hero of the hour – he just couldn't help it – although he wasn't sure that Lizzie believed him. He made a big thing about Mab and Rhett rescuing him, because Lizzie loved the dogs as much as he did. She listened so attentively that he got carried away, and was about to tell her about his near drowning in the River Conwy, when he saw something that made him stop…

"D'you see what I see?" William pointed to the hiring bay, where a red-haired drover was talking to a tall boy of about William and Lizzie's age and a scruffy-looking older man.

Lizzie's jaw dropped open. "It's them, isn't it? Mostyn and Cade?"

Just then, to William's astonishment, he saw Dad, striding towards the red-haired drover, shouting, "Don't take them on! They're good for nothing, those two…" When Mostyn saw Dad, he ran towards him, yelling abuse and waving his fist. Cade tried to pull him back, but he couldn't prevent Mostyn from grabbing hold of Dad's collar and shaking him.

"Stop that!" shouted William. He rushed to Dad's rescue but by the time he arrived other drovers had pulled the two men apart. "Dad, what are you doing?"

Struggling in the grip of two drovers, Dad jabbed his finger first at Mostyn and then at Cade. "He tried to steal two of my oxen last night and he bashed up my son!" he yelled.

"Prove it!" said Mostyn, spittle flying from his mouth. "Where are your witnesses?"

This silenced Dad. He appealed to William.

"He's right. Give us some proof," said the red-haired drover.

William shook his head. "Tom saw Cade attacking me, but Mostyn had left the oxen behind and gone by then," he told Dad.

"So, this is the murder victim, is it?" said the red-haired drover, peering suspiciously at William. "He's certainly got a black eye, but he doesn't look like he's dying." He pointed to Cade's bruised face. "Looks to me as though he gave as good as he got."

William scowled at Cade, but Cade was looking past him, with a stupid grin spreading over his face. "Hello, Lizzie Hughes. Come to do a bit of droving, have you?" he said.

"Ignore him," said William, pulling Lizzie away. "Come on, Dad. Let's get back to our cattle." And to his relief, Dad followed them.

"Good riddance! Clear off, you time-waster and let us find jobs!" shouted someone from the line-up.

"You'll be sorry for this Evan Evans – accusing an innocent man!" yelled Mostyn Jones.

By the time William, Lizzie and Dad had returned to the cattle pen, Mostyn and Cade were walking off with the red-haired drover, who had clearly decided to ignore Dad's advice.

Mr Hughes was waiting for them by the ox pen. "You just made a fool of yourself, Evan Evans," he said – and for once, William agreed with him. "Mostyn's a good drover," continued Mr Hughes. "You should have hired him yourself, instead of ranting and raving and holding up the hiring fair. Waste of good labour if you ask me." He frowned at Lizzie. "I don't remember giving you permission to go running off after William, daughter. Your mam needs help sorting out the wagon. Come with me now."

Lizzie blew a kiss to William and made a face at her dad's back as she stomped after him. William grinned as he watched her go. She clearly liked him, but if that was the case, why couldn't she just forget about Cade? And what did Dad think he was doing, trying to stop Mostyn Jones from getting a job? No good would come of that at all.

14

30TH MARCH 1848

Over the English border to Wentborough turnpike

It was a two-day trudge to the English border. For most of the time grey clouds sat low on the mountain tops and persistent drizzle meant that William never had a chance to dry out. The black mass of cattle squelched across the bottom of the sodden valleys and struggled over windswept hills.

They all slept in the open, apart from Lizzie and Mrs Hughes, who stayed cosily in the wagon that Mr Hughes had bought at Rhuthun Market. William thought this most unfair. Men and boys felt the cold just as much as women and girls, didn't they? So, why should Lizzie have shelter when he didn't? On the first night after they left Rhuthun, he made his bed under the wagon and cuddled up there with Mab. The ground was damp, but at least they were out of the wind. However, he couldn't forget that Lizzie was in the wagon just above him. He wriggled along on his stomach until he was under the steps and called, softly, "Lizzie, Lizzie!" When no answer came, he poked a stick under the wagon cover and wiggled it about. This got a reaction, though not the one he was hoping for.

"Ow! Who's there?" shouted Mrs Hughes. This was too much for Mab, who threw herself into a barking frenzy, causing uproar in the camp.

Mr Hughes came stumbling across the field with a lamp, so that Lizzie, who had just come out on to the wagon steps, spotted William trying to retreat underneath them.

"What are you doing there, William? You're all muddy!" she giggled.

"I just wanted to say goodnight," muttered William, feeling mortified.

"Goodnight! I'll give you goodnight! You can take over my look-out post, William. And make sure everyone else knows there's nothing to be alarmed about. You could have caused a stampede," said Mr Hughes.

Lizzie kept teasing William the next day: "Where are you going to sleep tonight, William?" or "You could sleep in that tree," or "Look there's an even muddier puddle for you to sleep in than the one under the wagon."

The wagon was heavily laden with goods and lurched about on the uneven ground. When William could leave his herding duties, he helped to push it up steep paths and carried bundles of goods on his back to lighten the load. He privately agreed with Dad that the wagon was nothing but trouble, but he enjoyed the excuse to be with Lizzie.

On the third day after they'd left Rhuthun, William was helping to keep the wagon going steadily down a steep hillside towards some woods, when Tom came running over. "We're almost in England! Can you see that road winding south in the distance? That's an English turnpike road – we'll be travelling on it soon."

"We're nearly in England, we're nearly in England," chanted Lizzie, dancing up and down and splattering her skirts with mud.

"There's a steam locomotive," said William, pointing at a plume of white steam filtering through the distant trees.

"That'll be on the new line from Sladsbury to Osforth," said Tom. "It won't be long before we're putting our cattle on a train in Ynys Mon and sending them all the way to Smithfield Market in London. That'll save us a bit of boot leather!"

Dad overheard this. "Never!" he said, in a voice thick as coal dust. "Never will my cattle travel by rail! My father travelled the drovers' routes to London, and my grandfather and my great-grandfather and my great-great-grandfather before him. If those routes were good enough for them, they're good enough for me!"

"But Sir Edward says steam power is changing everything, Dad," said William. "It takes weeks to walk our cattle to London, when a steam locomotive could get them there in a few days. Just think! You'd have more time to help Mam on the farm—"

"I don't care what Sir Edward thinks," interrupted Dad. "Droving is in our blood. It works. Why change it? I've never heard the like: forcing our cattle to be carried two hundred miles in an open truck. It's just plain cruel. They'll die of fright and their meat will be worth nothing. We'll lose our livelihood in a couple of years."

"But that's going to happen anyway if you don't keep up with the times," said Tom. "Lots of drovers are already using the new railways. They say that in London cattle trains will soon be running between Barnet and Smithfield Markets—"

"Spare me such nonsense!" shouted Evan. He jabbed Seren so hard with his heels that she lunged forward, almost unseating him, as he made for the head of the drove.

William ignored Dad and scanned the woods below for another sighting. "Do steam locomotives pull people as well as oxen?" he asked Tom. "I'd love a train ride. Imagine travelling at that speed! Have you ever done it?"

Tom laughed. "No, William, I haven't, not yet. But we'll see plenty more steam locomotives along the way. Businessmen are buying up land and laying railway lines all over the place. You never know, we might be lucky!"

That night they set up camp in England. By the next morning, the weather had improved, and William woke up to a clear, blue sky. However, this happy change didn't seem to cheer up Dad, who was full of warnings: "Remember, we're foreigners here. Keep your wits about you and your valuables hidden. The roads will be busy, and we might find some of our cattle joining other droves, if we're not careful." He beckoned to Mr Hughes. "Robert, make sure your wagon stays in the thick of the herd. If it's left with the women at the back, thieves are more likely to set on it."

"We can look after ourselves and the wagon, thank you very much!" said Lizzie.

"Quiet, Lizzie – know your place," said Mrs Hughes.

"We'll be going through our first turnpike at Wentborough," continued Dad.

"That'll cost us a lot. Why don't we keep to the hills?" asked Mr Hughes.

"You know as well as I do that would take two extra days, Robert, and there's a good inn near Wentborough. Besides, Jane said she'd send a letter on the mail coach to the Wentborough turnpike."

William couldn't wait to get to the turnpike when he heard that. He hadn't realised how much he would miss his mam when he'd left home.

Turnpike gates were to be found at regular intervals on the main highways. The turnpike keeper, or pikeman, collected fees from road users as they passed through. William was used to Dad and Mr Hughes grumbling about turnpikes – all drovers did. Pikemen cost drovers a fortune, because they charged a fee for every vehicle, beast and man. If a drover went through too many turnpikes on the road to London, he could end up making a loss. On the other hand, avoiding all the turnpikes made the journey longer and if the grazing was poor on the hill routes, it affected the health and value of the cattle.

The London road was surfaced with stones, for horse-drawn coaches, and was hard for the cattle to walk on. They snorted and swung their heads at the dogs as they stumbled along. At Wentborough turnpike, which they reached soon after midday, Dad called William to the pikeman's cottage. This was a small, white-washed dwelling with a half-open stable door. The pikeman came out of the cottage as William arrived, closing the lower part of the door behind him with a predatory smile. He wore a tall black hat and a white apron that stretched over his bulging stomach and hung down to the bottom of his breeches.

"Do you have a problem, gentlemen?" he asked Dad and Mr Hughes, who were staring in horror at the board of charges attached to the cottage wall.

"Yes!" snapped Dad. "These charges have gone up again since last year. And for no good reason, as far as I can see, apart from lining your pocket, Seamus Green. How am I supposed to make a living when you overcharge?"

"The charges have gone up because the road surface has been improved," said the pikeman evenly.

"Not for our cattle, it hasn't. You know well that the more stones you throw on that road, the harder it is for our beasts to travel!" complained Mr Hughes. "We should get a discount, not an increase!"

"I don't have the authority to reduce the tariffs. That would cost me my job!" said the pikeman, folding his ample arms across his chest.

"Huh! I bet you make a pretty sum out of us!" grumbled Evan.

"You don't know what you're talking about. Stick to cattle droving," said the pikeman. He took a sealed envelope out of his pocket. "Here you are, you can have this letter that I've been keeping for you, at no extra charge."

Dad snatched the envelope and tore it open. William held his breath, fearing the worst, but to his relief, a smile soon spread over Dad's face. "All's well at home, thank the Lord. There's a message for you, William. Read it later. I need you to tally now. Pick up a score of stones and stand here."

William pocketed the letter, happy to hear that all was well. He picked up a handful of stones and positioned himself by the tollgate. The land on either side was fenced off, so that this gate was the only access to the road. Animals had to pass through one at a time to be counted and the drover was charged by the score (every twenty animals). Drovers didn't trust pikemen, so they always did their own tally to make sure they weren't cheated. William prepared to transfer a stone from his left to his right pocket for each beast that passed through the gate. The pikeman, counting in the comfort of his cottage, sat by his front door and spread out his tally sticks on a table.

It was a long afternoon. No self-respecting ox wants to be driven through a gate when he could be grazing peacefully by the side of the road. There was constant bellowing as animals tried to escape and were nipped back in line by the dogs. Most oxen went through after one flick of Mr Hughes' stick, but not Big Beast. William could see him working himself into a fury as Mr Hughes drove him towards the gate. He reached for the coiled rope that Dad had left at his feet.

Sure enough, as soon as Big Beast reached the turnpike cottage and the gate posts, he lowered his one-and-a-half horns and kicked out with his back legs, catching Col, Mr Hughes' dog, and sending him flying. Then he refused to move any further. So, William threw the rope around Big Beast's neck, as a safety precaution, and with Mr Hughes' help coaxed him through.

"That damn animal's more trouble than it's worth. We should've sold it in Rhuthun," muttered Mr Hughes. He spat a large plug of tobacco in the direction of the pikeman, who was enjoying the show.

William returned to his tallying and notched up another seven score of black cattle on his tally stick. By the time they'd all gone through, he had lines of black oxen dancing in front of his eyes. Soon, Mrs Hughes appeared, leading Melfed and the wagon. The pikeman stood up, slapped his hat back on his head and sauntered around the wagon to calculate the toll.

"Anything chargeable in the wagon?"

"No," said Mrs Hughes. "All that's in there, is woollen goods for Barnet Market and personal belongings – and you're not charging me for those."

Where was Lizzie? William was about to ask, when Mrs Hughes put a finger discreetly to her lips. Her gesture wasn't discreet enough for the pikeman, however.

"Mm... I'll just make sure of that," he said and began poking the wagon cover sharply with his cane. After a couple of pokes, there was a squeal.

"Ow! Ow!" complained Lizzie, wriggling backwards out of the wagon, much to Mrs Hughes' dismay.

"I thought as much," said the pikeman. He turned to Mrs Hughes. "Hiding road travellers is a contravention of the turnpike trust regulations. I shall have to charge you extra."

"But my Lizzie's not a road traveller. She's not had her feet on the road all morning."

"Well, she's standing on it now," said the pikeman. "Come over to my office and settle up."

While the pikeman, Mrs Hughes and Lizzie were locked in a lively argument, William read his mam's letter. 'I miss you, William,' he read. An ache invaded his stomach. His mam went on to say she was fine and so were his sisters. Owain was managing the farm brilliantly, but it wasn't the same without William and his dad. Every day she prayed they were safe. Margaret and Owain had both added a note and Anne had drawn a picture of the piglets that had been born since he left, which made him smile and wish he were home.

He was still daydreaming when Lizzie crept up behind him and tried to slip an extra handful of tally stones into his pocket. "Oh, no you don't!" he exclaimed and slapped his hand over hers.

"Ow! Let go!" squealed Lizzie, almost doubled up with laughter.

"Give me those stones, then." William tried to unclasp each of Lizzie's fingers as she dragged him around in a circle.

"I'm only trying to help you, William."

"Ha! Ha! Very funny," laughed William, finally unclasping her fist so that the stones fell to the ground. At the same time, Lizzie lost her cap and her balance and fell against him, so that for a delicious moment his face was buried in her beautiful red-gold hair.

"Stop that, you two!" ordered Mrs Hughes, as she came out of the pike-man's office, very unhappy at the amount the pikeman had charged.

"Psst, William. Over here."

William looked around and saw Tom's head poking out from behind the turnpike cottage. He made sure the pikeman wasn't watching and sidled over. "Jump on my back. Let's see if we can have some fun with this old goat and save your dad a shilling." Tom squatted down and as soon as William was in position, began to creep jerkily past the office door with his head below the open half. William sat up as straight as he could, trying to look as if he always walked like that, and touched his hat to the pikeman as they passed. But the pikeman wasn't fooled. "That's the oldest trick in the book," he said, raising his eyes to heaven and adding two more men to his list of charges.

"It was worth a try," gasped Tom, as he and William collapsed in a heap, breathless with laughter.

Dad was not pleased when he saw the bill. "I'll make no profit at this rate," he grumbled to Tom as they followed the cattle along the road.

Their conversation was interrupted by the sounds of shushing and clanking and a piercing whistle. "There goes another locomotive," said William, pointing across the valley.

"So there does," grinned Tom. "You'd save money if you sent the cattle by rail," he dared to remind Evan.

"I'd rather be dead than use those outrageous inventions. I'll take Robert's advice after all – avoid the next turnpike by going across country again – and save money the old-fashioned way," Evan grumbled.

15

31ST MARCH 1848

A railway line, The Midlands, England

They followed England's ancient droving routes for the next part of the journey, ambling through green fields beneath a pale blue, cloud-flecked sky. The fine weather lifted William's spirits. It was so good to be with Lizzie again. His bruises and scratches from the fight with Cade were almost healed and Dad said they were over halfway to London.

Then, early one morning, the peace was broken by the sound of thundering hooves. Cries of "Stop!" stung the morning air as Seren came pounding towards them, nostrils flared, with Dad standing in the stirrups. Mr Hughes ran to meet him with William close behind.

"Someone's cut a railway line through the other side of those woods, right across our usual route!" Evan yelled. "I've been coming this way since I was a boy and I've never seen the like. It'll be one of those wretched railway investors that I've heard about. Disgraceful – blocking our path without warning!"

"I've heard about them too – businessmen buying up land and laying down railways all over the place," said Mr Hughes, grabbing Seren's bridle, to steady her. "But surely they can't just block drovers' paths? There must be a way around."

"I can't see one! Come and look!" Dad offered his hand to Mr Hughes, who leaped on to Seren's back and they galloped back the way he'd come.

Confusion broke out in the herd because the cattle were suddenly expected to stop. William ran to the front, whistling to Mab, who pranced about, yapping, as the animals bellowed and tossed their heads. Tom and his dog, Kyn, rounded up the beasts that were wandering off in search of juicier grass. Some of them objected and mooing and kicking broke out. "I feared this would happen. Didn't I tell you businessmen were having railway lines laid all over the place?" said Tom.

Soon Dad and Mr Hughes returned, arguing.

"It'll take the rest of the day to get the cattle through those gates and over the rails. We should go back to the turnpike!" said Mr Hughes as he dismounted.

"That'll set us back another day and cost us a fortune! You're the one who wanted to go this way in the first place! Now, we've got no alternative but to go on," Dad raged.

"But what if a train comes?" said Mr Hughes.

"It'll have to wait for us! Those devil's monsters are not going to put me out of pocket!"

"You think it would stop? Don't be foolish. Heaven knows how much those things weigh. We'd be crushed flat."

"What do you know about it?" stormed Dad. But he didn't want to hear Mr Hughes' answer. His mind was made up.

They got the herd going again and drove them past the edge of the woods. Soon the rails came into view. They were set neatly on wooden sleepers, with fencing on either side of them, obstructing the drovers' path. They stretched as far as William could see in both directions: from the distant blue horizon in the east, to the dark forests in the west. In front of him were two gates, providing the only way forward. Dad was right. They would either have to cross here or go back to the main road.

"Open the gates, William!" Dad's voice rang out, in a tone that had to be obeyed.

William slipped the catch of the first wooden gate, opening it wide. The two metal rails gleamed like swords in the sun as he stepped over them. To reach the second gate, he had to scramble up a low bank, created by the excavations for the railway. He quickly did this and once this gate was open Evan followed, leading Seren through. She carefully picked her way over both rails, up the bank and into the field beyond, where he tethered her to a fence post and returned to the railway line.

"We'll get the wagon over first!" he called.

Mr Hughes led Melfed and the wagon forward, frowning like a man who has lost a bet. Meanwhile Lizzie busied herself tying together the Bala blankets that they would sell in London. The wagon clattered and rocked through the first gate and over the first rail. The front wheels were soon over the second rail and lodged against the bank. Lizzie and Mrs Hughes took Melfed's reins and climbed to the top of the bank, calling words of encouragement. The horse strained with all her might to drag the wagon upwards. At the foot of the bank, Dad, Mr Hughes, William and Tom, formed a team behind the wagon, ready to push. As they did so, William noticed the cattle in the field behind them, edging nervously away from the line and heard the dogs growling, but there was no time to wonder why.

"Altogether now – one, two, three – heave!" shouted Dad. William pushed with all his might, wincing at the pain from his old bruises. The wagon moved upwards an inch. "And again!" cried Dad, through clenched jaws, his face turning purple with the effort. "Again! Again!" Each time he called, they lowered their heads and heaved. Each time, the wagon seemed to move hardly at all. They kept up the pressure to stop it falling back until William thought his legs would collapse beneath him.

"One last push and we'll do it! Ready to pull at the front?"

"Ready!" Mrs Hughes and Lizzie called back.

"Right!" William sucked in his breath and forced his shoulder once more against the wagon along with the other three. Melfed snorted. The wagon creaked and then suddenly lurched upwards, so that they almost fell on their faces as it stopped with its back wheels teetering at the top of the bank. In the same moment, William felt the earth tremble and, looking up, saw wisps of steam filtering through the trees. The smell of burning coal seared his nostrils, as a steam locomotive rushed towards him. "Dad! There's a steam train coming!" he yelled. The monstrous, black iron face of the steam locomotive roared out of the trees towards him at incredible speed, smut and smoke spewing from its chimney.

Terrified, William leapt backwards off the rails, into the field of cattle. As he did so a bundle of Welsh blankets fell out from the back of the wagon and on to the railway line. Next, he saw Lizzie flying through the air trying to grab them. She landed near the line with Dad close behind her, reaching out. Then William's view was blocked by the thundering locomotive, flashing fire, and spinning wheels. Hissing, booming, sparks fizzing, it flew past and rumbled away into the distance with its trucks rattling behind.

Moments passed. Silence.

William stared in horror at the railway line with his mind floating through an unimagined world. He saw a hump covered by his dad's coat, wedged up against the bank on the other side of the rails. As he watched, the hump shifted, and Dad propped himself up on one elbow. Lizzie was lying on her face, sheltered by his body. "She's still alive," Dad grunted. Then he toppled on to his back with a howl of pain. A thin, red trail of blood dripped on to the stone beneath his legs. Shreds of best quality Welsh blanket fluttered around him in the breeze.

William stood still, his eyes fixed on Dad's white, contorted face whilst others sprang forward to move Dad away from the rails. Mrs Hughes helped a sobbing Lizzie up the bank. Tom and Mr Hughes tied a tourniquet around Dad's leg, to stem the flow of blood. William watched the scene play out in front of him in slow motion, as if he were dreaming.

"William, Come here! We need you." Hearing his name, William stepped, still in a dream, across the railway line and joined the rescue.

"Hold his leg up." William knelt down and took Dad's wounded leg in his hands, whilst Tom slid a makeshift cushion of Welsh blanket underneath it. Blood from a hideous gash stained his palms and soaked into the wool. A white bone was jutting grotesquely through the flesh. "We'll take his weight. You keep that leg still," instructed Tom.

William fought back an urge to be sick. More than anything, he wanted to run away and pretend this wasn't happening, but he couldn't leave Dad. Mr Hughes and Tom crouched on either side of Dad, clasping each other's arms beneath his body to form a stretcher, while William cradled his damaged leg. "Ready? One, two, three, lift!" ordered Tom. The three of them shifted Dad slowly up the bank. He had his eyes tightly shut and moaned at each jolt. Somehow, they managed to get him into the back of the wagon. Mab and Rhett, sensing that something was wrong, ran around the outside, barking in sympathy with the groans and wails coming from within.

"Quick! We've got to get him to a doctor to set that bone and stitch up that gash!" said Mrs Hughes, seizing Melfed's reins.

"No wait! I can do it!" Tom threw off his coat and rolled up his sleeves.

"You're not a doctor, Tom. This is serious." Mrs Hughes was about to pull on the reins, but Tom stopped her.

"It'll be several hours before we can get him to a doctor," he urged. "My father was a bonesetter as well as a blacksmith. I used to help him with both trades. He taught me well." Mrs Hughes hesitated. "For God's sake woman – this might be our only chance to save Evan's leg. I'll ask him." Tom crawled into the wagon and put his mouth close to Dad's ear. "Did you hear, Evan? If I set this now, there's a better chance of saving your leg. Do you agree?"

Dad's eyes flickered. He nodded. William, who had crawled into the wagon from the other end, saw his lips moving. "He's saying 'yes'. Do it, Tom. Save his leg. Please help us, Mrs Hughes," he begged.

Mrs Hughes must have caught the desperation in William's voice, for she squeezed his shoulder. "Seems I have no choice," she said, climbing in beside him. "Come on, Robert."

"You two keep him steady," said Tom. "William can help me set the bone." He reached into his pocket and handed Mrs Hughes a flask. "Get as much of that down him as you can. It'll ease the pain."

Within the cramped confines of the wagon, they scrambled over each other to get into position. Mrs Hughes lifted Dad's head and trickled the fiery liquid down his throat. He spluttered and coughed, but swallowed most of it, moaning as Mrs Hughes laid his head back on the blankets. William wriggled backwards to Dad's feet, ready to help set the broken leg. His face was so close to the bone that stuck through Dad's flesh that he had to look away to stop himself from retching.

Tom's hands caressed the broken leg with expertise, feeling for the position of muscle and bone. "Put your hands here, William," he said cradling William's hands around the injury. Hold it steady when I pull."

"Ready Evan? This'll hurt."

"Do it!" muttered Dad.

"All right, William?" William nodded, clenching his teeth. "Now!" Tom pulled. Dad's roar of pain rose into a howl that set the dogs barking again, then faded to nothing, as he fainted. "Hold steady, William, while I see if it feels right. Got to make sure we've set it true." Tom ran his hands over the leg once more, tenderly feeling each bone and muscle. "That's the best I can do!" he said at last.

"At least it looks like a leg again," said William, his eyes full of tears.

Mrs Hughes crawled out of the wagon and returned with Rhett. "Get the dog to lick the wound clean, William," she said.

Rhett wriggled over to his master, licked the wound as directed, then put his paws on Dad's chest and slobbered over his face, whimpering. Mrs Hughes dressed the wound with hemp leaves. Then Mr Hughes handed her a splint, made from a tree branch that he had cut to roughly the right length, and she bound the splint to Dad's leg with rags. "Leave him with me, now. It's cramped in here and he needs air," she said when she'd finished.

Reluctantly, William slid away from Dad's pale, agonised face and crawled out of the wagon. He passed Lizzie, who was crouched on the steps, her hair matted with blood. On one side of her face was a red welt and her eye was swollen. Tears were running down her cheeks. For a second, William wanted to hug her, but then he felt angry. This was all Lizzie's fault. If she hadn't gone after those falling blankets, Dad wouldn't have tried to save her and neither of them would have been hurt. Why should William feel sorry for her when Dad might die because of her stupidity? In any case, there was no time to comfort Lizzie, even if he'd wanted to. He had to save Dad. He turned his back on her and walked over to Tom and Mr Hughes, who were waiting for him.

16

31ST MARCH 1848

The Drovers Rest, Tatlow, England

"This is the plan, William," said Mr Hughes. "You take Seren and ride on ahead to The Drovers Rest at Tatlow. Warn them that we're coming and get help. Tom will help Gwen to lead the wagon there with Evan and Lizzie."

"Don't look so worried, lad," interrupted Tom, throwing an arm around William's shoulders. "It'll be slow going, but we'll get there. Mrs Hughes and I will make sure your dad's well looked after on the way."

"I'm going to drive the herd back to the turnpike with Cefyn," continued Mr Hughes. "We'll find some farm labour to help along the way and, hopefully, get to The Drovers Rest by nightfall. There's a halfpenny green there, for the cattle. Tom will give you directions." He laid a hand on Tom's arm. "Good luck to you both. Look after my women, Tom."

Tom nodded and the two men shook hands. "I will. And you take care crossing back over that railway line." He turned back to William, as Mr Hughes strode off. "You shouldn't have any trouble finding The Drovers Rest, William. It's on the London road. See those Scots pines in the distance?" William nodded. "Keep them straight ahead of you all the way across the meadows. When you reach the London road, turn right and you'll see The Drovers Rest on the far side." Find the landlord, Joe Benson. He and his wife, Ada, are old friends of Evan. Tell them what's happened. Fetch a doctor. Get a bed prepared. Can you do all that?"

"Yes," said William, with forced confidence. He called Mab to heel.

"Good man," said Tom, giving him a handful of coins. "That's to pay for the doctor. Off you go then. The sooner we get Evan treated, the better his chances."

William called Mab to heel and went to fetch Seren, who was still tethered near the railway line where Dad had left her. She nickered when she saw William, then frisked sideways, showing the whites of her eyes. Mab ran backwards and forwards yapping, but William was not in the mood for games. "Sit, Mab!" he shouted, and she obeyed at once. He grasped Seren's bridle, running his hand down the horse's neck and keeping up a flow of talk.

"You know something's wrong, don't you, girl? Well, don't worry – you're going to help me put it right." He rubbed his cheek against her flank, just like he did when grooming her at home, until he felt her relax. It was good to be with an old friend at a time like this. He slipped his foot in the stirrup and swung himself on to her back. "We're going to find a doctor. Walk on!"

Mrs Hughes was in front of the wagon, adjusting Melfed's bridle, when William, Seren and Mab passed by. Her cap had slipped over one ear and her apron was splashed with blood. She looked up at William and patted his leg.

"How's Dad now?" he asked, ignoring Lizzie, who was propped up on the steps, wrapped in a blanket.

"Sleeping," said Mrs Hughes. "Take care, William. We'll get there as soon as we can."

"God speed lad!" called Tom. As William half turned to wave, he saw Mr Hughes standing amongst the cattle on the far side of the railway line, taking a swig from his flask.

The ground was dry and scattered with stones and molehills, so William resisted the temptation to urge Seren on. He knew she would gallop like the wind if he wanted her to, but the last thing he needed was a lame horse, so he let her find her way. He headed for the clump of Scots pines, as Tom had told him to, although as he rocked numbly in the saddle, the trees never seemed to get any nearer. He longed to escape from this terrible 'now': to go back to the moment before disaster struck or go forward to a place where everything was all right again. But that was impossible, so he kept going while images of the accident ran in and out of his head like a recurring nightmare.

At last, he arrived at the London road, Mab running eagerly beside them, and entered the village of Tatlow. Turning right, as Tom had instructed, William saw the sign for The Drovers Rest, swinging from a gibbet-like post with a weary-looking drover painted on it.

William steered Seren through a crooked archway into the stable-yard and demanded that someone should hold his horse. A ragged boy shuffled over and reluctantly took the reins. William dismounted, tied Mab to a post and plunged through the tavern door into a gloomy bar with a strong stench of tobacco. "Is there anyone there?" he called.

"She's gone to the pantry," croaked a voice from the gloom.

William waited impatiently, until a woman appeared behind the bar, carrying a delicious-smelling pie.

"Are you Mrs Benson?" William asked.

"That's me. Call me Ada," replied the woman, who wore a white lace cap and had a round, rosy face. "And who might you be?"

"I'm the son of Evan Evans, from Ynys Mon. You know him?" asked William, willing the woman to say 'yes'.

Ada smiled. She put the pie on the bar and wiped her hands on the apron tied around her plump body. "I certainly do," she said. "A decent man – not like some of the good-for-nothings we get here." She glared into the gloom, before inspecting William. "Mm, I can see a likeness, but you're not Owain, are you? He's older and taller, and if I may say so, less handsome." She stepped back with a grin.

But William had no time for flattery. "I'm Owain's younger brother," he said. "I'm here because Dad has had a terrible accident and we need help!" He explained that Evan had broken his leg in an accident involving a steam locomotive. He was bleeding badly and urgently needed a doctor. "Tom Morris and Mrs Hughes are bringing him in the wagon. They'll be here soon. I have money." William fished out of his pocket the coins that Tom had given him.

The landlady pushed his hand away. "Keep your money for now, young man. Let me get my husband. Joe!" she called through the door behind her. "Joe Benson, where are you? You're needed in the bar."

Joe Benson soon appeared with mud on his boots, wiping his hands on his breeches. When he saw William, he lifted his cloth cap and scratched his head. "What's going on?"

"Evan Evans is on his way, badly hurt. He was almost hit by a train."

"Almost hit by a train! How did he manage that?" said Joe.

"Never mind that now. Send the boy for Doctor Bell. Go on, hurry up. Evan is badly hurt. They're bringing him here in a wagon."

"Trains are a menace!" ranted Joe. "They should never have put down those tracks. It's not natural – heaps of iron tearing across fields causing death and destruction. Didn't I say so at the time?" He might have said more, but the look on his wife's face warned him not to, so he stomped out of the front door, muttering. William could hardly bear the waiting. He fidgeted from one foot to the other, his fists clenched by his sides, wishing that Dad had already arrived safely and was in the care of Doctor Bell. At last, he saw Joe, hurrying the stable lad past the inn and directing him up the road with a clip around the ear.

"The doctor won't be long," said Ada. "You can help get things ready."

They made up a bed on the floor of the snug, where the local farmers usually drank when the inn was crowded. Ada puffed up the pillows with two firm slaps. "Have you eaten, William?" she asked. "There's plenty of pie."

But William didn't feel like eating. He stood by a window for what seemed like hours, staring at the empty road until, at last, he heard wheels clattering on stones and saw Tom, Melfed and the wagon approaching the inn.

"Dad! Dad!" He bolted into the sunshine, colliding with Tom.

"Steady lad!"

A murmur came from the wagon. "Is that William?"

"I'm coming, Dad," called William.

"Wait a moment," said Tom, hanging on to him as he made for the wagon steps. "Let Mrs Hughes and Lizzie out first. Have you called a doctor?"

William nodded. "Joe and Ada have sent for Doctor Bell. We've made up a bed, as well."

Before he could say more, Ada brushed past him and wrapped Tom in her ample arms. "Tom Morris. How are you?"

"Worried," said Tom. "This a bad do, Ada." He released himself from her clutches and inclined his head towards William, raising his eyebrows.

Ada nodded and put an arm around William's shoulders. "Come on, William, let's get your dad inside."

In a daze, William helped Tom, Joe, Ada and Mrs Hughes to ease Dad out of the wagon and carry him into the snug. Dad looked pale and drowsy, but he touched William's arm and whispered his name.

"There – he recognises you," said Ada.

William didn't trust himself to speak. He'd never before seen Dad in such a helpless state.

Whilst they were settling Dad, the stable lad returned and announced, keeping well out of Joe's reach, that the doctor was on his way. He and William were told to take Tom's horse, Melfed and the wagon to the halfpenny green behind the inn.

Hurtling back into the bar when this was done, William was stopped in his tracks by the sight of Lizzie. She was being fussed over by Ada, who had made her comfortable with a pile of cushions and a mugful of warm milk. White bandages had been wrapped around her chin and head, making her look like a steamed pudding.

She grabbed his sleeve as he dashed past. "William – your dad – I'm sorry!"

William shook her off without a word and rushed into the snug. He found Dad propped up on pillows with his eyes closed. The golden rays of the evening sun slanted through the windows, lighting up his white face. He opened his eyes when William entered. "Come here, son," he murmured through cracked lips. He reached for William's hand and pulled him close, with a groan of pain. William laid his head on Dad's shoulder, just as he used to do when he was small and would cuddle up to him for comfort. How strange it seemed, now that Dad was the one in need of protection. What if he died? Who would look after Mam, and the new baby when it was born?

William's thoughts raced on until Doctor Bell arrived and ordered everyone, except Mrs Hughes, from the room. Then he crouched by the snug door as near to Dad as he could be, with his knees drawn up to his chin. After a while, the stable boy brought Mab into the bar. She nosed her way around the room, tail wagging, before finding William and resting her chin on his knee.

"She was pining for you," the stableboy said.

William rummaged his fingers through her fur, and she licked his nose. "I'm glad you're here, Mab."

Then, much to his surprise, William heard Dad's raised voice coming from the snug. "I'm not taking no for an answer! I'll be on that road in the morning, whether you like it or not! Do I make myself clear?" Maybe he wasn't so badly injured after all, if he could shout like that?

Shortly afterwards, the snug door opened, and Doctor Bell emerged, looking grim. "Are you Mr Evans' son?"

"Yes, Doctor."

"Follow me," said Doctor Bell. He found a settle in the bar and patted the seat next to him. William sat down, pulling Mab close. Doctor Bell scrubbed at his grey beard and cleared his throat. "The good thing is that the broken bone has been well set and should heal straight." He looked up at Tom, who had joined them. "I believe you're responsible for that, sir. Well done."

"William helped." Tom tousled William's hair.

"The wound is jagged but clean, thanks to the excellent skills of this lady." The doctor waved at Mrs Hughes, who had just come out of the snug. "However, it must be emphasised that there is a high risk of infection in these cases, so your father will have to be carefully nursed. The bad thing is that Mr Evans is still feverish. As I'm sure you could hear, he doesn't realise how serious his injury is and seems to think he'll be back on the road tomorrow."

"He can be unbelievably stubborn, at times," said Tom, shaking his head.

Doctor Bell put a sympathetic hand on William's shoulder and addressed Tom and Mrs Hughes, gravely. "You must prevent him from moving off his bed, let alone travelling to London. It's imperative that he be kept as still as possible for the next few days – otherwise he'll have no chance of recovery. I've given him a draught to make him sleep, for now. But, when he awakes, someone will have to talk sense into him, or disaster will surely follow."

"I'll make sure he does what he's told," said Mrs Hughes.

The doctor nodded. "Good. I'll be back in the morning. In the meantime – keep him still."

"Could you have a look at my daughter's injuries before you go, Doctor?" asked Mrs Hughes. "William can sit with his dad for a while."

"Certainly," said Doctor Bell. "In you go, William."

William did what he was told, but he felt nervous – having to look after Dad without Mrs Hughes' help. He didn't see why Lizzie couldn't have seen the doctor in the morning. There wasn't that much wrong with her. At least she could still walk.

17

31ST MARCH 1848

The Drovers Rest, Tatlow, England

Evan slept through the afternoon, on his back with his mouth open, snoring gently while William, Mrs Hughes and Ada took it in turns to watch over him.

At dusk, the clattering of hooves on the turnpike, men's shouts and oxen bellowing announced the arrival of the drove. When William and Tom ran out to help, they found Mr Hughes in a dreadful mood. He and Cefyn had had a tough time keeping the cattle on the road. They were tired from having to walk further than usual because of the detour and the hired boys were hopeless. Mr Hughes was too exhausted even to ask after Evan and staggered straight into the bar, leaving Cefyn, Tom and William to settle the oxen on the halfpenny grazing land behind the inn.

"You need feeding, young man," said Ada as soon as William got back. She ladled mutton and turnip stew into a bowl, from the cauldron hanging over the fire, and settled him into a fireside chair. Hungry at last, he downed the food and felt his strength returning. He was just polishing off a second helping when Lizzie sank into the chair opposite. Her face was still framed by a bandage, but her hair was neatly tied back, and she was wearing a clean apron. One eye was closed and swollen, but the other, still open and still a beautiful sky-blue, glared at him, causing a shoal of mixed emotions to swim around in his head.

Lizzie was first to speak. "Why won't you talk to me, William?"

William's anger boiled over. "Why would I want to talk to you after what's happened to Dad?"

"It was an accident," protested Lizzie.

"Was it? If you hadn't gone after those blankets, it wouldn't have happened. You could have both been killed. How would you feel if it was your dad who'd been injured? My dad might die."

Lizzie gasped. "Oh, William." She reached for his hand, but he pushed it away.

"Don't be mean. It wasn't my fault," said Lizzie indignantly. "I've never been near a railway before. I didn't know locomotives could travel that fast." She wiped her nose on the hem of her pinafore. "If anyone's to blame, it's your dad. If he hadn't decided not to go through the turnpike, we wouldn't have had to cross the railway line in the first place, and nobody would have been hurt!"

William scowled. "Dad's been using that shortcut for years. How was he to know someone had laid a railway line across the path?"

"Well, he still shouldn't have crossed the line. He should've taken my dad's advice and turned back. But he always has to have his own way. That's what my dad says."

"Oh, he does, does he?" Their voices were rising now.

"Hey, hey, you two. I don't like arguments in my tavern," said Joe Benson. He gave the tankards he was carrying to a customer and sat down beside them. "Falling out is not going to help your dad to recover, or heal Lizzie's wounds, is it, William? Stay friends and help each other, that's what I say." William exchanged a quick glance with Lizzie as Joe carried on, "We've all got to get used to railways, they're here to stay. I'm shocked by what I've seen in the last few months. I'd heard talk of railways, but I'd never expected one to be built near here."

"Did you see it being built?" asked William.

"I did indeed," said Joe. "One day, hundreds of men turned up with shovels and pickaxes and before we knew it, there was a railway line, paid for by some fancy toff from London. These folk with money – they think they can build railways anywhere. It doesn't matter to them if they injure honest people or threaten their livelihood. As a matter of fact, your dad's been lucky to get away with just a broken leg. I've seen a few reports in the newspapers of railway accidents where victims have had their legs cut clean off!"

Joe took a swig of beer and shook his head. "And that's not the only thing that's being reported. The railways will probably finish us." He referred to the bar, now filling up, with a sweep of his arm. "Customers won't stop here, if they're whizzing past on a train, will they? We could be out of business in a couple of years."

"That would be awful for you and Ada," said Lizzie.

"It would indeed," said Joe. "We'll just have to hope it doesn't happen, won't we?" He put his empty tankard on the table beside them. "But there is one thing of which I'm certain." He looked pointedly at William and Lizzie, his face glowing in the firelight, before taking one hand from each of them and enclosing them between his own. "Friends should stick together in difficult times and you two need to do that in the days to come."

Lizzie looked William in the eye and squeezed his hand, which was enjoyable. Then she gave him a smug smile, which was irritating. But he knew Joe was right and so he squeezed her hand back.

18

The Drovers Rest, Tatlow, England

Dad's face was as pale as candle wax when William visited him early the next morning.

"Good morning, Evan. I've brought something to help with the swelling," said Ada, bustling into the room. "Hold this, William." She pushed a bowl of herb mash into William's hands. He wrinkled his nose at the pungent smell, while Ada spooned the mash into a cloth and tied it into a bundle. Then she lifted the sheet to reveal Evan's broken leg. The bandage securing the splint was dark with congealed blood. The other leg was less bloody, but still swollen and bruised. "This poultice is to reduce the swelling on your good leg, Evan. I'll wait for Dr Bell's advice about the broken one," said Ada. She took the bowl from William and gave him the poultice, pointing to a large, purple bruise near Dad's knee. William obediently placed the poultice on this, trying not to feel sick at the sight of Dad's damaged body.

"Thank you for your kindness, Ada," said Evan, wincing.

Mr Hughes poked his head around the door. "Glad you're awake, Evan. We need a meeting."

"Evan isn't well enough for a meeting," said Ada.

"Well, I can't wait any longer. We need to get our cattle on the road." Mr Hughes came in with Tom and Cefyn. Mrs Hughes stopped him from closing the door and squeezed through, with Lizzie.

"This is men's business," said Mr Hughes, frowning.

"Nonsense, Robert, we're all in this together," said Mrs Hughes. "Lizzie and I can turn our hand to most tasks."

"Hmm…" said Mr Hughes.

"I'm as good as William, at herding cattle," added Lizzie.

"Gwen's right. Let them stay," said Tom.

More pillows were fetched, and Evan was eased into a sitting position, sweating and groaning. They crowded around his makeshift bed, the three men standing at his feet, while Mrs Hughes perched on a chair and William and Lizzie squatted on the floor.

"I'll come back when you've finished," Ada said, disapprovingly, as she left the room.

"I'll get straight to the point, Evan," said Mr Hughes. "We're leaving this morning. If we don't go today, we may not reach Smithfield Market in time to sell our cattle."

Evan looked dismayed, but his normally stern voice came out weak and breathless. "You can surely wait one more day. I'll be able to travel by tomorrow."

A clamour of protest broke out.

"Whatever makes you think that?"

"Don't be daft, Dad."

140

"You've got a broken leg. You'd be nothing but a burden."

"How can you think of travelling when you've still got a fever?"

Evan thumped the bed with a clenched fist. "I will be all right in the morning, I tell you. I should know – it's my body!" He glared at Mr Hughes.

"You can tell us what you like, Evan, but you're deceiving yourself," said Mr Hughes. "You couldn't walk two yards in this state, let alone one hundred miles! So, whether you like it or not, I'm taking charge as your deputy and we'll be leaving this morning. I'll be taking William and I'll need money from you, to hire a replacement drover."

"A replacement drover?" gasped Evan.

"Take a drink, Evan," said Mrs Hughes, holding a mug of beer to Dad's spit-encrusted lips, but he pushed it away. "A replacement drover, you say?"

"Of course," said Mr Hughes. "How else do you expect me to manage without you?"

Evan planted a hand on William's shoulder and eased his head away from the pillow. "I know what you're up to, Robert Hughes. You're just looking for an excuse to take on Mostyn Jones. As soon as you're rid of me, you'll be scouring the countryside for him. Well, I forbid it. That man is not to be employed on my drove ever again." He pointed a finger at Mr Hughes. "I'm not alone in this: Sir Edward agreed with me, as you well know." He collapsed back on his pillows, red in the face and panting.

"This is too much for him. He needs to rest," said Mrs Hughes. "Robert, go and get ready and come back later." She stood up and ushered all but William out of the room. Lizzie brushed William's hand sympathetically as she left.

"Dad, don't be angry, it's not good for you," pleaded William. "Mr Hughes wouldn't be able to employ Mostyn Jones, in any case. He's already working for someone else. You saw him going off with that drover at Rhuthun Market." He laid a hand on Dad's forehead and looked at Mrs Hughes. "He's boiling hot. I think his fever's getting worse. I can't leave him like this."

Fortunately, Doctor Bell arrived soon after that and, after a further examination, gave Evan a draught to help him sleep. His opinion was that his patient's wounds looked clean and with absolute quiet and rest, he had a good chance of recovery. However, if the fever was still as bad in the morning, Dr Bell would be very concerned. William listened bravely. He knew he had to keep going, for the sake of his family. So, he kept telling himself that Dad would be all right, even though he felt as if he was lost in an unknown land.

When Doctor Bell had left, everyone gathered in the bar. "You can't expect William to leave his dad yet – not when he's so ill, Robert," said Mrs Hughes. "We'll have to manage without him… and don't look so annoyed. If you were that ill, you'd want me and Lizzie to stay with you."

"Look on the bright side," said Tom, throwing a friendly arm across William's shoulders. "If Doctor Bell's right, there's a good chance that Evan will be showing signs of recovery by tomorrow. So, I suggest that William stays with his dad tonight and maybe another day. We can leave Seren here, Robert. You and I can share my horse. Then, if Evan recovers sufficiently, William can catch up on horseback. If Evan gets worse, William will have to stay with him and pay a rider to bring Seren to the drove with a message."

"What do you think, William?" asked Mrs Hughes.

"I agree with Tom," said William. "Dad needs me here, today. I'm not leaving him unless his fever goes."

"And how am I supposed to get this drove successfully to London without enough boys and drovers?" demanded Mr Hughes.

"We'll hire boys from here and find a drover soon enough," said Mrs Hughes.

"Yes, we'll manage, Dad. I'll help," said Lizzie.

Mr Hughes raised his eyes to the ceiling. "I see I'm outnumbered. You'd better get back to your dad, William. Let's hope, for all our sakes, that Doctor Bell is right about his chances of recovery." He pushed his chair back and stood up. "Come on, the rest of you. Let's get these cattle on the road."

William felt torn as he watched the others follow Mr Hughes out to the yard. Yes, he needed to be with Dad – to look after him and let Mam know what was happening, if he got worse. But if he didn't go to London with the drove, most of Dad's cattle, and therefore the Evans' family income for the next few months, would be in Mr Hughes' sole charge. Could Mr Hughes be trusted? He knew he shouldn't think like that – after all, Mr Hughes was Lizzie's dad – but something didn't feel right. Was it that Mr Hughes didn't seem to agree with Dad's views about how to run the drove? Or was William's unease just because he didn't want to leave Lizzie? He knew he would miss her when he stayed behind – but for the moment he had to put Dad first.

"Ah, there you are, William. Can you change the poultices for your dad, please?" Ada bustled out from the kitchen and thrust the aromatic bowl of herbs into William's hands.

Dad was in a deep sleep and hardly stirred when William changed his poultice. It was a relief to be helping. Better still,

Doctor Bell's sleeping draught seemed to be working because Dad had cooled down. When William finished tending to his wounds, he left the snug with a sigh and went outside to say goodbye to the others. As soon as he stepped into the yard, Lizzie flung her arms around him, laying her head on his chest. "Oh William, I do hope your dad gets better and you'll be able to join us soon."

"Thanks," said William. He touched the top of her head before pushing her gently away.

Mr Hughes was mounted on Tom's horse. "Look after Evan as best you can, William," he said briskly. "The sooner he recovers the better for all of us. And we really need your help with the drove. If Doctor Bell is right, you'll be able to leave Evan in Ada's care by the day after tomorrow and we'll see you at Lofton then. We'll be pasturing near The Bunch of Carrots inn. It'll only take you a day's travel on Seren. You should get to us before nightfall. You'll find us easily – just keep going on the London road."

William's stomach felt leaden as he waved them off. Mr Hughes was at the head of the drove, on Tom's horse, with Cefyn driving the middle section of cattle and Tom bringing up the rear on foot. With them were several local boys, who had been hired to go as far as Lofton. Mrs Hughes and Lizzie were leading the wagon at the back, Lizzie waving frantically at William as they passed. William watched in a daze, until Lizzie had stopped waving and the last of the bellowing cattle were trundling along the London road.

The rest of the day went by with him caring for Dad and being fussed over by Ada, who bustled in and out of the snug with fresh poultices, food and drink. By the evening, William was feeling calmer and looking forward to sleeping in a warm bed instead of in a damp field. But this all changed when he walked through the bar, on his way upstairs, and a newly arrived customer stopped him.

"Haven't I seen you somewhere before?" The speaker had a shock of red hair and a drover's badge sewn to his shirt. William recognised him instantly. "I know – Rhuthun Market!" said the drover. "You were with that man who tried to stop me hiring Mostyn and Cade Jones, weren't you?"

"Yes," said William. "That was Evan Evans, my dad." He could feel his heart thumping. "Where are Mostyn and Cade now?"

"I've no idea," said the drover. "Your dad was right. They're crooks. I sacked them. Found them trying to make off with a bunch of cattle. They denied it, of course. Insisted they was just doing the job they was paid for. Load of nonsense! But I couldn't prove anything against them. I should've taken your dad's advice. I've sold up to cut my losses. On my way to Wentborough Fair to start again." He picked up his tankard and took a long drink.

This was dreadful news. "Do you think they're still in this area?" asked William.

"Could be. I only sacked them a couple of days ago. Depends where they went to look for work."

By the time Doctor Bell visited Dad the following evening, his condition had definitely improved. He was in less pain and seemed to have regained his common sense. Most importantly, he accepted that he was too badly injured to travel. Doctor Bell declared that his patient was out of danger as far as he could tell and well enough to be nursed back to health by Ada. So, after some discussion, Dad agreed that William should leave him in the care of Ada and join the drove as soon as possible.

"Some advice before you leave, William," said Dad, once the two of them were alone. "The next stage of the journey is not going to be easy."

William didn't need to be reminded of that, particularly after what he'd been told about Mostyn and Cade Jones by the red-headed drover the night before. He had no intention of telling Dad what he'd heard, but it was adding to his anxiety. He perched on the edge of the bed, preparing to follow his instructions, but found himself arguing with Dad immediately.

"Whatever happens next, William, make sure Robert sticks to the roads and goes through the turnpikes. The countryside's not safe now that it's being taken over by those monstrous killing machines."

"Dad, they're not, monsters, they're steam locomotives. They're our future. That's what Tom says—"

"I don't care what Tom says! What does he know?" said Dad. Spit flew from his mouth as he propped himself on his elbows, ready for an argument. But William didn't want him to get upset and make his fever worse again.

"I'll do my best to keep away from railway lines," he said hastily. "I'll be going soon. Is there anything else?"

"One thing," Dad said, when he'd calmed down. "You'll need money, in case of emergencies. Lock the door." When William had done so, Dad patted his chest. "Help me get this packet out. That's it – there."

William thrust his hand inside Dad's vest and drew out a clump of sweat-soaked papers. Dad thumbed through them and passed William a wad of bank notes which William counted. "There's a lot of money here, Dad. Shouldn't Mr Hughes have it? He's in charge."

"I've already made sure Robert has enough to get by,"

said Dad, looking William in the eye. "What I'm about to say may sound disloyal, but you need to know. Mr Hughes is good with cattle, but not money, particularly when he's had a drink. That's why I want you to carry some of it, for safekeeping. I hope you won't need it, William, but you're the only member of the Evans family travelling with the drove now and I trust you. Now, let me see you put those notes away safely," he said, his voice cracking with emotion.

William stowed the notes deep inside his own vest and buttoned up his jacket. So, Dad trusted him, now that he had no other choice, did he? Like when someone handed you a newly sharpened knife – useful, but you had to mind not to cut yourself.

"One other thing – your mam – she's not to know anything about this accident. I'll write to Sir Edward to let him know what's happened and I'll ask him not to tell her anything yet – not until I know how well my leg is healing. You never know, I might get better quicker than expected. I don't want her upsetting herself for no reason, especially when she's carrying our child. Do you promise?"

"I promise," said William.

"Here's Sir Edward's business card. If you need help when you get to London, go to his office."

"Thanks Dad." William put the card in his pocket.

"And take my cudgel. The roads get more dangerous nearer to London." Unusually, Dad opened his arms for a hug. "Take care, son. I'd be with you if I could."

"I know, Dad. Please do what Ada and Doctor Bell tell you. Get better as soon as you can," said William. He wriggled out of Dad's grasp, picked up the cudgel and left the room, wiping tears from his eyes.

19

3RD APRIL 1848

The journey to Lofton, England

William went straight from Dad's sickbed to the stableyard. Here, he found Joe holding Seren steady whilst Ada stuffed the saddle bags with provisions. She slipped a barley cake into William's pocket. "That's for the journey." William nodded. "Oh, come here boy," she said, throwing her arms around him and hugging him as if she were his mam. "We'll do our very best for your dad."

William felt himself welling up. "Goodbye, Ada, and thanks for everything," he mumbled. Then he climbed into the saddle and walked Seren on. Soon they were riding up the hill beyond the inn, with Mab scampering beside them. William turned to wave when he reached the top, but by then Ada and Joe were out of sight. He was on his own: a fearsome thought. He pulled Seren to a halt, to give himself time to get used to it.

An unfamiliar landscape stretched before him. Below him, lay endless green meadows dotted with cows, sheep, clumps of trees, farm buildings and squares of brown earth. Such a vast expanse of flat land made him want to fly: to escape into the blue sky, leaving his troubles behind. But of course, he couldn't. Seated on Seren's back, poised for the journey, he faced the terrifying reality of his dad's accident and felt the weight of his new responsibilities. Images flashed through his mind – the roaring, iron locomotive, smoke and steam, blood on the railway line, Lizzie's bandaged head, Dad, white-faced and helpless in the wagon…

The memories sent shivers through him, but he pushed them away: for his family's sake, he had to be strong. He put his arms around Seren's neck and rested his head on her mane so that she nickered with pleasure. "Yap yap yap!" Mab, never keen to hang around, jumped up and nipped his foot, causing Seren to shuffle sideways and making William laugh – at least he had animal friends. He felt the reassuring warmth of Seren's sides between his knees as he squeezed her forward. "All right, Mab, we're on our way. Let's see how quickly we can get to Lofton."

At every opportunity during the day, William rode Seren as fast has he could without laming her or losing Mab, but the going was often difficult. Although this was a turnpike road, paid for by travellers, it was full of potholes. To make matters worse, horse-drawn coaches often lurched past, throwing up dust and stones. In spite of this, they made good progress and in the late afternoon William spotted a village in the distance that he judged to be Lofton. With great relief he urged Seren on and reached The Bunch of Carrots Inn in time to see his dad's cattle being driven on to the nearby pasture.

A few yards away, Tom was rounding up stragglers. He smiled when William rode up. "William, you've made it.

Well done, lad, well done. I'm so glad to see you! How was Evan when you left?"

"Well enough for me to leave him, but I'm still afraid he could get worse again," said William.

Tom patted his leg. "Try not to worry. He's in good hands and knowing that you're with the drove will help him to get better."

"How are things going?" asked William.

Tom frowned. "As good as can be expected, under the circumstances."

"What do you mean?"

But before Tom could say any more, Lizzie came dashing across the field with her hair flying and her skirts gathered above her ankles. "William! You're here!"

"Am I? Are you sure?" teased William.

But Lizzie looked serious. "My dad's got something to tell you. He wants to see you, now." She glanced at Tom, who sucked in his lips and raised his eyebrows.

William's heart thumped. Across a sea of black oxen, he saw Mr Hughes standing in front of the inn with two familiar, shabby-looking figures. The three of them were sharing a joke. So, Mostyn and Cade Jones were here already. The realisation was no surprise: but it filled him with dread. Well, at least Lizzie was with him. "Jump up, I'll give you a lift," he said grimly. Lizzie took his outstretched hand and landed behind him on Seren's back, clutching him around the waist.

When they reached the Bunch of Carrots, Mr Hughes grabbed Seren's reins. "There you are, William!"

William scowled at Mostyn and Cade. "What are they doing here?"

"I've hired them. And that's no way to talk to me," said Mr Hughes.

Cade stretched out his arms to Lizzie, with a devilish grin on his face. "Let me help you, madam," he said, in a mock, posh voice.

Much to William's annoyance, Lizzie giggled and joined in the pretence. "Oh, thank you, kind sir." She allowed Cade to lower her to the ground, but moved away from him quickly, when she saw the look on William's face.

Mostyn spoke. "I can see you don't want us here, William Evans, perched up there on your high horse, but you'll have to put up with it. Robert needs us now that your dad's put himself out of action by his own stupidity."

William's whip twitched in his hand. "My dad's not stupid. He saved Lizzie's life. You heard him say that he would never employ you again. You and Cade are bad news. Get away from here!"

"That's enough, William!" said Mr Hughes, through clenched teeth. "Now get down off that horse."

William stayed firmly in the saddle.

"Do as you're told. I'm in charge now and I expect to be obeyed. I can't run a drove without men to drive it. I've made a good choice in Mostyn and Cade, so you'd better get used to that and the fact that I will be riding Seren from now on!"

William stroked Seren's neck as she skittered and snorted, disturbed by their anger. He loathed the idea of Mr Hughes riding her, but he knew he would have to give her up. It was what Dad would expect. Whether he liked it or not, Mr Hughes was Dad's deputy and held a drover's licence and badge, which was a legal requirement for someone in charge of droving cattle. As William didn't have one, he would have to be supervised by Mr Hughes or even – William shuddered at the thought – licenced drover, Mostyn Jones. As he reluctantly dismounted, Seren nuzzled his forehead and a painful memory flashed through his mind, of Dad, riding her at the head of the drove before the accident.

"You're lucky we're here," said Mostyn. "We left our other job when we heard that your father was hurt." He removed his hat and clasped it to his chest. "We wanted to help. We're working for less money, but we don't mind. We Welshmen should stick together."

"That's a lie!" said William. "You were sacked! I met your old employer in The Drovers Rest. He says you're a couple of crooks. He told me he wished he'd listened to what Dad said about you at Rhuthun Market."

"How dare you!" growled Mostyn. He advanced on William with his hand raised, but Mr Hughes stepped between them. "Leave it, Mostyn. I'll speak to him. You and Cade get these cattle settled down for the night. And Lizzie, you get back to your mother and start making yourself useful. I don't know why you're hanging around here, where you're not needed."

"You'll be sorry for what you said, boy," snarled Mostyn. He turned on his heel and went off to move the remaining cattle off the road, with Cade following. Cade made sure William was looking at him, before blowing a kiss at Lizzie's back view as he left. She had scuttled off towards the wagon, without saying goodbye to either of them.

Once they were out of earshot, William rounded on Mr Hughes. "Why have you hired Mostyn and Cade when Dad specifically forbade it?"

"I don't have to justify myself to you, William, but we'd better get this straight," said Mr Hughes. "I happen to disagree with Evan about Mostyn Jones. I grew up with him. He's made some daft decisions in his life, but he's all right. What's more, he's first-class at handling animals. Look at him now." He pointed at Mostyn, who was driving cattle into the field in orderly groups. "Evan is no longer with us and if I'm to get these cattle to Smithfield Market on time, I need to run things my way." He sprang into Seren's saddle and kicked her on, pulling too tightly on her mouth for William's liking.

PART THREE

THE ROAD
TO LONDON

20

5TH – 9TH APRIL 1848

The London road, England

W illiam hated having to work with Mostyn and Cade Jones. No matter what he was doing, they always seemed to be there, sneering at him. As they travelled through the English Midlands, he was constantly watching his back. It was like leaping across a peat bog – you never knew when you might fall in. To add to his misery, Lizzie was still being friendly towards Cade.

One evening, he was walking amongst the oxen checking for any problems when he came across the two of them, huddled together, apparently examining one particular ox. "What's the matter with this one?" he asked.

Lizzie flashed him a sweet smile. "Nothing. Cade's just teaching me what to look for when making a purchase," she said.

Cade ran his hand over the animal in question. "Nice square backside and solid thighs. It'll travel well and produce sweet meat. There's a lot of good-looking oxen in this herd. Your dad's done well with his breeding, Lizzie." He gave Lizzie a look which made her blush.

"These aren't Mr Hughes' oxen, they're my dad's. Here's his mark – EE for Evan Evans. And Lizzie knows all about cattle already. She grew up on a farm, remember?" said William.

"I know I did, but I'm always willing to listen, William. You never know what you're going to learn," said Lizzie.

"What's the quality of my dad's cattle got to do with you, Cade Jones? If Dad was here now, he'd sack you," said William.

"Leave Cade alone, William," said Lizzie. "It's not his fault that your dads don't get on with each other." She pulled William's sleeve. "Come on, Mam's cooking broth tonight and you're invited. She sent me out to find you. Bye, Cade."

"What are you bothering with him for?" complained William as Lizzie dragged him away.

"I'm just being friendly. Cade's all right. It's Mostyn who's the problem – he forces Cade to do things he shouldn't. How would you like to have a dad like him? Anyway, they're here to stay, whether you like it or not. You might as well try to get on with them – it'll help us all to get to London safely, won't it?"

"I don't trust either of them," grumbled William. But when they reached the wagon, the delicious taste of Mrs Hughes' broth softened his mood.

The following evening, when they reached Thornfield, he found an ally in Tom. The other drovers had already gone to eat at the inn, but William had stayed behind to help Tom check the oxen's feet. The weather had been damp and cool since Lofton, and now a fine rain was penetrating his coat.

"Why aren't you in the bar with the rest of them?" he asked. "I'm cold and starving hungry. You could take me with you."

"I'm having nothing to do with that riff-raff," said Tom. "Evan would be devastated if he knew what was going on. I'm waiting until they're too drunk to notice we're missing, then we'll go and have a bite in the snug." He turned up an ox's foot and ran his finger around the shoe. "See, William. The nails are still in, but you need to make sure they're flush with the shoe. We don't want a load of lame cattle on our hands. You do the next one." He stood up straight and rubbed the small of his back, before driving away the cattle that he'd already checked.

William checked the hooves of another ox. "What's going on that would upset Dad?" he asked when Tom returned.

Tom bent down to pick up his tools. "A number of things. First of all, it seems to me that Mostyn Jones is a bad influence on Robert Hughes. For example, look at the poor quality of this pasture." He jabbed his heel on the ground. "This is cheap and soggy: not good for tired and hungry cattle. There's better quality, well-drained land down the road. Evan never stops here. I reminded Robert about that, but he wouldn't listen because this is where Mostyn wanted to stop. The grazing rate is cheaper and the beer's better here, apparently. Your dad always puts the welfare of his cattle first, so that they fetch the best price when we get to market. Secondly, have you noticed how much time Mostyn and Cade are spending on 'examining' the cattle?"

"Yes. I found Cade at it the other evening – showing Lizzie what to look for, as if she didn't know! Do you think he and Mostyn are up to something?" asked William.

"I don't know. But I don't trust them."

"Neither do I."

"So, we need to stick together and watch them carefully. It's not so much what Mostyn himself does that worries me; it's the way Robert is increasingly taking his advice. It could lead to him making some bad decisions." Tom closed his toolbag and slung it over his shoulder. "It's getting dark. Come on. Time for supper."

William felt good, having Tom on his side, as the two of them squelched across the field towards the inn. "I can hear a steam locomotive," he said. "Look, there's steam coming through the trees."

"Now, that would solve a lot of problems," said Tom. "If we transported our cattle by train, instead of driving them on hard roads, we'd have a lot less bother and we wouldn't need to employ Mostyn and Cade. But Evan won't accept that the old way of droving is dying out. He was against railways before his accident, so I'm damn sure we won't get him near one now."

"So am I," said William. "All he does if you mention steam locomotives, is shout." Thinking about Dad made him sad. "Do you think Dad's going to be all right, Tom?"

Tom put an arm around his shoulders. "There's every chance that he will, but it'll take a while, I'm afraid."

At noon the next day, when they stopped on a village common for the cattle to graze, Lizzie came sauntering over with a basketful of bread and cheese. "Want some lunch?" she asked.

"Thanks. I'm starving." William reached into the basket with both hands.

"You can't have all that, you greedy pig," laughed Lizzie, slapping his hands off the food. "This is for everyone, not just you." She passed him a hunk of bread and cheese.

"Sit down with me?" William pointed to a nearby tree stump.

"Not yet," said Lizzie. "Cade's waiting for his."

In William's view, Cade should fetch his own lunch. What had he done to deserve special delivery? Resentfully, he watched Lizzie carry on along the edge of the field, swinging her hips, with the basket hanging on her arm. There was Cade, not far away, leaning against a tree. William watched Lizzie offer him bread and cheese. Cade took the food, but then he grabbed Lizzie around the waist and tried to kiss her, while Lizzie struggled to get away.

William was at her side in no time. "Get your hands off her!" he shouted. Then he pushed Cade hard in the chest, separating him from Lizzie with such force, that he lost his footing and landed flat on his back. But he was on his feet again in no time, advancing on William with both fists clenched. William raised his own fists and prepared to attack, but before either of them could land a punch, Tom and Cefyn intervened.

"Get that idiot away from here. I'll deal with this one!" Tom shouted. He pinned William's arms to his side and pulled him away from Cade as easily as if he were a newborn lamb, while Cefyn did the same to Cade and marched him off in the opposite direction.

"What are you thinking of, William? We've got enough problems already, without you getting into a fight! You just listen to me…"

William did listen, because he knew Tom was right, but he kept his eyes on Lizzie the whole time Tom was speaking. He agreed that he should be ashamed of losing his temper and, if they were going to get their cattle successfully to market, he needed to act more responsibly.

Then, as soon as Tom had finished his lecture, William strutted over to Lizzie, who was picking up the remains of Cade's lunch from the grass. "Are you all right?" he asked. "No harm done, I hope." He smiled down at her with manly concern.

But Lizzie was surprisingly ungrateful. "There's no harm done, William Evans. But I don't need you or anyone else to fight my battles. I can look after myself, thank you very much." She picked up her basket, tossed her beautiful head and stomped off.

"You've picked a tough lass there. She's not impressed by fisticuffs, I'm glad to say. You'll have to try something more peaceful," teased Tom, coming up behind him.

"I don't want to impress her," said William, blushing.

"Oh no? Well, you could have fooled me!" laughed Tom, who had picked up William's lunch. "Let's share this. I'm hungry." He divided the food between them, and they sat on a nearby tree stump, stuffing their faces. "You realise Cade Jones will be after you now."

"Maybe, but he'd be after me anyhow. He's always hated me," said William. "I wish we could get rid of him and Mostyn." He kicked at a stone which was stuck in the ground and didn't move. "Ow!"

"Kicking stones won't help," said Tom. "And stop worrying. Something will happen to make them leave and even if they don't go, we'll get by."

"But we need to do better than that. My family need more money than ever now that Dad's injured. We have to make a good profit on our cattle sales. How much do we need to make, per head of cattle, for that?" asked William.

"Depends," said Tom. "There are overheads: grazing costs, lodgings, wages, turnpike fees, hiring help and more. Then the price you get for cattle varies by the day. You get twice as much at Smithfield as you do in North Wales – that's why we come all this way. But it's one big gamble when all's said and done. We'll have that challenge to face, whether or not Mostyn and Cade are with us."

Later that evening, after they'd settled the cattle on the halfpenny by the Bell and Bottle at Levensworth, William made a den under a damp bush. Mab crawled in and curled up next to him. William checked that no one was about, before fishing out of his vest the package that Evan had given him and counting the notes. There was also a list of expenses paid for up to the time of Evan's accident. William added this up and calculated that the money Dad had given him wasn't enough to get them to London. He realised that Mr Hughes held the rest of the expenses allowance, but Dad's view was that he liked his beer too much. With Mostyn influencing him, William couldn't be sure that Mr Hughes would spend his expenses wisely.

So, if they were going to make as much money as possible from cattle sales in Smithfield Market, they couldn't afford the risk of losing a single beast to Mostyn and Cade Jones. William knew he was right not to trust them. He'd caught them in the act of trying to steal from the herd at Rhuthun, hadn't he? He knew they were bad news, but Mr Hughes just wouldn't believe him.

"What can I do, Mab?" William mumbled into Mab's fur as he cuddled up to her. Mab explored the palm of his hand with her wet nose, but she had no answers.

21

10TH APRIL 1848

Clappington Turnpike, England

William kept a close eye on Mostyn and Cade Jones all the way to the Clappington turnpike tollgate. Both he and Tom noticed that Mostyn continued to check over certain oxen, usually the meatiest ones, when he got the chance. Several times, William caught him and Cade whispering together, but they moved off when they saw him coming.

To make matters worse, he'd heard nothing from Dad or Mam for over a week and he was worried. They passed through two turnpike tollgates on the way to Clappington and stayed the night near two more inns, but there were no letters awaiting him at any of these places.

They were travelling through low-lying countryside, between hedgerows covered with sprouting leaf buds. Clusters of yellow primroses, violets and white wood anemones decorated the banks. The weather was warmer, with a mixture of showers and bright sunshine. The cattle, used now to road travel and full-bellied with lush grass and plentiful supplies of water, were easy to manage. William should have been enjoying himself, but he couldn't shake off his gloom. It didn't help that, since his lunch-break scuffle with Cade, he felt embarrassed whenever he talked to Lizzie. However, the day they reached Clappington, she hopped off the wagon when he was passing and joined him.

"Where've you been, William? We haven't spoken for two days," she said.

William steered a stray ox back to the herd while he gathered his thoughts. "I thought you said you didn't need me," he said, giving Lizzie a sideways glance.

"Did I? When?" William raised his eyebrows. "Oh, you mean after you objected to me giving Cade his lunch," said Lizzie, looking up at him through her eyelashes.

"I didn't object to that," said William, although this wasn't true. "I just didn't like the way he grabbed you."

"I didn't like that either – but I can look after myself," said Lizzie.

"So you said."

"Well, it's true."

They walked a few paces in silence before Lizzie touched William's hand. "Thank you for caring," she said, smiling.

"I do my best," said William, suddenly feeling more cheerful.

"I'd better get back to the wagon, before Mam starts moaning," said Lizzie, running off.

As they drew nearer to Clappington, the landscape became more rugged. Craggy hills lay ahead of them against a background of thick, grey cloud. The road up to the toll house was steep, but William hardly noticed in his eagerness to get there. "There might be a letter at the turnpike for me or my dad," he told Tom.

"Go and find out then," said Tom.

The wind tugged at William's hat and storm clouds raced towards him as he ran up the hill. When he arrived at the toll hut, Mr Hughes was already with the pikeman, wrangling about fees. He handed William a sealed note addressed to Evan Evans. "Is that your mam's writing?"

"Yes," said William.

"You open it then," said Mr Hughes.

William huddled under the eaves of the toll hut, as large drops of rain began to fall, and broke the seal with a lump in his throat, dreading bad news. He skipped the first few embarrassing sentences about how much Mam loved Dad. Then he read that Mam was well and could feel their unborn child kicking. He learned that Owain, Margaret and Ann were being wonderfully helpful and rattled through details about farm business, which all seemed to be going well. But when he got to the last bit, he realised he had a problem: 'Let me know you are safe, Evan. I miss you.'

What was William to do, now? He'd promised Dad that he wouldn't tell Mam about the accident. If Mam didn't get a reply to her letter, she would worry. If he replied to the letter, instead of Dad, she would know something was wrong, even if he told her all was well. If he told her the truth, she might be so upset that she'd lose the baby. Worse still, she might put herself and the baby at risk by taking a coach to The Drovers Rest at Tatlow, to be with Dad… No, he wouldn't do any of those things. He'd re-seal the letter and send it to Dad, back at The Drovers Rest. The letter was addressed to Dad – let him deal with it.

Angry voices erupted behind him. Across the road, Mostyn, Cade and Mr Hughes were standing in the rain, arguing with the pikeman.

"If you lower your fee, we won't need to take any of the oxen off the road," Mr Hughes was saying.

The turnpike route took travellers through a gap between two hills. Just before the tollgate, where the men were standing, there was a narrow path winding up to the summit of one of those hills. The wind was howling now, and rain was bouncing off the jagged rocks that jutted out above this path at awkward angles. The pikeman was blocking the way.

"He's right," snarled Mostyn. "We can't afford your toll fees and you've got no right to tell us what to do." He advanced towards the pikeman, waving his stick. "Me and my son will take these oxen over the top for free, so that Robert Hughes can afford to pay your unreasonable price for the rest to go through the gate. Out of our way!"

To his horror, William saw that the oxen Mostyn referred to were a group of the most valuable in the herd, including Big Beast. He'd been right when he thought Mostyn and Cade were inspecting the animals for a reason: they'd been working out which ones would fetch the best price. He stuffed Mam's letter into his pocket, rushed across the road and grabbed Mr Hughes by the arm. "Don't let Mr Jones take those oxen up there. It's too dangerous. You know Dad wouldn't allow it."

"Be quiet, William! I'm in charge of this drove," said Mr Hughes, shaking him off.

"The boy's right," shouted the pikeman. "This path is treacherous, particularly in a storm. There's a sheer drop from up there. Your cattle could fall over the edge to their deaths. It's happened before now."

But Mostyn ignored the pikeman's warning and shoved him to one side with such ferocity that he almost fell over. "Drive 'em up, Cade. Keep away!" yelled Mostyn, brandishing his stick at William. Mr Hughes stepped in front of William with arms outstretched, blocking his path.

Soon Mostyn and Cade were whipping the animals up the hill. Determined to follow, William ducked under one of Mr Hughes' arms and rushed after them. "Come back!" he yelled.

Rain lashed his cheeks. The path was so narrow that in places there was hardly room for a man, let alone a dozen cattle. The cliff towered above it on one side and there was a sheer drop on to the road on the other. In the fading light, he could just make out Mostyn, way up ahead, beating the animals mercilessly. A flash of lightning lit up the figure of Cade, battling to control a large ox with a broken horn.

"Bring Big Beast back!" shouted William, but his words were drowned by a clap of thunder. He struggled on, blinded by driving rain. Then suddenly, someone thumped into his back, flattening him against the rock face as a large stone whizzed past his head.

"Keep away, William Evans, or you'll be sorry!" Cade's voice shrieked like a wraith on the wind as he and the stolen cattle disappeared into the storm.

William struggled against his rescuer, but Lizzie wouldn't let go. If he freed one arm, she grabbed the other, or his coat, or stood on his feet. He was surprised at her strength.

"Don't go after them, William!"

William desperately wanted to go after Cade and continued to fight her off, lunging forward, even though she hung on to his arm. But then her foot slipped over the edge of the path. "Lizzie!" he yelled and threw his free arm around her waist, grabbing a branch to steady himself as he used all his strength pulled her back. She clutched at his coat and they tottered at the cliff edge for a split second before he swung her back to safety.

"Lizzie! You could have been killed," William steadied them both against the cliff face, panting.

"I could see Cade was going to throw that stone," Lizzie said. "It could have killed you!" She threw her arms around his waist and hugged him tightly.

He looked into her upturned face. "Thank you," he said.

"I didn't want you to get hurt," whispered Lizzie. They clung silently to each other until a clap of thunder cracked overhead.

"We'd better go down. We're not going to catch them up now," said William.

They picked their way gingerly down the path, hanging on to each other and steadying themselves against the rockface. When they finally got to the bottom, a furious Mr Hughes was waiting for them by the toll house.

"Lizzie! Get back to the wagon. William! How dare you disobey me? Get over there and take over the tallying from Tom. He needs to be with the oxen that have gone through the turnpike – the storm's making them wild."

William was unrepentant. "We've just lost half our best stock! We won't see Mostyn and Cade again," he shouted over his shoulder as he ran over to Tom.

"I hope you're wrong, lad," said Tom, before going off to mind the remaining cattle.

22

10TH – 11TH APRIL 1848

Clappington, England

William knew Mostyn and Cade wouldn't be waiting for them on the other side of the turnpike, as Mr Hughes had said – and they weren't. Even after all the rest of the cattle were through, the dozen oxen that Mostyn and Cade had driven over the hill were nowhere to be seen. Two hours later, they had still not turned up.

"Where do you think Mr Jones and Cade have got to, Mr Hughes? Shall I go and look for them?" asked William.

"Certainly not, William. You stay here, where I can keep an eye on you. Mostyn will be sheltering from the storm, somewhere. I'm sure he'll be here by morning, if not before."

William didn't believe this and Mr Hughes' refusal to send out a search party made him angry. He needed all the money that the missing oxen would fetch in the market. He couldn't afford to lose any of them. He decided to search for them, without permission, at first light. He couldn't risk sharing this plan with anyone: even Tom might try to stop him, out of concern for his safety.

When he crawled out of his damp bed before dawn the next day, the storm had subsided, but the air was moist and the ground boggy. "Shh!" He clamped his hand over Mab's muzzle, because she was wagging her tail excitedly, before leading her over to Seren, whom he had saddled and tethered to a tree the night before. The horse sensed his need and allowed him to lead her to the road without making a sound. Soon he was riding her with Mab running beside them.

The outline of the ridge, over which Mostyn and Cade had driven the stolen cattle in the storm, loomed above them. But even when the sun appeared above the distant hilltops, there was no sign of the culprits or the cattle. It wasn't until the road curved around the end of the ridge, that William saw something that made him gasp and pull Seren to a halt. Beside them was a flat field in which were two black oxen, one grazing and one lying motionless on its side.

The grazing ox had one broken horn: Big Beast. William dismounted, tethering Seren and Mab to the gatepost, before approaching his old friend cautiously, so as not to spook him. "Big Beast, I'm so glad I've found you." He patted the ox's neck and Big Beast snorted a greeting, before carrying on with his breakfast.

William ran over to the other ox, still lying on the grass. It was dead. Limestone crags towered above it, leading up to the ridge. It had the EL brand mark of Sir Edward stamped on its rump. It must have fallen over the edge in the storm. He knelt down to examine the body. One leg was broken and there were deep gashes on its head and neck where it must have tumbled on rocks. Big Beast had been lucky to find a safe way down. So, where were the rest of them? He was about to start searching, when he heard the thud of hooves and swung around to see a gentleman on a fine bay horse trotting towards him.

"Caught you red-handed!" The gentleman pulled up and grabbed William as he jumped from his saddle. His fingers dug into William's shoulder. Over by the gate, Mab burst into a frenzy of barking, straining at the end of her leash.

"First thief of the season! What's your story? They all have one!" the gentleman demanded in a clipped, English voice. He was wearing a quality greatcoat and leather riding boots. His horse was a thoroughbred. This man had money and power.

William decided he'd better do some name-dropping. He forced himself to stay calm and look into the gentleman's eyes. They were ice blue, but not entirely unfriendly. "I'm not a thief, sir. I'm a drover's boy," he said, pronouncing his English slowly and clearly. "These oxen, and several others, were stolen from my father's drove last night. Some of them belong to Sir Edward Ellis-Lloyd of Ynys Mon. My father sent me to look for them. I know they're ours. You can check the brand marks – EL or EE, if you don't believe me. And here's Sir Edward's card." William pulled Sir Edward's business card out of his pocket and held it up. "We're on our way to Smithfield Market."

"Hmm. Well, you speak good English for a Taffy; I'll say that for you." The gentleman stroked his beard with his free hand. "Sir Edward Ellis-Lloyd – I've heard that name. Does he invest in railways?"

William seized the moment. "Yes, sir. He does, sir. He's investing in the new Britannia Bridge over the Menai Straits. He told me it's going to open up a new world for us all."

"Did he indeed? Quite right. Yes, I think I met him at a shareholders' meeting."

"Last time I was in his house he showed me his new painting of a steam locomotive: a Firefly, it was, sir," said William.

The gentleman looked amused. "Well, I can honestly say that I have never before caught a boy trespassing on my land who has told me about a Firefly steam locomotive." At that moment, Seren snorted and kicked the gatepost, attracting the gentleman's attention. "Whose horse is that?" he asked.

"My father's," said William. "He told me to ride her. He can't leave the drove himself, because we're short of men." He lied smoothly. If this gentleman found out that he'd taken Seren without permission, it would be harder to prove he wasn't a thief. He stood in front of him, sweating, with what he hoped was an honest expression on his face. The gentleman regarded him suspiciously for some time. At last, he spoke.

"How many have gone missing?"

"A dozen, sir, including these two."

"All right, I believe you." The gentleman loosened his grip. "This is a damn nuisance. We'd better get you to the police station."

"The police station?" squawked William.

"Yes of course. I'm no fool, boy. For a start, you're trespassing on my land. In addition to that, a dozen cattle have been stolen overnight, with one poor animal meeting a horrible death. The people responsible for this have committed a serious crime. Neither I nor other landowners around here want cattle thieves roaming about. It's really your father who should report the theft, but I'm needed elsewhere in an hour and I want to make sure this is done." He looked at William sternly. "You seem intelligent. I'm prepared to take you instead. Your father can call into the police station later if need be. Get on your horse."

He marched William over to Seren, untied the reins and guided him into the saddle. "I'll lead you – just in case you feel like running off." Mab burst into a paroxysm of barking. "That dog can stay here," he said, keeping well out of Mab's reach. "I can't hear myself think with that row going on. You can fetch her and the live ox later."

William had no choice but to sit tight whilst the gentleman mounted his bay horse and led him and Seren on to the road. "I'm coming back," William called to Mab, who was now growling at his captor with bared teeth. But he didn't know that for certain. He'd never been to a police station and didn't know what to expect. He was about to enter an alien world where anything could happen.

To his relief the police station, when they reached it, did not look alien. It was an ordinary stone cottage beside the London road. The front door was opened by a small girl in a white nightdress, who could only just reach the door handle. She called, "Papa!" then ran off giggling. Papa appeared at the end of the corridor. He was wearing a farmer's smock over a pair of breeches. On the way to the front door, he rammed a stove-pipe hat on his head and picked up a truncheon.

"Good morning, Mr Harcourt, sir. My truncheon has arrived at last, and my uniform is on its way." He stood to attention and raised the truncheon to his head, nearly striking himself on the nose. Then he held the weapon out for inspection. "My officer's number is on the handle, as you can see, sir."

"Yes, yes, very good, Whittle. I'm glad to have a constabulary in the village at last. Now we have an urgent case for you, so let us into the police station," said Mr Harcourt.

The police station was in the parlour. As Constable Whittle ushered them in, William caught a glimpse of a kitchen at the end of the corridor. It was filled with small children stuffing food into their mouths. The delicious aroma of home-baked bread made him hungry and homesick. However, his longings soon vanished when he found himself sandwiched between Mr Harcourt and Constable Whittle's desk. The constable sat down opposite William, placed a sheet of paper on his blotter, dipped a quill pen in the inkwell and began to write.

"Name?" William whispered his name and Constable Whittle wrote it down. "Occupation?" When William said he was a drover's boy, Constable Whittle raised his eyebrows. He recorded the fact that Mr Harcourt was reporting an incident and asked the gentleman to explain what had happened.

"The boy can explain himself." Mr Harcourt placed an influential hand on William's shoulder. "Tell your story, boy."

William was trembling. What if the constable didn't believe him? He opened his mouth to speak, but he was so nervous that his first words came out in Welsh.

The constable raised his eyes to the ceiling and muttered, "Another Taffy," under his breath.

"Speak English!" ordered Mr Harcourt.

William felt stupid: he'd be locked up, if he wasn't careful. He took a deep breath and began again, in English. He gave them an adapted version of what had happened in the storm, making it sound as if his dad and not Mr Hughes had been in charge. He hesitated a few times, searching for the right English word and the constable interrupted him frequently, to correct his pronunciation. But much to his relief, he got to the end of his tale without too many mistakes. Constable Whittle and Mr Harcourt then interrogated him, trying to catch him out. By the time they had finished, William was beginning to think it would be worth going to gaol for a rest.

"This is a sorry tale, indeed," said Constable Whittle, accidentally pushing his stove-pipe hat over one eye as he scratched his head. "The question is: do I believe the boy?"

"I'm prepared to believe him," said Mr Harcourt. "What's more, I'm acquainted with Sir Edward, who owns the land that this boy's father farms. I'm sure Sir Edward would not employ thieves to drive his cattle. As the boy says, his father made a mistake taking on these men. A foolish mistake, but understandable. The countryside's teaming with cattle thieves at this time of year. Let's give the boy the benefit of the doubt, Constable."

William felt a rush of relief. He was so glad he'd brought steam locomotives and Sir Edward into his story. It had made all the difference.

"Put out a search warrant for the thieves," continued Mr Harcourt. "Make sure it goes as far as Barnet Market. The cattle could turn up there, even if they've been sold – often happens."

"Yes sir," said Constable Whittle, noting down Mr Harcourt's instructions. "One other thing, sir. What about trespass?"

"Trespass?"

"Yes, sir. The boy was trespassing on your land. There's a fine for that, sir."

Now what was going to happen? William dug his fingernails into his palms.

"Hmm. You're right, Whittle." Mr Harcourt paced up and down the room, hands behind his back, and stopped in front of William, frowning. "I'll let you off on one condition, boy."

"What's that, sir?" William looked appealingly into Mr Harcourt's blue eyes.

"Your father must let me have that dead ox free of charge, as payment for my trouble. It will feed my hounds."

"Oh, I know he'll agree to that, sir," lied William. He was sure Dad wouldn't have agreed to that, but he was so overwhelmed with relief at not being charged, that he didn't care.

"Very well. I have to go. I'll leave you to give the constable the details he needs for the search warrant. Get your live ox and your dog off my land as soon as you can."

"Yes, sir. Thank you for your help, sir." William held out his hand to be shaken but Mr Harcourt was already on his way.

The clock on the mantelpiece struck eight, which filled William with horror. Mr Hughes would be wanting to move on and would be livid that he and Seren weren't there. He gave Constable Whittle the required details as quickly as he could. The constable advised him to check in at Barnet Police Station, when they got to Barnet, to see if Mostyn and Cade Jones had been caught. After that, William rode back to Mr Harcourt's land to collect Mab and Big Beast.

It was only when they were on their way back to the drove, with Mab driving Big Beast in front of Seren, that the seriousness of what he had done began to sink in. After all, he had no actual proof that Mostyn and Cade had stolen the missing cattle. Something else might have happened to them. If Mr Harcourt hadn't forced him to report them to the police, would he have done that on his own? Like Lizzie, he'd grown up with Cade in Ynys Mon, where people looked after each other. William didn't like Cade, but should he have given him and his dad a chance? Then again, he'd already caught them trying to steal Dad's cattle at Rhuthun, so the chances were that they were guilty of stealing them now. He couldn't bear to think what Mr Hughes would say if he found out that there was a warrant out for their arrest, though. He must keep that to himself.

The drove was just setting off when William reached it. Mr Hughes, who was leading the wagon, jerked the reins angrily, jabbing Melfed sharply in the mouth. "Where in Heaven's name have you been, boy?" he roared. "And who gave you permission to take my horse?"

"Seren is my dad's horse, not yours," William said rebelliously as he dismounted. "I've been trying to find Mostyn and Cade: seeing as they didn't turn up this morning like you said they would. All I found was Big Beast, grazing on the other side of the hill…" he hesitated. If he mentioned the dead ox, Mr Hughes might ask awkward questions. "I couldn't find Mr Jones or Cade or the rest of the oxen anywhere, so I just brought this one back."

"Well, that's worrying. What do you think has happened to them, Robert?" said Mrs Hughes.

"I shouldn't think anything's happened to them. They'll be waiting along the way somewhere," said Mr Hughes. "I expect they got lost in the storm, decided to rest up and couldn't see Big Beast wandering off in the dark: he's always been a troublemaker. They may have thought something's happened to us and decided to go on alone. They might well do, after all this unnecessary delay caused by William's disobedience." He snatched Seren's reins from William and climbed into the saddle. "Let's get this drove on the road. Join Tom at the back, William." He kicked Seren into action and rode off with the horse flicking her tail in annoyance.

"Don't mind him, William," said Lizzie, jumping out of the wagon. She flicked her head at Mr Hughes' back view with her mouth turned down and her eyebrows raised to heaven, in a way that made William smile.

"Don't be disrespectful, Lizzie," scolded Mrs Hughes. She picked up Melfed's reins and the horse moved off, pulling the rattling wagon behind her. "Mind you, I don't like the effect Mostyn Jones has on Robert. He's not his usual self when Mostyn's around. Please God, we get to Barnet soon. Then at least Rhys can give us some help."

"Rhys?" asked William, taking a chance to walk with Lizzie.

"Yes, my brother, Rhys Pryce – you know – the one who owns the cow-keeper's shop in Clerkenwell, where Lizzie's going to work. He'll meet us in Barnet and guide us into London. I told you that before we left home – remember?"

"Now I do," said William.

"Rhys is a good businessman and Robert will have to show respect, because we owe him a favour, with him taking on Lizzie for us," said Mrs Hughes. Her voice cracked and she wiped her eyes on her shawl. "It doesn't seem to matter how hard we work, we can't even make enough from the farm to pay our debts and feed our own child."

"Don't upset yourself, Mam. I'm looking forward to it," said Lizzie.

"Well, let's hope Mr Pryce can help us sell our cattle at a good price, Mrs Hughes. We're going to be way out of pocket unless Mostyn and Cade turn up with the oxen they took last night," said William.

"Rhys is a good man – you'll see," said Mrs Hughes. "I'm so looking forward to seeing him again and it won't be long now. Robert reckons it's only three days from here to Barnet, if we're lucky."

Only three days to Barnet – where there might be word from Dad. What's more, Barnet wasn't far from London and the end of their journey.

"Dad said he'd send a letter to The Bear and Billet at Barnet," said William.

"Let's hope it'll bring good news," said Mrs Hughes. "It's been tough for you since Evan's accident, William, but you've done well. Evan would be proud – whatever Robert thinks."

23

14TH APRIL 1848

Barnet, near London, England

They climbed the hill to Barnet village in the late afternoon. Now, they were only two days walking distance from London: no distance at all, compared to the two hundred miles that William had already walked. He leant against a tree trunk, taking a minute to rub his sore calves and wriggle his toes in his sweaty boots. What wouldn't he have given, just then, for a mug of beer and a slice of Mam's potato pie?

"William, over here!" shouted Tom, who was struggling to keep the cattle at the back of the drove from getting mixed up with other herds. With a sigh, William forced his aching feet to carry on with the job. Horses, sheep, cattle and other drovers were flooding into the village from all directions amid a cacophony of neighing, bleating and bellowing. It took all of Tom and William's skill and plenty of swearing, to manoeuvre their cattle through the narrow streets.

Sir Edward owned grazing land here, so that the cattle could feed on lush grass for a week and put on weight, to increase their value, before being sold in Smithfield Market. When they at last reached these pastures, William and Tom threw their hats into the air with cries of, "Hurrah!" The cattle, after weeks of being driven along stony turnpike roads and eating poor grass, bounded joyously into the rich meadow. William was delighted to discover a straw-filled barn in the corner of one field, where drovers' boys could sleep. Mrs Hughes and Lizzie had got there before them with the wagon and were handing out boiled onions, stale bread and small beer. William ate greedily, whilst Mab, after a lot of squealing and growling, emerged from a ditch with a delicious supper of dead rat in her mouth.

Mr Hughes declined the stale bread. "I'll sup at the inn," he said, waving away his wife's offering. "I need to find Mostyn. He's as like to be in The Bear and Billet as anywhere."

"That's the inn Dad said he'd send a letter to. I'll come along to see if it's arrived," said William.

"You're staying here, boy! You're needed to mind the cattle. I'll bring the letter back," said Mr Hughes.

"It won't take me long to fetch it," said William.

"No. Do as you're told, without arguing, for once."

"Let him come with you, Robert. He's desperate for news of his dad." Mrs Hughes touched her husband's arm, but he shook her off.

"And that's enough from you, as well," he said, striding off in the direction of the inn.

"Don't go after him, William. He'll come back in a better mood when he's had a drink," said Mrs Hughes.

William stormed off to the barn, slashing furiously at the grass with his stick. He couldn't believe Mr Hughes' stupidity. Did he really think that Mostyn Jones would be at the inn waiting to hand over the missing cattle? What's more he was so mean that he wouldn't even let William off for five minutes to fetch a letter.

However, before he had reached the barn, he heard Lizzie calling him. "Hey William, there's a fair!"

He turned to see her running towards him, her cap loose and her bright hair flying around her head like a halo. "Look over there." She waved at a field about half a mile away where heads were bobbing up and down behind a hedge. Then he heard drums beating.

"Let's go! Come on!" Lizzie grabbed his hand and dragged him back to Mrs Hughes. "Can we go to the fair, Mam? Please?" said Lizzie.

"Of course not. You know your father would never allow it," said Mrs Hughes.

"But we'll be all right together. Please, Mam." Lizzie snuggled up to her mam, begging with her eyes, whilst hanging on tightly to William's hand, behind her back.

"Let them go, Gwen. They deserve a bit of fun. I'll cover for William. It won't be dark for two hours. They'll be safe enough and Robert won't be back until late," said Tom.

Mrs Hughes looked first at Tom, then at Lizzie and shrugged. "Well, just for an hour. Be back before dark. And don't spend anything. Just look."

They were away before she could change her mind. "I've got money," William told Lizzie when they were out of earshot. "Dad gave me some for safe-keeping, he won't miss a few coins."

An explosion of sound greeted them when they arrived at the fair. A marching band with drums, trombones and trumpets was thumping out 'Rule Britannia' whilst children skipped at their heels. A fiddler scraped out a jig, and an organ grinder wound a tune and called for them to 'see the monkey dance'. Lizzie tugged William over to a table where three thimbles were being slid around by a man in rags. He wanted a farthing to guess which one had a pea inside. "Maybe later," said William.

They ran over to a roundabout with a double row of wooden horses fixed to the platform. Each horse was painted white with red, blue and green dots and had a fur mane and tail. The rides were a farthing a go. A man wearing a sparkling red jacket, with matching top hat and bow tie, was prancing about the platform, calling for customers. William fished a ha'penny out of his pocket. "Come on, Lizzie," he said. The two of them clambered on to a pair of horses.

Soon, the ride filled up with customers. Several scruffy boys tried to get on to the platform, but the red jacket pushed them back. "Ya haven't earned ya farthing yet. No rides till ya have. Get pushing!" He gave a signal, and the boys began to push the platform around, grunting and groaning as it gathered momentum. Cries of, "Faster! Faster!" came from the lucky riders. The red jacket joined in. "Get a move on. You need to go much faster than that if you want your pay." At this threat, the bigger boys increased their speed, sending the smaller ones flying in all directions to land sprawling on the grass.

"Wouldn't it be fun if we could ride these horses to London, William," shouted Lizzie, above the chaos.

"Yes," laughed William. He produced a second ha'penny. "Let's have another go."

The fun over, they wandered dizzily around the entertainment tents. Each of these had a dramatic poster in front of it, revealing a taste of what you could see inside. In front of one, stood a man with a gash of painted blood on his arm. He held up a sign entitled: THE WILDEST BEASTS YOU'VE EVER SEEN. Below this was a gory picture of a boy being savaged by a lion. Outside another tent they saw a living tableau: a terrified woman, a villain wielding an axe and a ghost in a winding sheet. The actors beckoned their audience into the tent with blood-stained fingers.

"Ah!" Lizzie gripped William's hand, pretending to tremble.

"Do you want to go in?" he asked.

"No! I'd faint with fright!" she said and they both burst out laughing.

Other advertised shows promised: THE TINIEST MAN IN THE WORLD; THE THREE-ARMED WOMAN; THE SINGING GIANT. Outside a covered wagon, a boy implored them to come and see an ancient wonder of the seas: A PIPE-SMOKING OYSTER.

"I could definitely eat an oyster as long as it's not smoking a pipe! Let's go to the food stalls!" Lizzie tugged William towards an enticing aroma of fish, pease pudding and roasting pork. Soon they were both gorging themselves on oysters, which slid deliciously down their throats.

"Isn't this wonderful, William, after all the travelling we've done? Thanks for paying."

William smiled into Lizzie's upturned face. "You've got oyster juice on your chin," he said, smoothing the juice away with his thumb.

"And you've got a crumb," she brushed his cheek. Her lips invited a kiss, but when William leaned towards her, she wriggled away, giggling. "We'd better get home, before my dad finds out we're here."

It was twilight now and showmen were lighting rag flares in front of their tents. As they were leaving, a young boy invited them to 'see the amazing adventures of Albert Montino unfold before their very eyes'. Beside him, a man was beckoning in the crowd. He had set up a Peep Show – a rectangular black box, with a number of small glass windows along one side.

William and Lizzie exchanged a look. "Go on then – one last treat," William said and thrust more coins into the showman's hand.

"Take a window each, my lovelies," said the showman.

William pressed his nose against one glass window, while Lizzie and six other people each chose a window of their own. At first, he saw only tallow candles flickering on a table. Then, as soon as everyone was in position, the showman slid a picture into the box, so that the candlelight revealed a young man on a prancing horse.

"Our hero, the amazing Albert Montino, a man of means who helped the poor," the showman said. He quickly removed the slide and replaced it with one of Albert Montino throwing gold coins to some ragged children. "What's so amazing about this? I've seen that happening on high days and holidays before, you may say. And perhaps you have."

The showman quickly changed the picture for a man holding a begging bowl. "The amazing thing about Albert Montino, ladies and gentlemen, is that he started off as poor as a church mouse. He had to beg for a living. Then one day, Albert Montino was wrongly accused of stealing a cow." Here, the showman slid in a picture of this event. "He was imprisoned in a hulk." A rotting ship on a river appeared. "And transported to Australia for life." Next came a ship in full sail on a blue sea, with Albert Montino reaching despairingly towards the shore. "But, ladies and gentlemen, our hero was different from other convicts. He knew he was innocent and he never gave up…"

William felt dreadful. He had his own pictures in his head now: pictures of Mostyn and Cade Jones. He'd managed not think too much about what had happened in Clappington, up until now, but the story of Albert Montino brought it all back. Because of William, Mostyn and Cade could be caught and convicted of cattle theft and possibly transported to Australia. Suddenly, he didn't want to hear the end of the story. He tugged Lizzie's arm. "This'll take too long, we'd better go." He pulled her away into the gathering dark.

"Why can't we stay till the end and get our money's worth?" she protested.

"Your mam wants you home before dark," William said, striding along so fast that Lizzie had to run to keep up with him.

After a few minutes, she grabbed his arm and forced him to stop. "What's wrong, William?"

William knew she wouldn't stop bothering him until he told her. "It was the thought of people being transported for cattle theft – like that Albert Mont… whatever his name was. It seems a drastic punishment," he said.

"But that's only a story, William. There's something else the matter, isn't there?"

William gazed across the darkening landscape, towards London, with the fairground drums throbbing in his head: *tell her – don't be afraid – tell her – don't be afraid.* "Do you promise to keep a secret – at least for now?"

"I promise," said Lizzie. "What's happened?"

William sighed deeply. "When I went off to look for Cade and Mostyn, the morning after the storm, I ended up having to report them to the police. There's a search warrant out for them."

Lizzie gasped. "William! Why?"

"Because when I found Big Beast, Mr Harcourt, the farmer whose land he was on, caught me and accused me of stealing. So, I had to tell him the truth – that I was looking for Mostyn and Cade and the cattle they'd taken – otherwise he would have arrested me. He believed what I told him, but then he forced me to go with him to the police station to report Mostyn and Cade for cattle theft."

"But there's no proof they've stolen those oxen, is there? My dad thinks still thinks they'll turn up with them," said Lizzie.

"No proof yet, but if they hadn't stolen them, they'd have brought them back by now, surely?"

"Probably," Lizzie frowned. "So, if they're guilty, you think they might be transported?"

"Looks like it, if there's any truth in that story," said William.

"Well, maybe Mostyn deserves that. He's been caught thieving before and he's a horrible man. But Cade? I know he's no angel, but he's only a boy. He's only one year older than us, William, and I know Mostyn forces him to do bad things against his will. Do you think it's fair for him to have his life ruined because of his dad's behaviour? How would you feel if you were sent away to Australia, for years, far from your family, for something you'd been forced into?"

"Oh, we're back to feeling sorry for Cade, now, are we? Never mind supporting me with trying to help my family. It's

Cade who really matters to you, isn't it?" said William angrily. He'd trusted Lizzie with his secret, and this was what he got in return. They were almost back now, and he could see Mrs Hughes standing by the wagon with a lantern. "Well, that's fine. You look after Cade and I'll look after myself. You're not the only one who can do that, you know. I'm going to see if there's a letter from Dad." He turned and stomped up the hill towards The Bear and Billet, ignoring Lizzie's pleas to come back.

24

14TH APRIL 1848

Barnet, near London, England

The Bear and Billet, an ancient inn with a thatched roof, was popular with Welsh drovers. William wrinkled his nose at the stink of beer and unwashed bodies when he reached the doorway, which was jammed with customers guffawing and exchanging news in raucous voices. They lifted their foaming tankards above their heads to make a space for William to squeeze through. Inside, the bar was lit only by tallow candles and a roaring fire. William peered through the haze of tobacco smoke for a sight of Mr Hughes, and spotted him with a group of drovers, huddled together in the far corner of the room. He weaved his way towards him through a maze of waving arms and swaying bodies. The foul atmosphere made him cough so much that by the time he arrived he could barely speak. He tapped Mr Hughes on the shoulder.

Mr Hughes looked up irritably. He had clearly had a lot to drink and slurred his words as he spoke. "What d'you want?"

"Were there any letters for me?"

"Yes. I said I'd bring them back."

"I want them now," said William. "Where are they?"

Mr Hughes fumbled awkwardly in his pockets. "Where've they gone? I know I had them. Has anyone seen those letters?" he asked the general company.

Drovers shifted about on the settles, shaking their heads. One of them lowered himself to his knees with a groan and peered underneath the benches. "Here you are, boy!" He brandished two sealed papers.

"Thanks," said William, snatching them.

"Steady on!" said the drover, hauling himself back on to his seat with much puffing and blowing.

One letter was addressed to William Evans, although his name was hard to read because the ink was smudged with beer. The other, addressed to Evan Evans, had a muddy toe-print on one corner. Taking advantage of the fact that Mr Hughes had already forgotten about him, William squeezed his way through to the fireplace. Here he could just make out Evan's uneven scrawl. The letter was written in Welsh, which was comforting.

'Dear William,

By the time you get this letter you will hopefully have had an uneventful journey to Barnet.

If only Dad knew!

'Ada and Joe have given me much care and kindness and thanks to them, the infection has gone. I am getting a little better each day, although I fear it will be a long time *before I can walk without a stick or ride a horse. I haven't heard any more from Owain or your mam, but then they don't yet know what happened. You will remember that we agreed to keep my accident a secret? If you find a letter from your mam at the Bear and Billet, please send it here post haste.*

'I have written to Sir Edward, telling him everything and asking him to break the news to your mam, in person. I think that will be less of a shock for her than finding out by letter. I haven't heard from Sir E yet, but knowing the man as I do, I think it's likely that he will come down to London to meet Mr Hughes and take charge of the finances, now that I can't.

'I have thought about you a lot whilst lying on my sickbed, my son. I hope you realise how proud of you I am. I know I can trust you to help Mr Hughes and Tom keep our stock healthy and sell at a good profit.'

Here, William's stomach muscles clenched: what would Dad think of him if it all went wrong?

'There have been rumours going around that Mostyn and Cade Jones are in the area. I can't warn you enough to keep away from those two crooks. Whatever happens, make sure they have nothing more to do with our business. Robert can be a bit of a fool about those two sometimes, but Gwen can usually talk sense into him.'

Nothing more to do with our business? It was a bit late for Dad to be telling William that!

'I hope you realise that you will have to sell Seren at Barnet. I know you will find this hard, son. I don't want to part with her, either, but it must be done. We need every penny we can get and she will fetch a good price to the right buyer. There's no point in paying out to stable her in London when you will be travelling home by coach. I have explained all this and more to Robert in a letter, which he should have got by now. Write with your news as soon as you can.

God be with you, William.
Your loving father,
Evan Evans.'

William hesitated for a second, before opening the letter from Mam to Dad. He broke the seal carefully and scanned the contents until he had read enough to know that Mam and the family were safe and well. What a relief. Then he jostled his way to the bar, where he borrowed a pencil and wrote a short note to Dad at the end of Mam's letter. He told him that all was well: they had reached Barnet and were enjoying a rest, before taking the cattle to London. He avoided telling him about Mostyn and Cade's arrest, after what Dad had written about them in his letter. After all, there was nothing Dad could do about them from his sickbed. He refolded Mam's letter and had it re-addressed and resealed. Then he paid the landlord and instructed him to send it back to The Drovers Rest in Tatlow, by the next coach. He really wanted to write to Mam himself, but if he did that, he would have to lie to her about Dad, which would be worse than not writing. He decided to leave it. 'No news is good news,' Mam always said.

The drovers in the doorway were now bellowing out bawdy songs. They tried to get William to join in, but he pushed on relentlessly until he was outside the inn and gulping down fresh air.

Now he'd read Dad's letter, it was clear that he had to do what he'd been dreading, whatever Lizzie thought. He'd have to go to Barnet Police Station to find out if Mostyn and Cade Jones and the missing cattle had been traced. He would need a qualified drover with him, so he decided to trust Tom with his story and ask him to help. If there was any chance of getting their cattle back, he had to take it. As Dad said, the Evans family needed every penny they could get.

25

15TH APRIL 1848

Barnet, near London, England

Barnet Police Station looked more business-like than the one in Constable Whittle's cottage at Clappington. It was an official, two-storey house used exclusively for police business, with a green-yard at the back for holding stolen livestock. William could see the white tips of oxen's horns, waving above the fence, as he and Tom rode up to the police station.

"They might be ours. I'll take a look," said William, as he and Tom dismounted from Tom's horse.

"Wait. First, we'll make ourselves known. You need to be cautious with policemen," said Tom.

William understood that only too well, after the interrogation that Constable Whittle had given him at Clappington. "You're right. I'm glad you agreed to come with me today," he said.

"I'd always agree to help you, William. You should know that. I'd have come with you to look for the oxen at

Clappington, if you'd asked me. Going off on your own like that was dangerous: you could have been injured or thrown into gaol."

"I see that, now," said William.

"Glad to hear it," said Tom. "Come on then." He marched up to the police station and bashed the black-lion knocker against the oak door.

His knock was answered by a police sergeant in full uniform which included a well-fitting black jacket with brass buttons. He was so tall and stern that the sight of him made William feel guilty even though he hadn't done anything wrong.

The police sergeant showed them into his office and recorded their details in his notebook. "How many cattle do you think you've lost, boy?" He looked William up and down like a wolf sniffing at its prey.

"Ten," said William. "There were two more but—"

"Describe their distinguishing marks," interrupted the sergeant.

"They're all Welsh Blacks. Five are branded with Evan Evans' mark – EE – and five have Sir Ellis-Lloyd's brandmark – EL."

The sergeant turned to Tom. "Are you registered? Can you vouch for this boy and his information?" Tom pointed to the drover's badge on his coat, pulled a tatty licence from his pocket and assured the policeman that William's story was true. The police sergeant noted this down. Then he leant back in his chair, stroking his bushy black beard, and scrutinised William suspiciously. This made William feel extremely uncomfortable, but he stood tall and met the policeman's gaze while his heart raced, and his toes curled up in his boots. He was beginning to think the silence might never end, when at last the sergeant spoke.

"You're in luck, boy. I've had notice from Clappington Police Station that you reported a theft. Your description fits the ten cattle that were brought here yesterday evening. In fact, I was about to send a boy out to Sir Edward Ellis-Lloyd's grazing land to find you."

"Where were they found?" asked William.

The sergeant gave a flicker of a smile. "Police Constable Adams spotted them at Medley, a few miles down the road. He arrested a man and a boy, who were trying to sell ten oxen, with EL and EE brand marks, to a local drover who is known for dirty dealing. The culprits are in our lock-up. You'll have to identify them, of course." He turned his head and called through the open door, "Bring up the prisoners!"

William felt as if someone had tipped a bucket of cold water over his head.

In the event, he didn't have to identify anyone because Mostyn Jones identified himself. There were sounds of scuffling in the corridor. Then he rushed into the room dragging a policeman behind him. Even though he was handcuffed, he got within touching distance of William before the policeman pulled him back and pinned him against the wall.

"Don't believe him. The boy's a liar!" bawled Mostyn, shaking his fist. "We weren't stealing. We drove the beasts over the hill to save Robert tollgate money. You know that, you varmint. We drovers from Ynys Mon should stick together. Tell the truth before I throttle you!" He spat at William and struggled so violently against the constable that the sergeant had to help restrain him. By the time they had succeeded, Mostyn's jacket was torn, and his hat trampled.

"If you weren't stealing, then why didn't you wait for us, like you told Mr Hughes you would?" asked William.

"We couldn't get back because of the storm, you idiot!" Cade's voice rang out from the doorway, where he was being held by a third officer. "We got lost on the ridge. One ox fell. It took us till dawn to find the rest."

"Oh yes?" said William. "So where were you at dawn, when I found Big Beast grazing by the dead ox in Mr Harcourt's field?"

"What do you mean?" A look of horror crossed Mostyn's battered face. But before William could say any more, the constable threatened Mostyn with his truncheon, and told him to shut his mouth.

After that, Cade was brought in to stand beside his father, so that William and Tom could formally identify them. Cade had a black eye and a swollen lip. For once, he looked defeated. When the identification was completed, he and Mostyn were taken back to the lock-up with Mostyn muttering objections under his breath.

"Well, I'm satisfied that there's a case for theft," the sergeant said, when they had gone. "Even if your story weren't true, and I'm inclined to believe you, the accused were caught red-handed in Medley. We have witnesses for that. I'll charge them and they'll be sent to prison to await trial. Cattle theft is a serious offence."

Prison! Although William had wanted Mostyn and Cade to be arrested, the word seemed so final. More importantly, what would Lizzie say? Would this be the end of their friendship?

"Don't look so shocked, William. You were right to report Mostyn. It's what your dad would have done," said Tom.

"I know," William sighed.

After that, Tom signed several documents for the sergeant and both he and William agreed to act as witnesses when the time came for the case to be heard. Then the sergeant escorted them to the green-yard to fetch their cattle.

When Tom and William saw the state of their oxen, they were angry. Although the animals had only been missing for a few days, they had lost weight and looked distressed. Some had whip marks on their hides and shrank nervously away from them. It took a lot of persuasion to get them rounded up and on to the road.

"We'll have our work cut out to get these cattle back into good condition in time for Smithfield Market," said Tom as they drove them back to the pastures. "What was Robert thinking of, letting those scoundrels take our best stock up a hill in a storm? He's going to get a piece of my mind when I see him!"

26

15TH APRIL 1848

Barnet, near London, England

William's pulse quickened at the sight of Lizzie running to meet them as they neared the camp, driving the oxen in front of them. "You've got them back. Where did you find them?" she asked, jumping off the road to avoid being trampled.

"In the green-yard at Barnet Police Station," said William.

"Oh!" Lizzie clapped her hand to her mouth.

"Cade's there too, with his dad – not in the green-yard, though. They're in the cells," said William, pushing past her. "Make way – we need to get these ill-treated beasts into the meadow."

They found Mr Hughes slouching against the wagon, picking his teeth with a twig. Lizzie, who had followed them to and from the meadow, crouched on the wagon steps next to her mam, with her arms crossed and her lips pursed.

"Where've you two been without my permission?" enquired Mr Hughes.

Tom towered over him, red-faced. William had never seen him so angry. "We've been to fetch the missing oxen. I hope you're pleased to have them back."

"Certainly, but I knew they'd turn up eventually," said Mr Hughes. He looked past Tom, toward the road. "Where are Mostyn and Cade?"

"Where they deserve to be – under arrest in Barnet Police Station, charged with cattle theft," said Tom.

"Under arrest? Cattle theft? What are you talking about?" Mr Hughes looked appalled.

"You should've listened to William at Clappington turnpike, when he told you not to trust Mostyn and Cade Jones and to keep those oxen on the road," said Tom. "As a result of your stupidity, one ox is dead, and the rest are in a sorry state." Tom pointed at the field where the cattle were grazing. "Take a look. They've lost half their worth in five days. You should be ashamed of yourself!"

"You think I should be ashamed?" said Mr Hughes, shoving his face close to Tom's and spraying him with spittle. "It's you, should be ashamed – reporting innocent friends to the police!"

William quickly squeezed between the two men. The last thing any of them needed was a fight. "Tom didn't report them – I did – at Clappington Police Station."

His confession worked. Mr Hughes took his eyes off Tom and grabbed William's arm. "Let me get this right, William," he said. "You've reported Mostyn and Cade to the police, for a theft they didn't commit?"

"They did commit it. There are witnesses. They were caught red-handed, trying to sell the oxen at Medley: except for the dead one, of course."

"They can't be guilty!" said Mr Hughes, squeezing William's arm until he winced.

"Let go of William, Robert," demanded Mrs Hughes, pulling her husband away. "Violence isn't going to get us anywhere."

"It does look like they're guilty, Dad," said Lizzie. "William told me what happened. He didn't want to report them to the police, but he didn't have any choice."

So, Lizzie was standing up for him now. Whose side was she on – his or Cade's? William felt confused.

"Tell us what happened, William," said Mrs Hughes, steering her husband away from Tom.

William repeated his story, beginning with the discovery of two of the missing oxen in Mr Harcourt's field. Then he explained how Mr Harcourt had made him report Mostyn and Cade Jones to the police and ended with Mostyn and Cade being charged with cattle theft at Barnet.

However, there are some people who only hear what they want to hear, and Mr Hughes was one of these. "Nonsense! There must have been a mistake," he said.

"There's been no mistake. You just don't want to hear the truth. What's wrong with you, man?" said Tom. "You should be grateful that William acted as he did. Go and ask at the police station if you don't believe him. At least we got all but one of the oxen back, even if they are in a dreadful condition. Some of them belong to Sir Edward and some to Evan. None of them are yours, I notice. What do you think Evan would say about these goings-on if he were here now?"

The sound of Evan's name made Mr Hughes even angrier. "I don't care what Evan thinks! I'm in charge now! What's more, I don't need you telling me what to do, Tom Morris. You're sacked. I've had enough of you. Go!"

"What?" gasped William. He, Tom, Lizzie and Mrs Hughes looked disbelievingly at each other. No one spoke. Mr Hughes stood his ground, legs apart, arms folded.

"Don't be silly, Robert," said Mrs Hughes, at last. "How will we manage without Tom?"

"It's all right, Gwen," interrupted Tom. "You'll be fine without me. I wasn't going to come with you to London, in any case. I'm wasting my time here." He held out a hand to Mr Hughes. "Pay me off and I'll go."

Mr Hughes turned pale. "I'm not paying you a penny, after what you've done to Mostyn," he said.

Did this mean he'd run out of money? William had noticed him spending more and more time in taverns since Mostyn had joined the drove.

"For goodness' sake, Robert! What's got into you! You must pay Tom," said Mrs Hughes.

But Tom put a hand on her arm. "Don't waste your energy, Gwen. I'll get my wages off Evan, in due course. I can get by for now." He turned his back on them all and led his horse over to the barn to collect his things.

William sprinted after him with Mab in close pursuit. "Tom! Don't go!" He inserted himself between Tom and his bedding roll. "Please don't go. I need you here." Mab joined in, pawing Tom's knees and letting out short, friendly barks.

Tom smiled as he pushed her down. "You'll be fine, William. You're doing what's needed to keep this drove going, already. You're like your dad – you don't give up."

"But Tom, what are you going to do?"

"Don't you worry about me, lad. I'd be leaving in a few days, anyway. Rhys Pryce will be here soon, to take you into London. I'm going up to Aylesbury to see my wife's parents," said Tom.

He moved William gently to one side and picked up his bedding roll. "Now, here's something to think about. Good things happen on droves as well as bad things, you know." William followed him out of the barn and watched him tie the bedding roll to his horse as he talked. "My father-in-law's a blacksmith – has his own smithy. He taught me all I know. I stopped there once, when I was droving, met his daughter, and never looked back!" He punched William playfully. "That's what happens when you go a-droving, lad. You want to watch that Lizzie. She'll be courting you before you know it!"

William felt himself blushing.

"I'll do a bit of forging for my father-in-law and then get back to the missus and little ones in Ynys Mon," continued Tom. "I'll be back droving with you before the summer's out – you'll see." He fastened a saddlebag to the saddle. "Evan always pays Rhys Pryce to guide him into London. Rhys knows the best routes. He's a sensible man and he can usually get Robert to see sense as well. What's more, he respects Evan and he'll want to help you out. So, cheer up. You'll be down in London with the cattle sold, and money in your pocket, before you know it."

"I hope you're right," said William, feeling a bit more cheerful. Then he remembered. "Money! I can pay you." He plunged his hand inside his vest. "Dad gave me money as well as Mr Hughes – just in case."

"Keep it, William. You're going to need it," said Tom.

"It's what Dad would want," said William. "Anyway, if you're right, I'll make loads more when we sell the stock. Take it, Tom. It's thanks to you that we got our best oxen back." He produced the package that had pressed against his chest for the past two weeks, counted out some bank notes and handed them over. "Here, take these."

"Well, I suppose Evan would have paid me if he were here," said Tom. He took the notes. "Ugh! They're greasy." He sniffed them. "Pooh! Pig's fat – all the way from Ynys Mon! Lovely!"

"You're lucky! You're the first to get a sniff!" said William as they both burst out laughing.

Tom stuffed the notes into his pocket. "Thanks, William. You keep the rest safe."

As William walked Tom to the road, Lizzie ran up. "Goodbye, Tom. I'm sorry you're going."

"Thank you, kind maid, but it won't be long before we meet again," said Tom. He stooped in an elaborate bow, which made Lizzie laugh. Then he shook hands warmly with William. "Remember! You did the right thing, reporting Mostyn and Cade Jones to the police," he said as he mounted his horse. William made a face. "Yes, you did, William, and Robert will agree, in time. If you hadn't reported them, they'd be stealing from someone else by now. You've done the world a favour. Robert knows that: he just doesn't want to admit it."

"I wish you were staying," said William.

But Tom wouldn't stay. William and Lizzie sadly watched him and his loaded horse trundling along the turnpike road. "What sort of state was Cade in when you saw him at the police station?" asked Lizzie, when Tom had disappeared around a corner.

William gritted his teeth: why did she keep harping on about Cade? Well, he wasn't going to tell her about Cade's black eye. That would really get her going.

"Not bad. He looked fed up, but then he's under arrest. He backed up Mostyn's claim that they're innocent, which is daft, when they're clearly guilty," he said, shrugging his shoulders. "Anyway, why are you always so interested in Cade?"

"I'm not. As I told you, I just feel sorry for him because of the way his dad treats him – and now this arrest." Lizzie raised one eyebrow. "Why, William? Are you jealous?" She smiled up at him, teasingly. "I didn't realise you cared that much!"

William's heart lurched but he couldn't look Lizzie in the eye. "Well, I do," he mumbled, staring at his boots.

"Oh, William!" Lizzie threw her arms around him.

But it was broad daylight. Mrs Hughes was probably watching, and she had eyes like a hawk so William pulled away. "Things might get difficult between me and your dad, now Tom's gone," he said, hastily changing the subject.

"Well, I'm on your side, William, and don't worry about my dad. Uncle Rhys will be here soon, and he'll talk sense into him," said Lizzie.

27

18TH APRIL 1848

Barnet, near London, England

It was two long days before Rhys Pryce arrived.

William was checking on the cattle when he heard a joyful cry from Mrs Hughes. He ran over to the wagon, where he found her tearfully hugging her brother while Lizzie hung on to his arm. Mr Pryce untangled himself and shook William's hand enthusiastically. "You must be William. You're very like your dad!" he said.

Mr Pryce had an abundance of curly, black hair. Sideburns sprung from his cheeks, black curls bubbled from under his hat and his eyebrows met untidily above his nose. Unlike William and the Hughes family, he looked well-fed and recently washed. His greatcoat hung open, showing a shirt and waistcoat in place of a smock, with the buttonholes straining across his belly.

"I was devastated to hear about your father's accident," he continued, cradling William's hand in both his own. "Tragedy. I'm so sorry."

William, momentarily unable to speak, nodded his thanks.

"We've been corresponding. I had a note from him yesterday, with instructions about our trip into London," continued Mr Pryce. "Your dad said to tell you he's a lot better and your mam and her unborn child are doing well."

William's eyes pricked with tears of relief. "Thanks for letting me know."

Mr Pryce touched his shoulder sympathetically, before turning to Mr Hughes.

"We may as well look at the stock straight away, Robert. You come too, William. Barnet Market starts tomorrow. We need to make some decisions."

"Can I come?" asked Lizzie.

"Certainly. I'd like to see how you are with cattle before you start handling mine, in London."

William was pleased to have his opinion valued. As he and Lizzie followed the two drovers into the field, he felt like an expert. They spent an hour corralling the cattle into groups for sale in either Smithfield or Barnet Market, depending on what Mr Pryce thought they were worth.

"We don't usually sell off so many cattle at Barnet, brother-in-law. Why the change?" asked Mr Hughes.

"Yes. Why don't we take them all to London?" asked William.

Mr Pryce gave him a conspiratorial smile. "Because I've got a plan," he said.

"And what might that be?" Mr Hughes folded his arms across his chest.

"It involves railways."

"Railways? After what we've been through? Is this a joke,

Rhys Pryce? Because if it is, I don't think it's funny," said Mr Hughes.

"No. I'm serious," said Mr Pryce. "Your views are only what I expected, Robert, but for the sake of business, you need to put them aside. Railways are our future. You surely noticed that I didn't arrive on horseback?"

William's jaw dropped. "You came by train?"

"I did. There's a railway station at Islington now, close to where I graze the animals for my cow-keeper's shop. I drove some of them up to the pasture and then hopped on a train to Sandford, which is only a mile from here." Mr Pryce looked down at William with amusement. "Shut your mouth, boy, before you catch a fly! Are you interested in railways, by any chance?"

"I certainly am," said William. "Tom Morris says they're our future, too."

Mr Pryce's eyes lit up. "And he's so right. What's more, riding on a train is like magic! You travel faster than you could ever go on a horse! It's wonderful! You just have to try it!"

Mr Hughes looked most unhappy with this turn in the conversation. "What have railways got to do with selling cattle? That's what you're here for: not joyriding around on railways!"

"We can now transport our cattle to London by train. That's what trains have got to do with selling them, Robert."

"Huh!" Mr Hughes fumbled for his tobacco in disgust.

"These steam locomotives pull cattle trucks," said Mr Pryce. They can carry the cattle to within two miles of Smithfield Market. Yes, you will pay a fare, but because the cattle are carried, they keep their price. Look at these animals."

He indicated the herd with a sweep of his arm. "They're in as good condition as you'll get them now. Even the ones that you tell me were stolen don't look too bad. If you walk them to London, they'll lose weight and get stressed on the busy roads – like they always do – but now, we have an alternative."

Mr Hughes chewed a plug of tobacco while he sullenly regarded his brother-in-law. "We always manage to sell them, nevertheless," he said.

"But not for the price you'll get if you take my advice," continued Mr Pryce. "Butchers like unstressed meat, as you know. I promise you, if you take your cattle to London on the train, they'll be worth more than any cattle that have walked there."

William surveyed the mass of black oxen stretching to the far side of the field. "How many trucks would we need?" he asked.

"I'm not suggesting we take them all," said Mr Pryce. "Another time we might, but I think we should try out a small group first. If we sell the less valuable animals here, at Barnet, with a bit of luck we'll get as much for them as they'd fetch in Smithfield after a long trek. We'll take the prime cattle into London on the train. You've got some good ones here – that big beast with the broken horn, for example."

"He's more trouble than he's worth, that one," grumbled Mr Hughes. "I don't like these new ways and I'm not putting my oxen on the railways: not for you or anyone else. I'll sell them all here, in Barnet, rather than do that. For now, I've got better things to do than stand here fantasising. I'll see you later."

But as he turned to go, Lizzie blocked his way. "Why don't we give it a try, Dad? No harm in that, surely? It sounds a great idea. I could go with Uncle Rhys and William and report back to you."

Mr Hughes put his hands on his hips and glared down at her. "And who do you think you are, my girl, to be advising your own father – an experienced drover of many years' standing – how to deal with his own cattle? Worse than that, what on earth makes you think I'd agree to you gallivanting all the way to London on a train?"

"But Dad…"

"She's right, Robert," said Mr Pryce, standing behind Lizzie and resting his hands on her shoulders. "Your daughter is talking common sense. I think you should listen."

Mr Hughes' neck reddened, and he tapped his stick rapidly against his leg, but he said nothing.

"Of course, what you do with your own oxen is up to you," continued Mr Pryce. "I wouldn't argue with that. But don't forget, Lizzie is my niece as well as your daughter. What's more, she's coming to work for me, and I want to keep up with the changing times. I'll be responsible for her, as part of my family, in your absence so I might as well start now. I think it would be a very good thing if she came with William and me on the cattle train to London. It will give us both a chance to get to know each other better before she starts learning to be a milkmaid in my cow-keeper's shop."

Lizzie grinned at William like a circus clown.

Mr Hughes pointed his stick at his brother-in-law. "You're telling me how to bring up my own daughter now, are you, Rhys Pryce?"

"Not at all. But once you return to Ynys Mon, and I'm responsible for her, I may not always make the same decisions as you would. If you don't like the sound of that, Robert, you'd better take her home with you."

"You know I can't afford to do that," growled Mr Hughes.

Mr Pryce shrugged his shoulders and opened his arms. "Your decision."

The two men glared at each other while William and Lizzie jumped up and down behind them with their fingers crossed.

"Oh, what's the point of me arguing? Gwen will take your side. Do what you like," snapped Mr Hughes at last. He turned on his heel and stomped off in the direction of The Bear and Billet.

Mr Pryce watched him go with a shake of his head. "If he doesn't keep up with these changing times, he'll regret it." He turned to William and Lizzie. "What do you think? Shall we have a go?"

"I think we should, but what if my dad finds out?" said William. "He takes the same view as Mr Hughes. Even before his accident, he disapproved of railways, let alone how he feels about them now!"

Mr Pryce leant towards William conspiratorially. "Your dad needn't know. And if my plan works, he won't care. I know him of old. If we make plenty of money, he won't ask too many questions, believe me."

But William still wasn't sure.

"Don't look so worried, boy." Mr Pryce put an arm around William's shoulders. "Your father has landed a lot of responsibility on you. I don't think he has a right to complain if something goes wrong. And in the unlikely event of that happening, I'll be there to stand up for you."

Both Mr Pryce's enthusiasm and his offer of support were hard to resist. There was always a chance that something would go wrong – but it could anyway – cattle droving was a risky business. And William was desperate for a ride on a railway. "All right, I'll risk it," he said.

"Excellent!" said Mr Pryce, giving him a hearty slap on the back.

The following morning, William and Mr Pryce walked to Sandford station to buy advance tickets for the steam train to London, for themselves and their cattle. Lizzie, much to her annoyance, was kept behind to help her mam, but Uncle Rhys promised to buy her a ticket.

They arrived just as a locomotive pulled up at the platform with an ear-piercing whistle and a blast of steam. William had never before been so near to a stationary steam locomotive, and there was so much he wanted to know. How did it move without a horse to pull it? How fast did it travel? Banishing the terrifying memories of Dad's accident from his mind, he ran towards it, weaving his way through passengers jostling each other for seats in the carriages.

As soon as he reached the locomotive, it let off steam with a deafening roar and he jumped back with his hands over his ears. From the safety of the platform, he looked up to see a shiny gold name plate screwed to the side of the engine: 'Lightning'. Standing on the footplate was the driver, pulling levers, and the fireman, shovelling coal into the glowing firebox. The searing heat hit William in the face and the smell of hot oil from the piston rods was intoxicating.

The fireman, a huge man with iron-grey hair and bulging arms, held out a grimy hand. "Want to come up, boy?"

"Yes, sir!" William put one foot on the step, grasped the fireman's hand and was propelled on to the footplate as if he weighed no more than a puppy. "Is that what powers the locomotive?" he asked as soon as he found himself standing two feet from the firebox.

"Partly." The fireman threw another shovelful of coal into the flaming furnace.

The driver wiped coal dust from his face with a greasy cloth. "We're due out in ten minutes. I'm going to check the couplings," he said, leaping on to the platform and striding off, carrying a large spanner.

"So, you want to know what makes this queen go?" said the fireman, pushing his cap to the back of his head.

"I do," said William.

"Think of the locomotive as a horse," said the fireman. "You feed a horse, right?"

William nodded.

"The food gives him power. The power makes his legs work and off he goes?" William nodded again. "This fire is like the horse's mouth. I feed it with coal, and it boils the water in the boiler here." The fireman stroked the wooden-clad boiler from which the locomotive's funnel rose. "The water turns to steam and builds up pressure which drives the pistons to move in the cylinders. The pistons turn the wheels with connecting rods and off we go. Clever, isn't it?"

"Yes," said William, who now had a picture in his head of Seren, with steam coming out of her ears, and wasn't sure if he had fully understood the fireman's explanation.

Soon, he heard Mr Pryce calling. "William! There you are. Looking for a job on the railways, are you?"

"Good day, sir. I do think I may have a recruit!" said the fireman, laughing.

"I wouldn't be surprised! I wouldn't mind joining you myself, but I need him back now," said Mr Pryce. "Come on,

William. There are spaces on the cattle train for our journey to Smithfield Market. Let's buy the tickets."

William reluctantly climbed down from the footplate. "How do you become a fireman, Mr Pryce? Could I be one? Do they employ boys on steam locomotives?"

"Whoa, whoa! I can't answer three questions at once," laughed Mr Pryce. "I'll deal with the last one. I've never seen a boy driving a steam locomotive, but I've seen boys doing jobs at Camden Engine Sheds, near my cow-keeper's shop: cleaning, running messages, that sort of thing. You'll have to ask your fireman friend if you want to know more."

They joined the queue of customers at the ticket office, which was a hastily constructed shed at one end of the platform. William shifted from one foot to another, hoping to get out in time to ask the fireman more about his job before the train departed. But nobody else was in a hurry. A couple of farmers bought tickets for cattle trucks; the businessman in front of them made a fuss because there were no first-class carriages available; and at last, it was their turn. Mr Pryce booked four cattle trucks as well as places in a second-class carriage for himself, William, Lizzie and Mab. The Clerk picked up his quill pen, wrote out the tickets in perfect handwriting and slid them across the counter. But it all took far too long. By the time they came out of the ticket office, Lightning was moving off.

William couldn't take his eyes off the locomotive as she barked out of the station, clanking and shushing. He hated to think what Dad might do to him if he found out that he'd just bought tickets to take his cattle to London by train. But soon he was lost in the excitement of seeing Lightning panting up the hill, whistling wildly, and he ceased to care.

28

20TH APRIL 1848

Barnet, near London, England

Barnet Market throbbed with sound: the thundering of hooves, the bleating of sheep, the neighing of horses and the bellowing of cattle, as hundreds of animals were separated into enclosures, ready for sale. William and Mr Pryce shouldered their way through the heaving crowds, doing their best to keep their cattle together. Drovers and boys jostled each other for prime positions in order to get the best prices for their livestock. Scuffles broke out. Barking dogs lost their owners in a forest of thrashing hooves. The Bear and Billet overflowed with beery customers, boasting about successful sales to their friends.

Luckily, Mr Pryce knew the market and many of its drovers well: who to dodge and with whom to deal. Before long they had sold, for a reasonable price, all the animals they didn't want to take to London.

Then came the task that William had been dreading: Seren had to be sold. Any other time, he would have tried to persuade Dad to keep her, but Dad wasn't here to be persuaded. William was already going against Dad's wishes, by secretly agreeing to transport his cattle to London by rail, wasn't he? The least he could do for Dad was to sell Seren. After all, why would Dad want to keep a horse that he might never be able to ride again? And anyway, the family needed the money.

William told himself this as he walked over to the field where Seren was grazing. She'd been part of the family for several years – so long, that selling her felt like a betrayal. He flung his arms around her neck and she nudged his cheek with her silky nostrils. "I'll do my best to find you a good owner, old friend," he said, tracing the star on her forehead with his finger. "We've been through a lot together, you and me."

Mr Pryce found them, still making a fuss of each other, a few minutes later. "No time for that, boy," he said, slipping a halter over Seren's head. "You can't afford to be sentimental in this business. She'll fetch a good price, this one."

"I know, but I still don't want to part with her," said William.

Mr Pryce tutted. "Your dad shouldn't have kept her so long. It doesn't do for a drover to get attached to his horse. Horses often get injured on a journey and have to be put down or sold for a less demanding job." As he spoke, he ran his hands down Seren's legs and examined her feet. "She's not in bad condition, but she's past her best for long-distance droving." He stood up and adjusted his hat. "Come on, let's see what we can get for her. Your dad needs every penny, now that he's injured."

"I know," said William. Gloomily, he led Seren to the horse market, where many fine animals were lined up in rows. Gentlemen dressed in top hats and tails and ladies in satin skirts were parading up and down, viewing them.

"This is the fancy end. We need to be over the other side," said Mr Pryce. He explained that rich people came to this section to buy hunting horses or matching pairs for their swanky carriages. William stopped to admire a beautiful pair of greys. They stood a hand higher than Seren and were decorated with shining brass ornaments. But Mr Pryce hurried him on.

In the drovers' section, there were a lot of Welsh cobs. The breed was valued by both English and Welsh drovers because of their hardiness and tough character. But none of the cobs William saw were as fine as Seren and he wasn't the only one who thought so. He and Mr Pryce were soon surrounded by eager buyers. He bartered with customers whilst William held Seren's head steady and fought back the urge to leap on to her back and ride her to freedom. Before long, she was sold for a fair price to a drover who, to William's relief, at least seemed to care about horses. The man intended to ride her to Suffolk with the cattle he'd bought – but then, for all William knew, he might sell her on to some unscrupulous dealer. He swallowed the lump in his throat and tried not to think about it.

"Cheer up, boy," said Mr Pryce. "I'll treat you to lunch at The Bear and Billet. A full belly should help to take your mind off your horse."

But even this generous offer didn't comfort William. "Thanks, but I'm not hungry," he said. "I'll see you later." He left Mr Pryce outside The Bear and Billet and went off to look for Lizzie. He found her with her mam at a stall in the goods market, selling woven blankets and socks knitted by her uncle in Bala.

"Poor William," said Lizzie and squeezed his hand.

"No time for messing, you two," said Mrs Hughes. "Make yourself useful, William."

Welsh woollen goods were highly prized by London society. Traders came to Barnet Market especially to buy them. There were now a number of customers, fingering the blankets, and haggling with Lizzie over the price. At first, William just watched with his arms folded while he moped about Seren. But when he saw the prices Lizzie was letting the goods go for, he couldn't resist interfering. Before long, he'd squeezed himself between Lizzie and the customer she was serving.

"That can't be a serious offer, madam. Have you not felt the quality and thickness of this beautifully woven material? The warmth of this wonderful wool keeps Welsh mountain sheep alive through the winter snows. I can guarantee it will keep your customers cosy in bed," he said with an irresistible smile.

"Go on with you!" laughed the woman. But she paid a higher price for the blanket than Lizzie had been asking. The same approach worked for the next customer and the next, as William practised his charms and, as he thought, superior sales technique. By the time they were down to the last blanket, they had made a good sum.

"It takes a man's touch," William said, pushing his hat to the back of his head.

"Rubbish, William Evans. I'd have done just as well without you," scoffed Lizzie. She flung the last blanket over William's head and pummelled him with her fists.

"Hey! Hey! Ow! Stop it!" William shoved her arm away so that she lost her balance, knocked William and the blanket to the ground and landed on top of him.

"Get up you two! You're ruining valuable goods." Mrs Hughes bustled over and wrenched the blanket away. "This is stained now. You'll have to pay for it!"

But William and Lizzie were helpless with laughter. "Sorry," they said as they struggled to their feet. But they weren't sorry at all. William ran off to find Mr Pryce, with the happy memory of Lizzie in his arms and the loss of Seren temporarily forgotten.

29

25TH APRIL 1848

The journey to Smithfield Market, London, England

Once Barnet Market was over, they all set off for London. Mr and Mrs Hughes, having sold their livestock, wagon and Melfed the horse, took the road coach. Their only reason for travelling into London now was to meet up with Lizzie and the Pryce family, at the cow-keeper's shop, for a family reunion. After they had settled Lizzie with her uncle, they would return by coach to Ynys Mon.

Meanwhile, William, Lizzie, Mr Pryce and Mab drove a select group of fine-looking Welsh Blacks, including Big Beast, into the waiting pens at Sandford Station. The smell of coal-fired steam sent shivers of excitement through William. A locomotive was already waiting at the end of the platform, wisps of steam wafting from its tall funnel and cylinders. William read its name plate. "That's Lightning, Lizzie, the same locomotive I saw before."

He was about to take Lizzie up the platform for a closer

look when the station policeman arrived to check their tickets. That done, the policeman lowered the sides of four trucks, so they rested on the platform, forming ramps.

"Is this the first time you've driven cattle into trucks?" he asked. William nodded. "Get on with it, then." The policeman stood back with his arms folded expectantly.

William began with Big Beast, hoping the rest of the oxen would follow his example, which they did. Big Beast leapt forward at William's command, took an instant dislike to the wooden slats under his hooves and backed up, bellowing. The other animals copied him, scattering along the platform, much to the alarm of Mr Pryce and the waiting passengers. Mab made matters worse by running around in circles yapping so that the distressed oxen didn't know which way to turn.

Eventually, the station policeman tired of his own joke and came to their rescue. He tied Mab to a post and helped William and Lizzie coax the nearest cattle into the trucks, while Mr Pryce rounded up the stragglers. Once the oxen were all in, the policeman lifted up the ramp for each truck and slid the bolt closed. The animals protested with moans and brays, but they were secured.

William and Lizzie ran up the platform to see Lightning. They stopped by the locomotive's gleaming wheels, two of which were nearly as tall as them. "Feel the heat from her firebox," said William.

But Lizzie backed away. "I nearly fell under one like this. Look at the size of it! No wonder your dad was hurt. It's amazing we're both still alive!"

"I see you can't keep away young man, can you?" said the fireman in a familiar, gravelly voice. "I've got a minute – hop up!" He stretched out a grimy hand and pulled William on to the footplate once again. "Does your friend want to come up too?"

Lizzie shook her head vigorously. "I'm just getting used to it."

"Wise decision," laughed the fireman. "Bit dirty up here for a pretty maid." He turned to William. "I'm stoking her up." He flung a shovelful of coal into the firebox, which glowed like a dragon's mouth. Triangular tongues of white-hot flame flickered hungrily amongst the coals. "She's ready to go now. Feel the power." The fireman closed William's hand around a lever above the firebox door.

William grinned as the vibrations buzzed through his body.

"When the driver moves that regulator lever, the pistons will start to move and off we'll go," said the fireman.

William pointed down at Lizzie. "My friend nearly fell under a steam locomotive like this, that's why she's looking so worried. My dad went after her and caught her just in time, but he broke his leg jumping away from it."

The fireman raised his eyebrows. "I'm sorry to hear that," he said. "These locomotives are dangerous and that's a fact. Accidents are pretty common, I'm afraid. The maid and your dad are both lucky to be alive. How's your dad now?"

"He's getting better, but his leg was mangled, so I don't know how well he's going to be able to walk." It was the first time William had voiced this fear to a stranger and his words came out wobbly. The fireman patted his shoulder, before tactfully busying himself with the firebox.

"Where's the brake? Why didn't the driver stop? He must have seen Dad," said William when he could speak again.

"This is the brake." The driver grabbed another lever. "But it doesn't work that well."

"That's reckless!" said William. "No wonder my dad got hurt."

"You're talking about tons of metal hurtling along, son," said the fireman. "No one has yet invented a brake that can quickly stop a train travelling at speed. Once she's slowed down enough, this brake will stop her but, for their own safety, people and animals just have to keep out of our way." The fireman wiped the sweat from his forehead with the back of his hand and checked his watch. "Time to go. You'd better get into your carriage." He looked up at the darkening sky. "We're going to get soaked again, by the look of those clouds. The wind's getting up. What a life!" He buttoned up his jacket. "Are you in second-class?"

William nodded.

"Well then, unlike us, you'll have a roof over your head. It's all right for some!"

"Thanks for showing me how it works," shouted William, jumping off the footplate as the driver climbed on. He and Lizzie ran back to join Mr Pryce, who was waiting by the carriages with Mab straining on her leash.

There were three carriages between theirs and the locomotive, Lightning – an open third-class and two second-class, each of which had a roof on poles but no glass in the windows. They got into one of these and sat on a wooden bench with Mab wedged between William and Lizzie.

"You need to train this dog properly," said Mr Pryce. "She made a nuisance of herself, worrying the cattle like that." Mab whined and thumped her tail as William squeezed up to make room for more drovers and a young couple with two children.

The station policeman was striding down the platform, slamming doors. "Everyone here for Islington station?" he yelled. Everyone agreed that they were. "Enjoy your journey," shouted the policeman. He locked the carriage door with a large key.

After that he waved a green flag and blew a whistle. Seconds later, the carriage jolted and rumbled forward with a clanking of metal on metal. Lightning gave a deafening shriek as she left the station. The noise set the children sobbing and the cattle clamouring in their trucks.

William clung to the side of the carriage in awe. He had once travelled with Mam on the top of the road coach from Bangor to Chester, but that had been nothing like this. This was sensational. The carriages rattled rhythmically through the countryside with exhilarating speed. Fresh air rushed past him, stretching the skin over his cheekbones as he clutched at his hat. Sheep in the fields became white blobs. Houses flashed by. William had never in his life travelled so fast. It seemed only a moment before Lightning was pulling into the next station. Here, a station policeman unlocked the carriages of the passengers whose journey had ended and hurried new passengers to their seats.

As Lightning set off again, it began to rain. Listening to the drops landing on the carriage roof, William remembered what the locomotive driver had said about it being, 'all right for some'. This made him feel snug and dry – but not for long. As Lightning gathered speed, the rain lashed through the open sides of the carriage, stinging their faces and soaking their clothes. Mab retreated under the seat, whimpering, while the mother of the small girls covered them with a rug.

Worse was to come, as Lightning began to labour up a gradient, belching out red-hot cinders. Shrieks of dismay came from the passengers in the open third-class carriage. Mab rocketed out from under the seat, barking and then let out a howl of pain as a smouldering cinder landed on her back. William picked it off with his coat sleeve over his hand and flung it away.

"There's a spark on my skirt," shouted Lizzie, shaking off the glowing ember, stamping on it and then losing her balance and falling against William.

Uproar resounded from the cattle trucks. William reluctantly pushed her away and stuck his head out of the carriage, but he couldn't see anything.

"Do you think our cattle have been burned, Mr Pryce?"

"We'll soon find out."

At the next station, Mr Pryce yelled for help, rattling the carriage door until a policeman ambled up.

"Are you hurt, sir?" he enquired.

"No, but my cattle may be. Let me out! I need to find out why they're making all that noise!" said Mr Pryce.

"Were you intending to finish your journey here, sir?" asked the policeman. "Because if not, I'm afraid I can't unlock you. It's against company law, sir."

"That's ridiculous!" protested Mr Pryce.

The policeman shook his head. "More than my job's worth, sir. I'll check on the cattle myself and give you a wave if they're all right. Have to go now, sir, or the train will be delayed." The policeman touched his top hat and marched down the train to the cattle trucks. William and Mr Pryce craned their necks out of the carriage window, waiting. They soon got a wave from the policeman, followed by a whistle.

"He'd say they were all right even if they were dead!" spluttered Mr Pryce, as the train moved on. He adjusted his hat and raked smut out of his sideburns with his fingers. "Disgraceful! Locking in passengers! We've paid good money. We should be able to do as we like – including checking our own cattle!"

"They'll be all right," remarked one of the drovers. "I transport mine regularly. It's more the smoke than the cinders that upsets them. They've got thick hides. They don't notice a spark or two." And indeed, the cattle soon stopped complaining.

William and Lizzie clung to the side of the carriage, watching fields and rivers, bridges and farmhouses, people and horses, roads and coaches flash past.

"What a speed – faster than Big Beast!"

"Faster than galloping horses!"

"As fast as Lightning." They both laughed.

"I told you, you'd enjoy the journey," said Mr Pryce.

As they neared London, the landscape became more populated. Instead of isolated farmhouses, they raced past clusters of ramshackle dwellings – some brick-built, others like piles of rubbish with holes for doors. Then came a stretch of green fields and muddy lanes. Eventually, they shot past a mansion with beautiful gardens. After that they saw nothing but a clutter of buildings spreading out to the horizon with church spires and smoking chimneys pointing at the sky.

"Is that London?" asked Lizzie.

"It is. We're almost there," said Mr Pryce as the train began to slow. "Those fields beyond the station are near Islington, where I graze my cows. Beyond that is Clerkenwell, where I have my cow-keeper's shop… and that reminds me…" He fumbled in his waistcoat pocket and took out two cards, giving them one each.

"This is the address – Peter Street – just in case."

"In case of what?" asked William.

"In case we get separated. It'll be a free-for-all when we get off the train. Smithfield Market starts tomorrow, and drovers will be pushing to get their cattle into the best pens. So, we need to stick together. You'd better carry a lasso. I brought a spare." Mr Pryce picked up one of the two coils of rope that lay at his feet and handed it to William. "Just in case, but don't worry, we should be fine. If the worst happens and you lose sight of me, just follow the crowd to Smithfield. If you can't find me there, send a boy to my cow-keeper's shop for help. It's only half a mile away."

William slung the rope across his body. "I've got Sir Edward's business card here, as well. Dad gave that to me, in case," he said, pulling the card out of his pocket.

"I know Sir Edward well: he's a good man," said Mr Pryce. "I look after his grazing land. He sent word yesterday that he was on his way to London and wants to talk business." He nodded at the card William was holding. "You won't need that today, William. All will be well, I'm sure."

If they did get lost, would finding Smithfield Market without Mr Pryce's help really be that easy? William didn't think so: he'd make sure they stayed close. But his fears were drowned by excitement as the train drew up at the platform of Islington station in a cloud of steam. "We're in London, Lizzie – the great city of London." He pulled Lizzie into the middle of the carriage and they danced a clog dance until the other passengers protested.

"Remember those stories about London your dad used to tell us around your kitchen fire when we were small?" said Lizzie.

"I do," said William. "And now, we're actually here."

30

25TH APRIL 1848

The journey to Smithfield Market, London, England

In spite of Mr Pryce's optimism, William found getting the cattle out of the station even harder than driving them through the mountains of Wales. As soon as the ramps were lowered, they burst out of the trucks, bellowing loudly, and shot off in all directions. Then, when Mr Pryce, William and Lizzie finally got them on to the highway, they were faced with a new set of problems. They had to steer their cattle into an endless stream of animals being driven up the London road. This was also the main route for the coaches, loaded with passengers and luggage, that were trapped amongst the waving horns and bobbing drovers' hats slowly moving towards the city.

Mr Pryce took control of one side of their herd and William, Lizzie and Mab the other, with William making sure to keep Big Beast close, in case he tried any of his tricks. The recent rain had made mud-soup of the road surface, causing hooves to slither and slide and oxen to bounce off each other, bawling and bellowing.

"Help, William! Get Mab off me!" shouted Lizzie as Mab dived to avoid an ox's hoof, skidded beneath her skirts and splattered her with stinking mud.

"Mm… you smell lovely!" laughed William, grabbing Mab and attaching her leash.

Eventually, their oxen settled down and ambled along at an easy pace, with Mr Pryce shouting encouragement to William and Lizzie from his side of the herd. It was only when they reached a place where the road was wider and lined with large, ornate houses, that the trouble started.

Now that there was more space, drovers urged their herds forward with cries of, "Go on, get along," so that the cattle spread out and moved faster. Taken by surprise, William and Lizzie tried in vain to keep their half of the herd close to Mr Pryce's until, to William's horror, he saw a mass of brown and white Herefords hurrying towards them. Before he and Lizzie could stop them, they had trundled straight through the middle of their Welsh Blacks, dividing his and Lizzie's half from Mr Pryce's. William could see Mr Pryce frantically waving his hat and pointing straight ahead. But then, as he, Lizzie and their oxen were pushed towards the far side of the road, he lost sight of him altogether.

"We've got to get back to Uncle Rhys," called Lizzie.

"How can we?" shouted William. "We'll have to carry straight on like he said and hope we meet up with him later. Have we lost any? Where's Big Beast?"

"Over there with two others," said Lizzie. "I'll get them."

William watched admiringly as Lizzie caught up with the strays just in time and headed them back into the herd.

It pained him to admit it, but she was probably better at herding than him. Between the two of them, they should make it to Smithfield.

But soon they faced another difficulty. They came to a road junction with four roads fanning out in front of them. Which way should they go? Some drovers were choosing one way, some another. William touched the arm of one drover as he strode past. "Which road goes to Smithfield Market?"

"Any of these – depends where you want to be in the market square – ask your boss," said the drover, hurrying on.

But William and Lizzie had lost their boss. William could see some Welsh Blacks disappearing down the street furthest away from them, but there was no way they could get across there and he wasn't even sure that those animals were Mr Pryce's. He looked glumly at Lizzie, who shrugged and made a face. "We'll just have to guess."

William nodded. "I'll lead, if you keep the back in order." He looked around for Big Beast, wanting to be near him to keep him calm. Unfortunately, the ox was now nearer to Lizzie than him, but William couldn't do anything about that.

They followed the Herefords in front of them, down the nearest of the four narrow roads that led to Smithfield Market. Here, crooked houses leant in from both sides of the street, with lines of washing strung between their overhanging gables so that only a strip of grey sky could be seen above. Ahead of William, a woman in a white cap leant out of an upstairs window and emptied the contents of a chamber pot on to the backs of the cattle below. A cry of fury rose up from nearby drovers, followed by a hidden cackle of laughter. Women defended their doorsteps with brooms: sweeping off cattle muck and yelling insults. Skinny children shivered in doorways. William felt sick from the stink of rotting rubbish and slime beneath his feet. But just when he was beginning to think they would be trapped there for ever, they came to a T-junction.

"Move on!" yelled a drover from behind.

"Which way to the market?" shouted William.

"Turn right and carry on round, past the slaughterhouses; you'll find roads into the market a quarter of a mile up on your left."

Following the drover's direction, they came to a place where butchers' shops, with slaughterhouses in their cellars, lined both sides of the road. Mr Pryce had warned Lizzie and William about these, so they would be prepared. But William didn't feel at all prepared for what he now saw.

Carcasses of slaughtered sheep and cattle hung on giant hooks in front of the shops and blood dripped from them into the gutters. Beside the door of each shop were chutes leading into cellars, where, Mr Pryce had told them, butchers slaughtered the live animals they had bought in the markets. The stench of stale blood coming up from these cellars brought bile into William's throat. He swallowed it down and looked back at Lizzie, who had her hand over her mouth. Ahead of them, a terrified sheep squealed as it was forced down one of the chutes by two burly men.

William and Lizzie had grown up on farms. They were used to oxen, sheep and pigs being killed for meat, but not like this, with no apparent regard for decency or respect for the animals. William hurried their oxen on, desperate to get away from it all.

At last, the butchers' shops came to an end and they reached the first entrance into the market square, but they couldn't get near because of the queue of drovers and cattle trying to get in, so they carried on to the next one, where there was less of a crush.

"I'll take a look before we go any further. Maybe I'll see Mr Pryce," William called back to Lizzie, miming his words in case she couldn't hear. He did a quick count of their oxen. None were missing and Big Beast was near the back, with Lizzie keeping an eye on him. Then he edged forward to get a glimpse of the open square that was Smithfield Market. It was a relief to get his nose out of that stinking alley, even for a moment. Here there was plenty of sky to be seen, but still no peace. Sheep and cattle were being driven into vast numbers of pens from all directions. Horse-drawn carriages jolted across the cobbles with vendors running alongside, holding trays of pies under the windows. Hungry children ran around the wheels, risking their lives for a bite. Ponies reared and cows kicked out. Laughter, yelling, mooing and neighing filled the air.

William scanned the muddle of people and animals for a glimpse of Mr Pryce, but he couldn't see him anywhere. They would have to find him once they were in the market. He looked back at Lizzie, shaking his head and gesturing her to move the herd forward, but she was pointing at the sky with a look of awe on her face. William followed her gaze with a gasp of wonder. In the distance, beyond the square, he saw a vast dome towering high above the grimy roof tops. This must be the dome of St Paul's Cathedral that Dad and Old Griff had told him about. They had made it sound grand, but he hadn't expected anything as beautiful as this. He watched with wonder as the dome shimmered in the light of the watery sun, like a magical gift.

But there was no magic in Lizzie's sudden scream of dismay. "Oh no, William – Big Beast's running off!"

31

25TH APRIL 1848

Clerkenwell Police Station, London, England

Another disaster was the last thing William needed, but it was too late to stop Big Beast. The ox had got away and was trundling further up the butchers' alley, towards an open square. Even worse, the rest of the oxen were following him.

William raced down the side of the herd. "We'll turn them in the square and drive them back," he called to Lizzie. But there was no chance of this. A crowd of rowdy drovers were drinking in the square, outside the inn, and their mouths dropped open with alarm as Big Beast trotted towards them. The nearest drover jumped out of the way, swearing loudly, which spooked the already nervous ox. Howling like a mountain wind, Big Beast kicked out with his back legs and rampaged around the square with the other oxen racing after him.

Just when they'd almost got to the market! William couldn't believe this bad luck. He unfurled his lasso and prepared to throw it over Big Beast when he got the chance. Some of the drovers set down their beer mugs and chased after the oxen, waving sticks and trying to restore order. In an attempt to escape, Big Beast charged at the dark cave of the inn door, scattering the remaining customers. Someone inside quickly slammed the door shut, so that his lowered head collided with a wall of solid oak. This stunned him long enough for William to throw the lasso over his head. He hung on to the rope with all his might until, with the help of one of the drovers, he got Big Beast to stand still, his sides heaving. Several drovers trapped the other oxen in a corner of the square, while Lizzie and William dealt with the complaints of angry customers and furious staff from the inn.

"What do you think you're doing, boy? My dress is torn, thanks to that animal!" shrieked a barmaid, rustling the hem of her scarlet dress at William.

"You shouldn't be on your own, boy. Where's your boss?" said the drover who was helping to restrain Big Beast.

"I'll wager these oxen are stolen! Lock him up! He's spilled my beer!" roared a drunken customer, shaking his fist at William and staggering sideways like a crab.

The square was full of outrage.

Lizzie rushed to William's side with Mab, still on her leash but barking hysterically. "William, what shall we do?"

Her question hung in the air as William, to his dismay, saw a police officer pushing his way through the crowd.

"What's going on here?" enquired the policeman.

"Stolen cattle!"

"This boy's caused a riot!"

"I'll hold the ox while you talk to the bobby," said the drover helping with Big Beast. He pushed William forward.

The crowd closed in on William, Lizzie and Mab. Soon William was so close to the policeman that he could read the words on the bottom button of his jacket: 'Metropolitan Police'. The same message was on each button all the way up to the policeman's chin. Above this were two flared nostrils with a dewdrop hanging from them and above that, a pair of clenched eyebrows.

"Are you in charge of these oxen, boy?" the policeman asked.

"Yes, sir," said William.

"I see. Show me your badge."

"I don't have a badge, sir."

"Of course you don't. You're not old enough. Who gave you permission to drive these oxen?"

"Mr Pryce," said William.

"Uncle Rhys," said Lizzie, at the same time.

"I see you have an assistant," said the policeman, glaring at her. "So, which of those two owns these oxen and why isn't one of them with you?"

Lizzie spoke first. "It's not two people, it's only one, 'cos Uncle Rhys…"

William put his hand over her mouth. "My father owns them."

"So, where is your father? He should be with you," said the policeman.

"He's injured," said William. "He's in The Drovers Rest at Tatlow."

There was some sniggering in the crowd, which the policeman dismissed with a wave. "Not a convincing story so far, young man. It's illegal to drive cattle through London unless you're a badge holder or have the permission of a badge holder to do so. On top of that, you're underage. I'm taking you in for questioning."

"But, I do have permission from Mr Pryce, who's a badge holder, and so is my father," protested William. But the policeman ignored his words and grabbed his arm. As he did so, William twisted sideways and grasped Lizzie's hand.

"Run Lizzie! Take Mab! Find Mr Pryce! He'll know what to do!" he hissed.

Lizzie yanked at Mab's leash, but Mab didn't want to leave William and dropped on her haunches beside him, growling. "Go Mab! Now!" ordered William desperately.

"Do you want this one as well?" called one of the drovers, leering down at Lizzie and blocking her path.

"Get away from me!" screamed Lizzie.

Sensing her terror, the confused Mab flew to her rescue and sank her teeth into the drover's leg.

"Go on Mab!" shouted William again.

This time Mab obeyed him, releasing the drover and dragging Lizzie away on the end of her leash, as the man doubled over with pain. Meanwhile, two drovers held William steady whilst the policeman handcuffed him.

"You two! Take these animals to the police station green-yard!" ordered the policeman, waving at Big Beast and his fellow oxen.

"What's in it for us?" one drover asked.

"I'll tell you what's in it for you, if you don't do as I say," said the policeman. "I can have you run in for refusing to assist an officer of the Metropolitan Police in the execution of his duty." He watched the drovers gather the oxen and move them off, before shoving William forward roughly, so that he stumbled and almost fell.

"I've done nothing wrong!" William protested.

But the policeman ignored his objections and marched him out of the square and along the road to Clerkenwell Police Station.

32

25TH APRIL 1848

Clerkenwell Police Station, London, England

The policeman's name was Constable Runnadey. When they reached the police station, he pushed William into an examination room. Another officer, Constable Cooper, banged the door shut and stood on guard. Through a barred window, William could hear the click of metalled hooves on stone and Big Beast's moans.

"That'll be the cattle that were causing havoc, being driven into the green-yard," Constable Runnadey told Constable Cooper.

Sweat was stinging William's eyes, but he couldn't wipe it away because he was still handcuffed. His thoughts flashed back to the police station at Clappington, where he had reported Mostyn and Cade Jones for stealing cattle. Then he remembered Barnet police station, where he had identified them as thieves. He pictured Mostyn lunging at him and recalled the fear in Cade's eyes. Now here he was, in the same predicament! It was hard to take it in. He felt sick in his stomach and light-headed.

Constable Runnadey plonked himself down at his desk with a notebook, quill pen and ink. "Right, let's have your details," he said, before hammering question after question into William's buzzing head.

William answered them as best he could, but nothing he said seemed to improve his situation. No, he hadn't seen his father recently. No, he'd never been to Mr Pryce's cow-keeper's shop. No, Mr Pryce wasn't a relative, just a family friend. How long had he known him? A few weeks. Where was he now? William didn't know. No, he hadn't seen his mother recently. She lived two hundred and fifty miles away, in a place that Constable Runnadey had never heard of. William thought Mr Hughes, his father's deputy drover, was probably at Mr Pryce's cow-keeper's shop by now, but he couldn't be sure. All through the questioning, William kept glancing at the police station door, willing Lizzie to walk through it with Mr Pryce. But it remained closed. His situation did not look good, and it soon got worse.

"Right, Constable Cooper, time to search the suspect. Remove his handcuffs," said Constable Runnadey.

"Yes, sir," said Constable Cooper eagerly. He grabbed William's arms roughly and unlocked the cuffs. When William almost lost his balance, he gave him a clip around the ear.

Constable Runnadey delved into William's coat pockets, where he found a plug of tobacco, a hunk of stale bread, a spare dog-leash and a handful of small change, which he placed on the desk.

William was outraged at having his personal possessions taken from him. "You don't need to search me! I've done nothing wrong!" he shouted, trying to wriggle free.

Constable Runnadey pulled him up by his collar. "Behave, boy! Unless you want your other ear warmed. And just for the record, you have done something wrong. You've already committed one offence: driving cattle without a licence. Now, I'm investigating the possibility that you've committed another." He shoved William backwards, so that he fell against Constable Cooper, who pushed him upright again. "Remove his coat and jacket and search him."

William rubbed his sore wrists as he faced both policemen in his shirt sleeves. Constable Cooper patted and poked him as if he were an ox in a beef market. He found a hoof-cleaner, a snotty handkerchief and half a mouldy onion wrapped in a cloth.

"Nothing incriminating here, sir," he said.

Why would there be? All William had been doing was droving cattle to Smithfield Market. It wasn't his fault he'd been separated from the licence holder, Mr Pryce, and surely it wasn't a crime if an ox got out of control by mistake? That often happened to drovers…

"Just a minute. There's something not right here. His chest's an odd shape. Lift your arms up, boy!" Constable Runnadey took a step back, scrutinising William from head to toe.

William's heart sank as his shirt and one of his vests were whipped over his head. A rough hand plunged between his winter vest and his skin. It pulled out the packet of bank notes that Dad had trusted him with; the ones he had concealed so well, for so long.

Constable Runnadey wrinkled his nose and held the packet at arms' length. Then he took out a handkerchief, wiped off the pig's fat and opened up the packet, gleefully laying the bank notes on the desktop. "My word! I thought he might be hiding something, but nothing like this. This boy is no petty thief, Constable Cooper. I would say we have a serious criminal on our hands."

"What do you expect? He's a Taffy," said Constable Cooper.

William clenched his fists but forced himself to keep calm. He looked Constable Runnadey in the eye and spoke calmly in English. "I haven't stolen anything. The money is from cattle sales and I'm looking after it for Evan Evans, my father, who works for Sir Edward Ellis-Lloyd of Ynys Mon."

Constable Runnadey roared with laughter. "Did you hear that, Constable Cooper? The boy's a name-dropper as well. Oh, we've got a clever-stick here and no mistake."

"But it's true! You've got to believe me!" protested William.

"I've GOT TO believe you, have I?" Constable Runnadey lifted William by his ears, so that they were face to face. The constable's breath smelt of rotting onions. William tried not to retch and supressed a squeal of pain. "I haven't GOT TO do anything you tell me to do, boy. You're the one in the GOT TO position." Constable Runnadey let William go, so that he staggered backwards and almost fell over.

"In any case, it's not me that has to do the believing, it's the magistrate," Constable Runnadey continued in an official tone when he had returned to his desk. "Tomorrow, you'll appear in court and you can tell the magistrate your story. Now, he may believe you but if he does, I'll be very surprised."

William tried to speak, but Constable Runnadey stopped him with a raised hand and turned to Constable Cooper. "Give him his clothes back and lock him up," he ordered.

33

25TH – 26TH APRIL 1848

Clerkenwell Police Station, London, England

The police station lock-up was in the cellar. William was clutching his clothes to his chest as he was propelled down the steps by Constable Cooper, so he couldn't see where to put his feet. Only the iron grip of the policeman's hand on his arm kept him from falling. When they reached the cellar, he saw a door with a grille in it glimmering in the dim light of an oil lamp. The constable opened this door and shoved William into the empty cell. "You'll get supper later," he growled, then banged the door shut and locked it. His boots clattered on the steps as he went back upstairs.

William stood in the middle of the cell, shaking. Gradually his eyes got used to the gloom. Like all the cellars that he'd seen at street level, there was a supply chute coming down from the pavement. This one had iron bars fitted at both ends, to prevent escape, but a little light filtered through. There was a wooden bench with a blanket on it along one wall and a pisspot in the far corner, from which came a nauseating stink of urine and mould.

His instinct for self-preservation had helped him to keep calm during Constable Runnadey's investigations, but now panic set in. He flung his clothes on to the bench and began pummelling on the door. "Let me out! I'm innocent! Why won't you believe me?" On and on he yelled until the light was beginning to fade and he was sobbing and exhausted. But nobody answered and nobody came.

By this time, his teeth were chattering with cold. He put his jacket and coat back on and wrapped the damp blanket around himself, wrinkling his nose at its rotting smell. Then he perched on the edge of the bench, shivering, and listening to the muffled street noises coming down the chute: the clip-clopping of horseshoes on sets, street hawkers' cries, the rattling of carriage wheels – his only links to the outside world. None of his family and friends knew he was here – not Dad, not Mr Hughes, not Mr Pryce, not Sir Edward. Even Lizzie didn't actually know where the police station was, and she might not be able to find Mr Pryce and… he clutched his head in his hands as dark fears overwhelmed him.

After a while, he heard footsteps on the stairs. The grille cover in the door shot back. "Supper!" said Constable Cooper, pushing through a metal bowl. As soon as William grabbed it, the constable's hand disappeared. "Constable Cooper!" yelled William.

"Eat your gruel and get some sleep, boy," said the constable as he slammed the grille cover shut.

William was hungry, but the food was the colour of vomit. He scooped up a morsel on the end of the spoon and sniffed it. It smelt disgusting. "I'm not eating this!" he shouted and flung the bowl at the wall, from where it bounced on to the floor, leaving the gruel to slowly slide down the stones to join it. He returned to the bench, where he sat hugging his knees and rocking backwards and forwards. How could this have happened? It was such bad luck when they had almost got their cattle into Smithfield Market… Now here he was in this cell, accused of being a thief by a stupid policeman who wouldn't even listen to him! Oh, where had Lizzie got to?

A movement near the cell door caught his eye. Cockroaches. Enormous cockroaches. He slid off the bench and crept towards the black, thumb-sized creatures that were running over his discarded supper. When he was near, he lifted his foot above one insect and stamped hard. He missed the cockroach but sprayed his boots with vomit-coloured mush. The cockroaches fled through a crack in the wall.

They might smell the food on his boots and come after him! He jumped around the bare floor in disgust, scraping his boots on the stones until they were streaked with green slime. Only when he was utterly exhausted and too tired to care, did he sink on to the bench with the blanket pulled up to his chin. Something must have happened to Lizzie or she'd be here by now… maybe he'd never see any of them ever again… maybe… What was that?

A door banged. He heard boots tramping across the floor above his cell: muffled voices, shouting. Was that Mr Pryce come to find him? He sat motionless, hardly breathing in anticipation. Then another door banged, followed by a long, long silence and no further signs of rescue.

Well, help would come in the morning. He had to believe that. He lay down on the hard bench, with his face to the wall, and tried to think of calming things – like home. He pictured

Owain, keeping the farm going and having to do both sets of chores – his own and William's – by himself. This made him smile. He thought of Mam making butter in the dairy, the unborn child swelling her belly, and of his sisters, Margaret and Ann – he missed them all so much. He wondered if Old Griff was still trying to help out on the farm and getting in the way. It seemed so long since they'd all been together.

He thought about the day the drove had left – he and Dad cantering over the Menai bridge on Seren – blue sky and a salt sea breeze. He had been so proud. He had wanted so badly to go droving then, even though he'd had no idea what he was letting himself in for. And then there was his train ride – what an experience! He shut his eyes and recalled the sound of the locomotive, Lightning, puffing along the rails; smelt the acrid smell of coal smoke and steam; pictured the landscape rushing past at incredible speed… until at last he fell into a half-sleep.

Street sounds awoke him at dawn, and he opened his eyes to find a rat sitting on his chest, cleaning its whiskers. "Yah!" William swiped it off and leapt to his feet in one movement. With a squeak, the rat jumped at the wall and scuttled through the bars, up the chute and into the outside world.

Next, William felt the urge to scratch. He found red marks on his arms and tiny lumps on his neck. Bed bugs. Could things get any worse? "Ugh!" He jumped about, slapping himself. Why didn't he start a vermin circus with rats, cockroaches, and bed bugs? He put his hands on his head for horns and bared his teeth like a monster, stomping around the cell until he became alarmed by his own weird behaviour. Then, he flung away the bug-ridden blanket and squatted on the bench with his knees drawn up to his chest, waiting.

34

26TH APRIL 1848

Clerkenwell Police Station, London, England

William lost track of time, curled up on the bench in his cell. The sounds of the waking world – clogs clacking on cobbles, bleating, barking, the scritch of knives being sharpened – penetrated his gloom. He listened, but he didn't stir. He stayed tucked up, tight as a ball of string, until he heard doors banging and voices rumbling overhead, followed by footsteps clumping on the stairs.

This must be his breakfast coming. What would it be this time? Crushed cockroach and rats' tails?

But it wasn't breakfast. A key grated in the lock and Constable Cooper flung open the door. "You're in luck, boy. You've got friends." He flicked his head in the direction of the stairs. "Up we go."

As Constable Cooper manhandled him up the stairs, William hardly dared to believe that Lizzie had arrived. But he thought he heard Mab's bark, and was propelled into the police station office, to find a rescue team. Not only were Lizzie and Mab there, so were Mr Pryce, Mr Hughes and, most surprisingly, Sir Edward Ellis-Lloyd himself – looking grand and official, in a top hat and tails. Constable Cooper pushed William in front of the great man as Mab broke into a frenzy of barking.

"Keep that dog quiet!" thundered Constable Runnadey. Lizzie immediately clamped her hand around Mab's jaws and shortened her leash.

"Do you recognise this boy, sir?" asked Constable Runnadey, who was safely positioned behind his desk.

"Just about," said Sir Edward. "Good morning, William."

"Good morning, sir," croaked William, his voice hoarse from shouting.

"This is William Evans, my chief drover's son," said Sir Edward, glaring at the constable. "Look at the state he's in. Is this what you call 'looking after' your prisoners? You should be ashamed of yourself." He looked down at William sympathetically. "Are you all right, William?"

William nodded, swallowing back tears of relief, until he could trust himself to speak. "I haven't done anything wrong, sir," he blurted out at last.

"They all say that!" remarked Constable Runnadey.

"Oh, they do, do they, Constable?" said Sir Edward. "An important fact, as I hope you know, is that in English law, alleged offenders are innocent until proved guilty. So, tell me, Constable, with what offence are you charging William?"

Constable Runnadey sniffed, then opened a drawer in his desk and took out a document. "This charge-paper states that William Evans stands accused of droving cattle without a badge and without the permission of the owner."

The constable let this sink in and then fixed Sir Edward with a look of triumph. "There may also be a charge of theft."

"Theft! Have you been stealing, William?"

"No, sir," said William. "Dad gave me that money. And why would I want to steal our own cattle?"

Sir Edward guffawed and gave William a friendly slap on the shoulder that nearly sent him flying. "Well said, William. Never short of an answer. Just like your father."

"This is no laughing matter, sir," interrupted Constable Runnadey. "The cattle that this boy was found with yesterday are in the station green-yard. As yet, I have no proof that he had permission to drove them. Nor do I have evidence to suggest that the drover in charge is licensed, if indeed he exists at all."

"He certainly exists. I employ three licenced drovers and here are two of them." Sir Edward indicated Mr Hughes and Mr Pryce. "Rhys Pryce, here, is not only a licensed drover, he also runs a cow-keeper's shop nearby. And he is acting in place of William's father: licenced drover, Evan Evans."

"I gave William permission to drove the cattle you have in your green-yard, Constable," said Mr Pryce, waving his licence at the constable.

"Very well. I accept that William had your legal permission, but we're not finished yet," said Constable Runnadey. "Returning to the question of theft: how do you explain this considerable sum of money which I found in William's possession?" He slapped the bank notes taken from William on to the desk with a flourish.

"Easily," said Sir Edward. "I can vouch that William is telling the truth. His father is recovering from injuries at The Drovers Rest in Tatlow. When I called in to see him on my way to London, he told me that he'd given William money to cover expenses for the rest of the drove."

"I didn't know that!" interrupted Mr Hughes. "As Evan's deputy drover, I should be in charge of all expenses."

William opened his mouth to speak, but Sir Edward signed to him to say nothing and glared at Mr Hughes. "I'm sure Evan would be willing to sign an affidavit confirming my statement, Constable, if you won't except my word for it."

"So would Tom Morris. I paid his wages out of my expenses when you sacked him, Mr Hughes," said William, unable to stay quiet any longer.

"What?" said Mr Hughes, taking a step towards William.

"That's enough," said Constable Runnadey, leaping to his feet. "This is not the place for you to sort out your personal grievances. I shall consider whether I need proof of this evidence before we proceed."

"Certainly, you shall… In the meantime, will someone bring this boy a chair? William, you look as though you haven't eaten for days. Are you hungry?" asked Sir Edward.

"Yes, sir."

Constable Cooper pursed his lips as he pushed a chair forward. "The prisoner was given a meal last night."

"I couldn't eat it. It was disgusting," said William, sitting down at last. "It stank. I fed it to the cockroaches and even they didn't finish it."

Sir Edward gave Lizzie a handful of coins from his pocket. "Find a pie shop and buy William some breakfast, Lizzie. And take that dog with you before it explodes."

"Thank you, sir. I'll be back soon, William." Lizzie rushed out of the police station, tugging Mab behind her.

Sir Edward turned back to Constable Runnadey. "I can vouch for this boy's character. His father, Evan Evans, has been a tenant and employee of mine for years. He's a respectable family man, good at his job. As for his son," he beamed at William, "this boy's a hero! From what I've heard he's done his very best to make sure our cattle arrived safely in London, in spite of a number of difficulties." Sir Edward paused and looked at Mr Hughes accusingly. "And if that doesn't convince you, I have a letter of good character from an independent witness." Sir Edward pulled a paper from his waistcoat and waved it under the constable's nose before showing it to William. "Do you remember Mr Harcourt, William?"

"The gentleman farmer at Clappington, sir?"

"That's the one – an old acquaintance of mine. Shares my interest in steam locomotives," said Sir Edward. "He wrote to me about the arrest of Mostyn Jones and was very complimentary about you." He turned to Constable Runnadey. "William had to deal with a difficult incident on the way to London after his father was injured. Listen to what my gentleman friend, Mr Harcourt, says about him:

'I was struck by the bravery and clear thinking of this young man. I would be proud to have him as an employee and I'm sure he will make a very good drover in the future.'

Sir Edward folded the letter and replaced it in his waistcoat, without taking his eyes off Constable Runnadey. "Now, I'm sure Mr Harcourt would be willing to stand as a character witness, if it came to a court case, Constable. Add that fact to the evidence, which several people can provide, that William is not guilty of droving without permission, or of cattle theft. Don't you think a magistrate would consider that bringing this case was a waste of time?"

Constable Runnadey flopped into his chair, wiping beads of sweat from his forehead with a grimy handkerchief. "I suppose so."

At that moment, Lizzie and Mab returned with a steaming potato pie.

"Thanks, Lizzie. Food at last!" As Lizzie passed him the pie, William caught the scent of her rosy skin and sweet-smelling hair, fresh from a wash under a pump. He sank his teeth into the pie voraciously, delighting in the taste of rich gravy and salty potato.

Soon, matters were settled. In the absence of any incriminating evidence against William, Constable Runnadey had to agree to his release. Mr Pryce and Mr Hughes prepared to fetch the cattle from the police station green-yard and take them to sell in the market. However, Sir Edward had arrangements to discuss with them, first, and told Constable Runnadey that they would be back to collect the cattle soon.

Free at last, William followed Sir Edward down the steps of the police station into the street, with Lizzie, Mab, Mr Pryce and a disgruntled Mr Hughes close behind.

35

26TH APRIL 1848

Clerkenwell, London, England

William blinked in the sunlight as they emerged from the gloomy police station. "Last night, I thought I'd be stuck in that stinking police station forever. I might have been, if you hadn't come along, sir."

Sir Edward adjusted his top hat and smiled down at William. "Glad to help. London's a dangerous place, particularly round here when Smithfield Market is open. Mind your back!" He snatched William out of the way of a hansom cab that dashed past, the horse kicking up muck. "We'll find a tavern in that square at the end of the street: somewhere where we can talk," he told Mr Hughes and Mr Pryce.

'That square' was the one in which Big Beast had gone on the rampage and caused William to be arrested, so William made a grim face at Lizzie when they reached it. But Sir Edward soon cheered them up by ordering beer for everyone while William found benches to sit on in front of the inn. He made sure he sat next to Sir Edward, so that he could ask a very important question. "How's my dad, sir? You said you'd visited him on the way here."

Sir Edward looked grave. "I imagine he's a lot better than when you last saw him, William. His fever's gone and his wounds are healing. He asked after you, of course, and told me how proud of you he is. He's anxious to get back to work as soon as possible, but…" Sir Edward sighed and flicked a spot of mud from his cuff.

"But?" prompted William.

"He's not yet able to put weight on his broken leg and I fear it will be a long time before he can. His claim that he'll be back droving before the end of this season is wishful thinking, in my opinion."

Mr Hughes and Mr Pryce exchanged an anxious look. Lizzie squeezed William's hand.

"How will we manage without him?" William asked.

"Good question. I asked myself the same thing, on my coach journey down here, and I have a plan. Gather round so you can hear me – the noise from that market is deafening." William and Lizzie shuffled their bench nearer so they could hear Sir Edward above the din of shouting men, bellowing oxen and bleating sheep.

"The question is: how are we going to drove another herd of cattle to London by the end of the season, without Evans to lead it?" continued Sir Edward.

"I'm his deputy – I'll take over," said Mr Hughes.

Sir Edward looked at him disapprovingly. "I'm afraid I don't see that as a good solution, Hughes. I'll explain why, shortly." He turned to William. "Mr Pryce, here, tells me that the two of you took some of our cattle from Barnet to London by train."

William glanced at Mr Pryce, who nodded encouragement. "That's right, sir, Mr Pryce thought it best. Lizzie helped as well."

"Excellent. Railways are our future. What did you think of the journey?"

William's memories zoomed around his head, all trying to break out at once. "Incredible! Our steam locomotive was called Lightning, sir, and it certainly moved like lightning. It makes its own power and travels faster than a galloping horse. You pass everything in a flash – trees, horses, houses, people and miles of land – all gone before you can blink…"

Sir Edward threw back his head and laughed. "I see you're hooked, boy. I think you might like my plan to transport some of our cattle to London by rail. You would still have to walk them to England: the railways don't come as far as Ynys Mon yet. But once you're over the border you could have a go." He turned to Mr Hughes. "I know Rhys Pryce agrees with me, Hughes, and I'm sure Tom Morris will be up for it. What's your view?"

Mr Hughes looked shocked. "I want nothing to do with railways, sir, as Rhys well knows. Look what happened to Evan. Give me good, old-fashioned walking any day."

"Yes, I expected you to say that." Sir Edward exchanged a knowing look with Mr Pryce. "Which brings me to the question of your future employment. I've heard some disturbing things about the way you managed the drove after Evans was injured and unable to continue. I realise you were in a difficult position, but that doesn't excuse some of the things you did."

"What do you mean?" asked Mr Hughes.

As if he didn't know! William raised his eyebrows at Lizzie, but she was staring at her dad with her hand clapped over her mouth.

"I've heard several worrying reports, Hughes. But the thing that most concerns me is that you employed Mostyn and Cade Jones when Evans had specifically told you not to. The result was disaster. I'm told that if it hadn't been for William's quick thinking, you would have lost twelve good oxen before you got to Smithfield. Thanks to him, you only lost one, but that's bad enough."

"What else was I supposed to do? I had to find another drover to replace Evan—"

Sir Edward silenced Mr Hughes with a wave of his hand. "We can talk this through another day. However, you need to know that, because of what happened when you were in charge of the drove, plus your reluctance to use railway transport, I have decided not to employ you as a drover, for the time being."

Lizzie gasped and Mr Hughes went red in the face.

"I'll employ you as a farm labourer – I won't let your family starve. But I can't take the risk of sending you off on another drove this season, I'm afraid. Come and see me when you're back in Ynys Mon." Sir Edward glanced at the gold watch in his top pocket. "I must go. I've got business to see to."

"That's ridiculous…" began Mr Hughes, but Mr Pryce stood up hastily and took his arm.

"Robert and I should get going, sir. We need to collect your oxen from the police station. The sooner we sell them and get back to my cow-keeper's shop, the better." He rammed his hat over his curly black hair and picked up his stick. "Lizzie, you can find your way back to the shop with William, can't you?"

"Yes, Uncle. After searching for you last night, I think I could find my way to quite a few places around here."

"Good. In that case, you can show William the way. Your mam and your aunt are waiting for him and he needs a good wash." He swiped William's coat playfully with his stick so that dust flew out of it. "And William, follow Lizzie's directions carefully. We don't want to lose you again."

"Yes, Mr Pryce." William elbowed Lizzie, for sniggering.

Mr Pryce turned to Sir Edward. "How shall we get your share of the takings to you, when we've sold the cattle, sir?"

"Ah, yes. I haven't mentioned the rest of my plan. I've arranged with Evans to take both him and William back to Ynys Mon in my private coach. William and I will pick him up from The Drovers Rest on our way home. Your dad will need your help on the journey, William, and I know he wants to see you as soon as possible."

"And I want to see him, sir," said William. He also liked the idea of riding in Sir Edward's private coach all the way back to Ynys Mon, but he kept that to himself.

"Good. So, Pryce, I'll call by your cow-keeper's shop in my coach this afternoon, to pick William up and collect any takings due to me from the cattle sales."

"Certainly. See you later, sir. Come on, Robert." Mr Pryce steered an angry Mr Hughes in the direction of the police station green-yard before he started arguing with Sir Edward and making matters worse for himself.

"One more thing, William." Sir Edward leant forward, confidentially. "Don't say anything to your dad about our plans just yet. Wait until he's better. He's had a bad experience with railways. They upset him – quite understandably. Let's wait a bit before we mention them, shall we?" He stood up, ready to depart, but was prevented from going by Lizzie, who pushed in front of William.

"Excuse me, sir. Could I ask you something about Mr Jones and Cade?"

Sir Edward looked amused. "Yes, my bold young woman," he said. "Ask away."

"Well, if the judge says they're guilty of cattle stealing, they could be transported for it, couldn't they?"

Sir Ellis-Lloyd raised his eyebrows. "Knowledgeable, as well! Yes, you're right, they could be."

"That seems drastic, sir. Mr Jones may be guilty, but he bullies Cade. I've known Cade all my life and he can be stupid, but he's not wicked. His dad will have made him steal those oxen. I don't feel right about it, sir. Is there anything you can do to help him – like you've helped William?"

William gritted his teeth. So, Lizzie was comparing him with Cade now! What was she thinking of, bothering Sir Edward about Cade's future? In any case, it was none of her business.

But Sir Edward didn't seem to mind Lizzie's request. "Um. That could be a problem," he mused. "If found guilty, they both deserve such punishment in the eyes of the law. I don't know if there's anything I can do…" he stroked his beard thoughtfully for a while. "But then Cade is only a boy. If he showed remorse… second chance… I've always thought he had potential." He looked at Lizzie. "The only thing I could do, is get a good character reference to the right people. After all, he is the son of one of my tenants. He'll be given a prison sentence, at the least, but maybe I can keep him and his dad in this country."

"Anything would be better than transportation, sir. They might never come back, and I don't know how Mr Jones' wife and children would survive without them. As you say, they live in our village, sir. They're part of our community."

"Well, I'm impressed by your caring attitude, young woman. I'll see what I can do if the need arises," said Sir Edward. "Now, I have business to attend to. I'll see you later, William."

"I'm sorry your dad has lost his job as a drover, Lizzie. He'll earn less as a farmhand. That'll be hard for you and your mam," said William as Sir Edward strode away.

"I don't want to talk about it," muttered Lizzie, busying herself with untying Mab from the bench. She wiped away a tear as she stood up. "You'll be amazed when you see the cow-keeper's shop – we've got nothing like it in Ynys Mon. They keep cows in stalls at the back. When customers come in to buy milk, Aunt Cerys or Cousin Ellen milk the cows while they wait... come on." She started to tug Mab towards a narrow road on the far side of the square.

"Wait a minute," said William. "I need to get something straight, first. Why were you asking Sir Edward to help Cade? I thought I was the one you cared about, not him."

"Sit, Mab!" Lizzie yanked Mab's lead with such force that the dog sat down at once with her ears flattened. "I do care about you, but that doesn't mean I can't care about Cade in a different way, does it? You and I aren't courting, are we?"

William blushed. "Well, no..."

"So, why can't you trust me, William? I'm a caring person. I'm only trying to make sure Cade gets fair treatment. I'd do the same for you." She pointed at him. "In fact, I have done the same for you. Think about it: I put myself at risk last night to get you out of prison. What do you think it was like for me, trying to find Uncle Rhys in that place?" She waved at Smithfield Market. "I had to force my way through the crowds. I got pushed and shoved and spat at. Men frightened me with insults. When I finally found Uncle Rhys, it was getting dark. We went straight to the police station, which was a waste of time because they said it was too late to see you. I was exhausted by the time we finally got back to the cow-keeper's shop. Then, this morning, Uncle Rhys took me to Sir Edward's office, so I could explain what had happened and get his help. And I got you a potato pie, which you didn't even offer me a single bite of. On top of that, we've both just heard Sir Edward say he won't employ my dad as a drover anymore. And all you can think about is whether I care about Cade!"

"Don't get upset." William reached out to Lizzie, but she pushed his hand away, leaving him battling with conflicting emotions as the facts sank in. "So, it was you I heard last night when I was in the cell. I thought I heard voices overhead and I hoped it was you, but then nothing happened," he said at last.

"Well, you would hope. Anyone would hope to get out of a prison cell. That's why I'm trying to help Cade," said Lizzie, crossly.

This was all very well, but Cade was most probably guilty of theft and William wasn't. The comparison felt like an insult. However, the look on Lizzie's face warned William to keep that thought to himself. "I did think about Cade when I was put in that cell. It gave me an idea of what it was like for him when he and his dad were arrested," he said.

"But, fortunately for you, you only had to put up with it for one night!" said Lizzie.

"I know, and that's all thanks to you. I might still be there if you hadn't come to my rescue. Please don't be angry," said William. He squeezed her free hand and at last she smiled.

"That's better," she said. "I just wanted to know I was appreciated. So, can we both forget about Cade for the moment?"

William nodded.

"Good," said Lizzie. "Let's go to Uncle Rhys' cow-keeper's shop, then."

36

26TH APRIL 1848

The cow-keeper's shop, London, England

Mr Pryce's shop had a bold white sign above the door:
    RHYS PRYCE COW KEEPER
Purveyor of dairy products. Fresh milk delivered daily.

William and Mab arrived there with Lizzie, after following her down several winding lanes and across the Clerkenwell Road, narrowly avoiding horses and cab wheels.

On one side of the open door was a small window, in which were displayed a wooden cow, a jug of milk, a pat of butter and a hunk of cheese. Standing at a counter, just inside the door, was a woman in a white cap, pouring milk into the jugs held out by a line of customers. "That's my Aunt Cerys," said Lizzie, waving. "There's my Cousin Ellen in the back."

In the gloom at the back of the shop, William saw a girl, a bit older than Lizzie, milking a cow, whilst the cows on either side of her chewed hay and flicked away flies with their tails.

He wrinkled his nose at the strong smell of dung, creamy milk and human sweat.

"Cousin Ellen's a milkmaid, like I'm going to be. She milks the cows, serves the customers and delivers milk to rich people in the city. They just sit at home and wait for it to arrive. Have you ever heard of such a thing?"

"No, but everything seems different in London," said William.

Mrs Hughes appeared, wiping her hands on her apron. "William! There you are at last. Freed without charge – and so I should think. I couldn't believe it when I heard you'd been arrested. What a state of affairs. And your face! Did they hurt you?" She touched William's bruised cheek.

"Nothing I couldn't handle."

"Mam, William's going back to Ynys Mon with Sir Edward, in his private coach, this afternoon," said Lizzie.

"My word, you're going up in the world," said Mrs Hughes.

"We'll pick Dad up on the way," said William.

"Uncle Rhys says William's got to get cleaned up before Sir Edward comes."

"I quite agree. There aren't many squires who would help their tenants like this. The least you can do is be clean, William," said Mrs Hughes. "Has Sir Edward seen your dad? Is there any news?"

"Yes. He stopped at The Drovers Rest on his way down," said William. He told Mrs Hughes what Sir Edward had said about Dad's condition.

Mrs Hughes looked upset. "Poor Evan. What a state of affairs. How your mam is going to cope, I don't know." She wiped her eyes with a corner of her shawl and set a smile back on her face. "You'd better give yourself a good scrub, William. And you need clean clothes. I'll see if Rhys can lend you some." She bustled William through the shop and into the back yard. "There's the pump. Lizzie – come with me."

Lizzie followed her mam indoors. As she did so, she looked back at William with a silly grin on her face, hugging herself and pretending to shiver. William soon found out why. He hadn't washed under a pump for some weeks and was not keen to do so because his well-travelled garments, though smelly, were warm and comfortable. When he pushed the pump-handle experimentally, freezing water gushed out, soaking his boots, and he let out a yell that disturbed the cows in the yard.

Getting undressed was surprisingly difficult. He was so stiff and sore from his night in the cell, that when he bent down to remove his boots he felt like an old man. His ears throbbed where Constable Runnadey had grabbed them, and his joints ached. His socks, unchanged for many a mile, seemed to be stuck to his feet. He was trying, unsuccessfully, to peel them off when Lizzie appeared with a slab of soap and clean clothes.

"You'll need to soak those socks off, William. Sit down and put your feet under the pump," she said.

William obediently sat on the cobbles and stretched out his feet. Lizzie seized the pump handle and doused his socks relentlessly, while William complained, "Ow! Stop! My feet are cold as ice."

Lizzie squatted down and tried to remove his socks. "Ugh! They're still stuck to your skin. I'll see if rubbing your feet will loosen the wool."

"Thanks," said William gruffly.

He supported himself on his elbows and lifted up one foot, then another, for Lizzie to massage. The sensation was extraordinarily pleasant. It sent shivers up his spine. He watched drowsily as her strong hands worked their way up and down from his ankles to his toes and sunlight shimmered in the strands of golden hair that had escaped from her cap.

But all too soon the blissful sensation came to an end. "That's loosened them," said Lizzie. "I'll try pulling them off now. Ready?" William nodded sleepily, a smile on his face, as Lizzie grasped the toe of his left sock and whipped it off with a flourish, along with a flap of skin.

"Ahh!" roared William, leaping to his feet and hopping across the yard.

"Hey! I haven't done the other one yet. Come back." Lizzie ran after him, laughing.

"Get off my leg," shouted William, dodging her outstretched hands. But he was helpless with laughter now, in spite of the pain.

The commotion disturbed the cows, set Mab barking and brought Mrs Hughes bustling crossly into the yard. "Whatever are you two doing? You should be ashamed of yourself, Lizzie, behaving like a hussy. Get inside!" She grabbed Lizzie's arm and swung her through the kitchen door. "Hurry up, William. The men will be back from the market soon and it won't be long before Sir Edward arrives."

William was only just ready by the time Mr Hughes and Mr Pryce returned, looking pleased with themselves. It was embarrassing, limping into the shop on his sore feet, wearing an enormous pair of Mr Pryce's old breeches and an outsized shirt. "You're an interesting sight, William," laughed Mr Pryce. "But at least you look clean enough to ride in

Sir Edward's coach. Here – I've got good news for you." He produced a wad of notes from his waistcoat pocket and laid them on the counter. "That should pay the bills, even after you've given Sir Edward his dues, eh?"

William seized the notes and quickly counted them. "Thank you, Mr Pryce, that's more than I expected. Did Big Beast fetch a good price?"

"He did. A fine ox, that one. A nightmare to handle, though. I should think you're glad to see the back of him. He was the reason you were arrested, wasn't he?"

William nodded. "He often caused me a load of trouble, but I'll still miss him. He was a great character."

"You can't be sentimental in this business, boy." Mr Pryce patted William's shoulder. "So, what do you think of Sir Edward's plan to transport his cattle by train?"

"Exciting. Do you think he'll employ me to go with them?"

"I should think so. He has ambitions for you, William. And quite right too," said Mr Pryce.

"Does he?" William's thoughts raced ahead. Maybe Sir Edward could find him work with steam locomotives. "Mr Pryce, you know you said you've seen boys working in Camden locomotive sheds – do you think I could get work there?" he asked.

"Maybe, William, but you'd have to start at the bottom on low pay. Your dad's going to need your wages and the profits from droving cattle for some time to come."

"I know that, but there's no harm in finding out more about it, is there? Do you know anybody in Camden sheds whom I could ask?"

"Perhaps…" Mr Pryce stroked one of his sideburns thoughtfully. "Tell you what, next time you're down, we'll pay a visit to Camden sheds and see who we can find. Will that do?"

"Yes, thanks. That would be great," said William. "Sir Edward might be able to help, as well. I'll ask him on the way home." He started to think of questions that he might ask Sir Edward, but Lizzie interrupted him.

"Here are your belongings, William. Mam says to put them by the door in case Sir Edward comes." She struggled across the shop dragging his bag with one hand and towing Mab with the other.

"Thanks." William placed the bag out of the way of Aunt Cerys and her queuing customers, who were passing the time by looking him up and down and whispering to each other.

"What about Mab? Sir Edward won't want her in his coach, will he?" said Lizzie.

William bent down to make a fuss of the excited dog who jumped up at him, barking. "Shh, girl, shh." He looked up at Lizzie. "No, he won't. She'll have to follow the coach and make her own way home when she can't keep up. You can do that, can't you, girl?" He stroked Mab's velvety ears. "After all, she crossed the mountains all by herself and tracked me down in Rhuthun, on the way here. Once I'm on the coach, let her off the leash. She'll follow until we get ahead and her instincts will direct her after that. She'll most likely get home before me."

"But what if she gets lost or someone kidnaps her?"

"That would be sad but she's a drover's dog now, she has to take her chances like the rest of us." William stood up, brushing dog hairs from his over-sized breeches. "Besides, I've got to make the most of my time with Sir Edward, before we collect Dad, so I don't want Mab getting in the way. I'm hoping he'll agree to employ me direct as a trainee drover. I need to earn more money to make up for Dad's lost income." He sighed under the weight of this responsibility, anticipating Lizzie's admiration, but she didn't show any.

"You're not the only one with that problem, William." Lizzie folded her arms across her chest. "As you pointed out earlier, my dad will earn less money working as a farm-hand and our village shop doesn't make much. That means Mam and Dad are going to be relying on my wages from Uncle Rhys."

"Yes, but at least you've definitely got a job. I can't be certain of that yet," said William.

"I know, but what if I can't do it? I've never been a milkmaid before. Have you seen those great yokes they have to carry and the enormous buckets of milk that hang on them? I don't know if I'm strong enough."

William put a protective arm around Lizzie's shoulders. "I'm sure you're strong enough. Your cousin Ellen manages it and she's not much bigger than you. Anyway, with luck, I'll be back in a few weeks, so I'll be able to help you if you're struggling. I've always wanted to be a milkmaid."

Lizzie pushed him away, laughing. "You're not taking me seriously."

"I don't need to. I know you can do it," said William. At that moment, Sir Edward's gleaming coach, pulled by four sleek brown horses, rumbled into view and stopped in front of the shop. This set the waiting customers twittering with excitement as it was an unusual sight in that part of Clerkenwell. Mr Pryce and Mrs Hughes heard the commotion and came out to say goodbye as Sir Edward's coachman jumped down to open the door.

"I'll stay here," said Sir Edward, sticking his head out and waving at them. "Put William's luggage up and we'll be on our way."

"I've got the money Mr Pryce owes you, sir," said William, as he handed his bag to the coachman.

"Excellent, William. Hop in, then. You can travel inside on the way to the Drovers Rest. We need to discuss your future employment."

"Good luck, William. We'll see you in a few weeks," called Mr Pryce.

Mrs Hughes drew him into a hug. "Give my love to your mam. I'll be home to help her soon."

"Take care, William," said Lizzie. Then, in front of everyone, she flung her arms around his neck, planted a big kiss on his lips and jumped away, laughing.

William hid his red face with his hat brim as he climbed into the coach. But once he was seated opposite Sir Edward, he pushed aside his desire to kiss Lizzie back. Suddenly it seemed much more important to convince his prospective employer that he knew how to transport cattle on the railways.

AUTHOR'S NOTE

I grew up in London but have lived much of my life near North Wales. Walking along drovers' routes through the mountains of Snowdonia inspired me to find out more about the drovers who used these routes and the hardship and danger that they endured along the way. I wondered what it might have been like to be a drover's boy or girl in Victorian Britain, walking cattle all the way to the London markets.

In the mid-nineteenth century, railways brought enormous changes to Great Britain which still resonate to this day. For drovers, although the changes provided opportunities – enabling cattle to be transported more economically and efficiently by train – they also brought the ancient practice of long-distance cattle droving to an end. How would this have affected the drovers of North Wales and their families?

The tales I discovered, about the brave drovers who made this journey, inspired me to write *The Speed of Lightning*.

This book is a work of fiction. Names, characters, places and incidents are either imagined or have been used fictitiously whilst keeping as close to the historical context as possible.

Many thanks go to all who have helped me to write and publish this novel.

To Peter, Mark and Julie for giving up their time to share their invaluable skills with editing and historical guidance. To Vic, Sam, Emma and Andrew for their enthusiasm, advice and encouragement. To all my other readers for their helpful feedback: particularly, Jude W, Jude R., Jane, Susan, Lucy, Jo and Year 6 children from Rock Ferry Primary School. To Antonia Prescott, of The Literacy Consultancy, for her insightful manuscript assessment.

Finally, much love and gratitude to Peter, who has walked every step of the way with me as well as giving me the belief, knowledge and support that I needed to finish the book.

Jennie Richmond April 2021

jennierichmondauthor.com

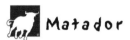 Matador